Troy's Possibilities

Troy's Possibilities

Rodney Strong

LoreQuinn Publishing

Published by LoreQuinn Publishing
Author website: www.rodneystrongauthor.com

A catalogue record for this book is available from the National Library of New Zealand.

To Mum and Dad, who were there at the start of the dream, but couldn't be there to see it come true.

Contents

The one where I opened the door

It starts, and ends, with love. Okay that's not true. As I lay writhing on the floor the thought foremost in my mind was definitely not of love.

They say that love is blind, but no one talks about it being excruciating.

Rewind 30 minutes.

That morning I'd woken, slowly becoming aware of sounds and smells and light pushing against my eyelids. I wondered how old I was. Most days it's hard to tell. Eyes still shut, I moved first one leg, then the other. No pain. Flexed my fingers; they felt strong and supple. Finally I opened my eyes and stared at my hands. They looked young, wrinkle free, yet slightly callused. I sighed. It narrowed the age down but not enough. My phone lay on the bedside table. The screen confirmed the date, and my age.

Hauling myself out of bed, I glanced at the corner of my room. Nothing had changed. I shuffled into the bathroom, rubbing sleep from my eyes. Staring at me in the mirror was the face of a young man, and I despised it.

My name is Troy Messer and I'm twenty-five years old. Again –

or still, I think. It's complicated. I'm an average-looking sort of guy, a shade under six foot, with short brown hair. Plus blue eyes that according to my flatmate and best friend, Emily, never smile. Several women have accused me of being handsome, but I usually dismissed them as drunk, which some of them were; deluded, which in one or two cases was also true; or just plain mistaken. I'm quite bright when I want to be, and athletic if I work hard at it, which rarely happens. In short, there is almost nothing extraordinary about me. Almost.

Having turned away from the mirror, I briefly flirted with the idea of going back to bed, but general apathy has its limits, stopping just short of not paying the rent. I wandered down the narrow hallway into the kitchen. We lived in a bungalow with the original wooden floors and doors, and small rooms with tiny windows – built when people were shorter. Ours was one of many along the street; in fact if it wasn't for the second-hand BMWs parked on the road you might think you'd stepped through a rip in time.

The bedroom walls were covered with a sickly mustard wallpaper that looked sixty years old, but had been selected by the landlord's three-year-old daughter. It could have been worse. Her first choice had apparently been Peppa Pig wallpaper. However the kitchen had been updated with modern appliances and a spacious pantry.

There was a note on the kitchen bench: *Fridge*.

I sighed. We'd been friends for ten years and Emily had what could best be described as boundary issues – she was constantly trying to fix me. Not that she knew what was wrong, but she'd decided a man of my age shouldn't spend his time drifting through life with a weariness reserved for returning soldiers suffering from post-traumatic stress disorder.

She'd experimented with a range of diagnoses for my problem, and offered up a bunch of potential solutions with varying results:

Bored with job ... Emily had left the newspaper on the bench with several adverts circled. Everything from a waiter to the CEO of a power company.

Too much time ... She'd dragged me to dance lessons, pottery classes, and one failed attempt to learn sign language.

Relationship ... Not with her, of course – that'd be weird – but she'd set me up with several women, assuming that if I had someone in my life then I would actually have a life. I did admittedly sleep with some of them, so it wasn't a complete bust, but the experiment stopped when I jokingly called Emily my pimp.

Mental stimulus ... This was her latest. She had decided I needed to challenge my brain. So for the past two weeks she'd been leaving puzzles and treasure hunts around the flat in the hope it would spark some enthusiasm.

I opened the fridge with a little trepidation – I never really knew what to expect. Nothing exploded or leapt off the shelf. Apart from plastic containers filled with leftovers, some eggs and a bottle of expired milk there was nothing out the ordinary. As I went to shut the door I saw one of the eggs had writing on it.

Next door is the lowest clue.

I briefly thought about frying the egg but rebellions are pointless if someone isn't around to witness them. Assuming next door meant one of the neighbours, I exited the kitchen and was nearly at the front door where two thoughts stopped me. One was that I knew Emily was usually literal. The other was that I still had my dressing gown on.

Retracing my steps, I reread the egg, and thought about it from an

Emily perspective. I crossed to the kitchen door and looked down. Something was written on the bottom of the door. Not 'next door' as in the neighbours, but the next door I would open. Shaking my head, I squatted and squinted at the tiny writing.

Stop and smell the roses.

That was puzzling. I didn't know if it meant the next step in the game or a suggested lifestyle direction. I decided to consider it while having a shower – I do some of my best work there. And yes, sometimes that refers to masturbation.

I padded into the bathroom and turned on the water. In most houses this would be a simple task of rotating the mixer. Unfortunately, along with the original floors and doors, the house had the original bathtub, the original plumbing, and quite possibly the original shower curtain. To get the water to the right temperature is akin to cracking a safe. Rotate the hot tap twice, cold tap once, hot tap three times, cold tap once, hot tap back the other way twice, wait one and a half minutes, and there you go – water at the perfect temperature emitting from the showerhead with the same ferocity as sweat dribbling down your neck on a hot day. But if you lay down in the bath and let the water fall on you it was like a gentle massage, with the added bonus that sometimes you got clean as well.

While waiting for the water to reach optimum temperature I stared at myself in the slightly cracked mirror. Nothing had changed in the last five minutes – or ten years – but one day it might.

It took some manoeuvring to get comfortable in a bath made for someone five inches shorter than me but finally I was able to relax with my left leg bent and my right leg leaning against the wall. Water misted down, hitting my chest and slowly spreading across the torso, while I wondered what excuse to use for being late to work. I don't particularly hate my job – in fact sometimes working as an analyst at the second largest bank in the country was quite rewarding. But it's hard to muster enthusiasm for another day, another meal, another conversation, another one of everything I'd done endless times before.

After pondering the problem for a while I decided things would be easier all around if I called in sick and spent the day in bed.

Extraction from the bath was trickier than getting in but eventually I managed it with minimal damage to knees and elbows. Drying myself was interrupted by a knock at the front door. I ignored it and continued with the tiresome process of making sure every part was dry. It seemed like no matter how hard I tried, there was always one spot missed which gleefully soaked into my clothes. It was like a battle between my brain and body; the score was 6,000 to nil in favour of my body. It didn't help that the towel was five years old with the softness and absorbency of sandpaper.

The knock came again. I wrapped the towel around me, wandered down the hall, took the security chain off and opened the door.

The girl standing on my front porch was slim with long blonde hair and blue eyes. She would have been about my age, and slightly shorter than me. She wore figure-hugging faded blue jeans, a plain white T-shirt, dark boots, and carried a large shoulder bag. The sun streamed across her face, filtering through strands of hair that left rippling shadows when she talked.

'Hi,' she said.

'Hi.'

'Do you know you're naked?'

'I have a towel on.'

'Barely,' she replied with a grin.

I looked down. The towel had come open, leaving things poking out that were best kept hidden. I readjusted the towel. 'Can I help you?'

She was struggling to keep her eyes locked on mine. 'Do you think you could put some pants on?'

'I could close the door,' I replied, already over the encounter.

'Can I use your phone? My car died.'

'Don't you have a cell phone?'

'That died too.' She gave a helpless shrug.

'Unlucky.'

'Not really – it was a piece of shit.'

'The car or the phone?'

'Both. So can I use it?'

'Um, use what?'

'The phone.' She said this like she was talking to a two-year-old, and I didn't know whether to be amused or insulted.

I sighed. 'Sure. Come in.' I led the way down the hall, followed by the hollow echo of boot heels. In the kitchen I turned back around. She was pointing something at me.

'What the…?' was my last rational thought for several minutes. My eyes erupted in burning agony and I fell to the floor, writhing like a crazed marionette doll being operated by two drunk monkeys. My eyes refused to open, and they felt like they were being stabbed by millions of little needles.

Through the pain I became aware of sounds from the other rooms of the house, then footsteps approaching. Instinctively I scrambled backwards, eyes still glued shut, and smacked my head on a cupboard. The floor was cold against my arse so my towel must have come off. I tried to rub my eyes, my head, and cover myself at the same time, failing on all three counts. A door opened and closed, then someone grabbed my hand. I jerked it free.

'Don't be a baby,' she said, putting something cold in my hand. 'Pour this on your eyes. Then come and get me.' Boots retreated, and the front door slammed shut.

What? No goodbye? No thanks for falling for my stupidly clever trick and by the way your penis is the biggest I've ever seen.

I groped around with my free hand and found she'd put the milk container in my other one. My addled brain hoped it wasn't Emily's soy milk since she hated wasting things. I fumbled the lid off and poured the entire container over my face, accidentally inhaling some, coughing and spraying milk around the kitchen, but kept going until it was empty and I lay in a growing pool of dairy. I might have made a crack about crying over spilt milk but I was too busy actually crying. And it was Emily's soy so this woman had even more to answer for. Eventually the pain subsided enough for my eyes to slit open.

The phone was inches away from my hand; the rational thing would be to call the police immediately. Instead I stumbled into the bathroom, ran a basin full of water and plunged my head into it. Coming up for air, I checked my appearance. My eyes were puffy and angry red, but at least I could see out of them. Water streamed off my face and after three more dunks the pain subsided to manageable proportions. I stumbled back into the kitchen in search of painkillers, slipped in the puddle of milk and skidded into the island bar, unfortunately at groin height. Fresh pain erupted, and a stream of swear words shot into the air.

Cradling my injured genitals, I explored the house, looking to see what was missing. I tried my room first, where organised chaos was completely destroyed. Casual observers might not have noticed the difference, but there was usually order beneath the clutter. An assortment of pillows, currently strewn across the room, usually formed a vague person like shape in the centre of the king-size bed, my oasis in the desert sized mattress. Piles of clothes typically dotted the floor, seemingly carelessly dropped, but there was a system. Pants over by the drawers, agonisingly close to their destination, T-shirts by the door, undies and socks in the top drawer. Some things are best kept off the ground. Now a tangle of everything littered the carpet.

My eyes went to the corner of the room. I went over to the canvas leaning against the wall, untouched, unfinished.

After a few minutes of searching I realised my iPhone was missing from the bedside table. Swearing, I went into my roommate's room. Fortunately it was spotless – Emily was a neat freak, thinking if she started every day with a clean room it was like starting the day fresh. The thief obviously hadn't gone through her room at all. Which made no sense. Emily's stuff was worth way more than mine, so why only target my room? And what did that girl mean, come and get her? I shook my head, another in a long list of bad ideas.

It was then I noticed Emily's jewellery box open and empty on the top of her dresser.

Which leads us back to my original starting point – recently pepper sprayed, naked, and extremely pissed off. Logic dictated that the next move would be to call the police, closely followed by a call to Emily. While I had every intention of calling both the police and Emily, it didn't matter whether it was now or in a few hours. In the meantime I planned on taking my visitor up on her invitation. The loss of my phone wasn't a big deal, but no one fucks with my friend.

I retained enough sense to put on trousers and sunglasses.

Rummaging around the pile of pillows on the bed, I pulled out my iPad. Thank God for technology – the Find My Phone app pointed to a spot halfway across the city. A search of every pocket came up with $32. More than enough to get a bus into town. Normally I would have walked into the city, just me and my thoughts without distraction from unimportant people doing unimportant things. But the thirty-minute walk might cool my anger, and I was determined to keep the fires stoked.

I slammed the door shut behind me and stormed to the bus stop. Three doors down from our place an elderly couple stood outside their gate having an argument. I'd seen them around before, just a casual hi in passing. This time the woman grabbed my arm.

'You there, settle this for us. This one or this one?' She held up two paint samples.

'Um, for…?'

'The house, son, obviously,' the man told me.

Both options were horrible. One was a sandy grey colour and the other bright green. I pointed to the grey as the least offensive. The man looked triumphant and the woman waved me off in disgust.

The bus was half full with an assortment of retirees, unemployed and student artists accompanying me on my search for revenge. The student artists annoyed me the most, carrying their large portfolio bags and eyeing up the rest of us with a critical painter's eye as if they were trying to capture our true essences. I'd wanted to be one of them, but life had taken several unexpected twists. Now I looked at them with a mixture of envy, annoyance and disgust.

I checked several times during the journey, but the phone hadn't moved in the fifteen minutes it took to cover the distance between the house and the place marked by my screen's blinking light. As the bus travelled closer I began to have second thoughts. I've been shot several times, beaten up more than my share, and suffered through excruciating and sometimes fatal illnesses. Until today I'd never been pepper sprayed, and looking to get it done twice in one morning bordered on sheer stupidly.

But I needed to get Emily's jewellery back.

When the bus pulled over I queued up behind a young mother with two crying children. For a moment something shifted in my heart, before I stifled it behind a curtain of indifference. She gave me an apologetic smile and I returned it with a look of encouragement. As the bus rumbled off I paused on the edge of the pavement to get my bearings. The air smelled of diesel, fried food and – as of ten seconds ago – baby vomit. The mother looked mortified, but I just shrugged. With the start I'd had to the day, baby vomit wasn't an issue.

The sun reflected off the screen of my iPad, making it impossible to see, so I stepped into the doorway of a shop. My phone was about 100 metres up the road. I walked slowly, letting the bustle of pedestrians pull me along, trying to seem relaxed and nonchalant while my heart beat faster. I didn't know what I was going to say to her. Obviously 'Give back our stuff' was high on the list, but apart from that I didn't have a plan.

Suddenly I realised the blinking light was now behind me. Retracing my steps, I stopped outside a café. Several tables sat on the pavement but she wasn't at any of them. Tinted windows reflected the street back at me. There was no choice but to go inside.

It was one of those small, intimate places with minimal space between the wooden tables. Only two were occupied – one with a couple of girls about my own age sipping their drinks and gossiping, the other by an elderly gentleman wearing a suit and tie and reading the morning paper. A blackboard above the cash register set out a standard café menu – pretty much anything, with a side of chips – and I caught the top of a head moving around behind the coffee machine followed by the sharp sound of steam. Jazz music played softly and the pleasant smell of coffee blanketed the room like a thin layer of fog.

Next to the counter I spotted an arrow pointing to a toilet down a narrow hallway. Maybe my assailant was back there. I picked my way through the tables and headed past the counter.

'Won't be a second,' came from behind the espresso machine. The voice, though muffled by the machine, was vaguely familiar. 'What can I get you?' she asked, emerging into view.

We stared at each other for a moment. 'How about our stuff?' I asked her.

She didn't blink. But then someone who enters your house, assaults you, steals your stuff and then goes back to work has a lot of nerve.

'What took you so long?' she asked with a cheeky grin.

'It's hard to mount a pursuit when you can't see,' I retorted.

Now I was paying attention she was prettier than I remembered. A small scar below her left eye, barely visible beneath a thin layer of makeup, only enhanced her look. One of her teeth was slightly crooked, somehow making her smile more appealing.

With an apologetic smile she pulled her handbag out from under the counter. When she put her hand inside I instinctively took a step back. She laughed and had enough decency to look a little ashamed. 'Relax,' she said handing over my phone and a small plastic bag filled with Emily's jewellery.

'Hard to relax when your eyes are on fire.' I took my sunglasses off and she winced.

'Damn. What's that like, by the way?'

'Hand it over and I'll show you.'

She laughed again and this time I took notice of the way her eyes filled with humour when she smiled. I shook my head at my own stupidity. This woman assaulted me, and here I was thinking she was cute.

'Why?' I asked.

'That's all we agreed on,' she replied.

'What?'

'You still don't get it, do you?'

I opened the camera on my phone and snapped a picture of her to show the police. 'Get what? Wait, I don't care. Thanks for the phone,' I muttered and turned to leave.

'You know, you won me fifty dollars,' she called out.

I stopped and turned back. 'For what,' I asked instinctively.

'For the bet.'

I stared blankly at her.

'You think I spend my time stealing people's stuff?'

I shook my head. 'Still don't care.'

She laughed. 'If that were true you wouldn't have won me fifty bucks.'

I couldn't help myself. 'I don't get it.'

She tutted in mock dismay. 'You're not the sharpest knife in the block. I bet Emily fifty dollars if I stole something from you, you'd come and get it.'

I looked at her in shock. 'That's insane.'

'It worked.'

'You could have maimed me for life,' I protested.

She waved a hand dismissively. 'Want to help me spend the fifty dollars?'

For a few seconds I considered it, then I shook my head and it broke the moment. 'Is that part of the bet? No, I've got our stuff. See you never.' This time I made it to the door before she spoke.

'You know, when you opened the door wearing just the towel I almost forgot the bet and shagged you in the hallway.'

I'm not so vain to think I'm the most attractive man in the world, especially when naked; there's something generally unattractive about naked men – lots of dangling bits. However when a cute girl says something like this to you, you stop and listen. Turning back, I realised the two girls at the table were staring at me – and it wasn't my face they were looking at. I shifted uncomfortably, inching behind a chair.

'Just a coffee,' my thief said.

I stared at her for a while longer before reluctantly taking a step back into the shop.

'Not here,' she said. 'The coffee's terrible.' She yelled something through the door to the kitchen, grabbed her bag and came to meet me, pausing at the girls' table. She leaned in and winked at them. 'Whatever you're thinking, think bigger.' Then she took me by the arm and guided us out onto the street.

'You still haven't told me your name,' I pointed out.

'It can be whatever you want it to be,' she smiled.

'Christ, I'm not being charged by the hour, am I?'

She wasn't offended. 'No, although I did consider it once. I'm an actress – can't you tell?'

'Don't actresses have names?'

'Oh, yes, but it keeps changing with the parts. It can be difficult keeping track – get it?'

'I've got a headache.'

'That's probably the after effects of the pepper spray. Let's get some caffeine into you.'

She linked her arm in mine and in a slight daze I left it there. From the outside we could have simply been another couple strolling down the street. We didn't talk again until she led me down a short alleyway and into a small, dark coffee shop. I hadn't even known it existed until we walked through the door, and given the lack of customers neither did anyone else.

Music played softly through hidden speakers and the walls were covered in an eclectic collection of art that to an art critic would no doubt have represented some sort of retro, post-modern statement on society, but to me looked like someone gave a fifteen-year-old some cash and said decorate the walls. There were five small tables, each with two chairs, none of which matched. For a moment I couldn't figure out what was missing, and then it struck me. There was no counter, no coffee machine, no food cabinet. I thought we might have accidentally walked into someone's house. Then my companion/attacker sat down at one of the tables.

As I slid into the chair opposite, a woman appeared from a discreetly placed door in the back wall. She stood silently next to the table.

'Trim mochaccino with whipped cream and a cinnamon twist,' the blonde said.

The woman turned her gaze onto me.

'Coffee.'

She remained still.

'Please,' I added.

She didn't move.

I glanced over at the blonde who regarded me with amusement. 'What am I missing?'

She grinned. 'If you want coffee you go to Starbucks. What you get here are creations. Try again.'

I sighed, just wanting coffee. 'Okay, I'll have what she's having.'

The woman seemed less than satisfied at my lack of creativity, but she disappeared into the back without a sound.

'Okay, seriously, what is your name?'

'I told you, whatever you want it to be.'

'Okay, I'll call you Psycho.'

She laughed softly. 'And you wouldn't be the first.'

'How do you know Emily?'

'Oh, we volunteer together at the SPCA.'

Emily goes there every Saturday morning. For a sensitive soul like her it's probably the worst possible thing to do. Every Saturday afternoon she comes home with grand plans to adopt homeless animals. If I didn't constantly put my foot down we would have enough cats, dogs, chickens, guinea pigs and rabbits to repopulate the earth. Kitten season was particularly hard on her. Every weekend brought fresh tears at the prospective fate of cats that couldn't be rehomed. Something told me the woman sitting opposite me didn't have the same problem.

'Ok I'll call you Cat.'

She nodded thoughtfully. 'Cat. Cool, I like it.'

'So what, you and Emily got talking and she asked you to assault me?'

'Not quite. She told me about her efforts to get you interested in something, anything, and we came up with the plan to rob you. To see if that would be enough to get you out of this rut you're in. I thought it was important to raise the stakes, so I took her stuff too. The pepper spray was my idea.'

'That's insane.'

'Little bit,' she agreed. 'You know, Emily cares about you a great deal.'

'I care about her too. She's my best friend.'

'Do you love her?'

'Of course.'

'Are you in love with her?'

'Not that it's any of your business, but no, I'm not.'

Before she could reply the woman appeared at our table and set our drinks down. I blinked a couple of times. To say they were cups would have been generous. They were ceramic and at least cup like in shape, but looked like someone had given a lump of clay to the fifteen-year old's much younger sibling and left them to it. There wasn't a straight line to be seen and my handle could fit my entire fist through it, while Cat's could barely fit her little finger.

'What is this place?'

'The best-kept secret in Wellington,' she replied.

'That's not an answer.'

She laughed. 'I know,' she mocked.

I reluctantly tasted the coffee, but it was surprisingly good.

Cat gave a satisfied nod when she saw the look on my face, like she'd made it herself. 'So what's your deal?' she asked.

'What do you mean?'

'You're what? Twenty-four? Twenty-five? I've met some pretty apathetic guys, but from what Emily has told me you don't seem to care about anything.'

'Not entirely true. I care about getting pepper sprayed,' I quipped.

'Okay, I think we need to move past that.'

'It only happened a couple of hours ago.'

She waved her hand, dismissing my statement as irrelevant.

'Where do you even get one of those?' I asked.

'Us single girls can never be too careful. The world is full of perverts.'

I didn't know what to say, so we sat in silence for a while, sipping our drinks and listening to the music.

She broke the silence. 'You didn't answer my question. How'd you get this way?

I looked down at my half empty cup, searching in the swirls for the right words. Not the truth, of course, but something to say. Finally I looked at her. 'It is what it is.'

She looked expectantly, waiting for more. Eventually she realised there was no more. 'It is what it is,' she repeated. 'That's the stupidest thing I've ever heard.'

I shrugged, 'Well, that's what it is.'

'But it doesn't even mean anything.'

'That's why I thought it would appeal to you. You haven't said anything that means anything since I met you.'

Cat laughed. 'Touché, but something must have happened to make you like this.'

'Maybe there is no why – it's who I am. Maybe it's genetic.'

'It's genetic that you have no motivation to do…anything?'

'Look, the thing is, we've just met and this isn't a movie. There's no immediate connection here where I sense you're my soul mate and spill my guts to you about everything that's wrong in my life.'

'Wow, how's that nerve?'

'This was a mistake.' I made to stand up.

'There's a difference between being a drifter and being a dick. You leave before we've finished our drinks, it makes you the latter.'

I sat back down and silence fell, but it was the comfortable sort of silence from sitting with an old friend, not the awkward silence of a first date.

Suddenly she leaned forward. 'So what's your walk-away song?'

I looked at her blankly.

'You know, the end of the movie where the hero has won the day and puts on his sunglasses and walks off into the sunset. They play a song as he leaves. What's yours?'

'I can safely say I've never thought about it.'

She looked disappointed.

'Okay, so what's yours?'

She grinned. '"Don't wait another day" by Greg Johnson.'

'I haven't heard it.'

'Then there's no future for us, Troy,' she said seriously before giving me a sly look. 'You need to figure out your walk-away song.'

'So you're an actress? What have you been in?' I asked to change the subject.

'Mostly extra work on commercials and TV. Some plays. Nothing big yet.'

'Are you any good?'

For once she didn't have a quick answer and I sensed it was a touchy subject.

'What about you?' she asked instead. 'Was it your life ambition to work at a bank?'

'It pays the bills. Better than acting, anyway.'

She ignored my gibe. 'Does it make you happy?'

'Paying the bills makes me happy,' I replied.

She rolled her eyes in disgust.

The truth is I did have other ambitions when I was a teenager. The evidence of that sat in the corner of my bedroom. But Possibilities got in the way.

'Tell me a story,' she demanded.

'What sort of story?'

She waved a hand. 'Anything. Entertain me.'

I sighed. 'When I was twelve –.'

She stopped me. 'Not a real story. We're not bonding over childhood experiences here.'

'What are we doing here?' I shot back.

'Drinking coffee and talking.'

'That sounds like a date. I don't date people who physically assault me.'

She gave me a wicked look. 'As you shouldn't. It's a terrible way to start a relationship. But this isn't a date.'

'Then what is it?' I insisted.

'Let's call it a pre-date. To see whether a date will work.'

I stared at her in disbelief. 'You're crazy.'

'So we've established. Now tell me a story. Make one up.'

'I don't know any made up stories,' I sulked.

'Don't be stupid, of course you do.

I figured it wouldn't matter, so I told her the story about the moon and the sun. 'Thousands of years ago there were no beaches. Just mirrors where the sand is – strips of perfect glass between the water and the earth. In the daytime the sun would shine down on the mirrors and her light would be reflected back at her magnified a hundred times. And the sun was happy because she knew she was the most beautiful thing in existence. But at night the moon would look at himself in the glass and be incredibly sad. All he saw were his imperfections, the darkness and cracks on his face. Sometimes he would only peek at the earth and his sadness was diminished. But once a month he would gaze fully upon the mirrors and his ugliness would return in its full glory. One night he couldn't take it any more. He reached out and pulled at the water in the oceans and seas, sending it crashing onto the mirrors again and again. At first nothing happened. Then a single crack appeared. He intensified his efforts. Wave after wave hit the mirror until more cracks appeared, and suddenly the glass shattered into millions of pieces. Even then he wasn't satisfied, constantly pushing the water onto the beaches until the glass was nothing more than sand. Still he was afraid that if he stopped the water the glass would reform and he'd have to look at himself once more, so the tides continue, constantly moving, all so the moon doesn't have to see himself.'

Cat looked at me. 'Wow, that's an interesting story. So which am I? The sun or the moon?'

It took a moment to realise she was asking me if I thought she was pretty. 'It's a bit early in our relationship for me to be assigning you astral bodies.'

'So we're in a relationship?'

'You blinded me. I feel like there's a connection between us.'

Cat laughed. 'Have dinner with me.'

I glanced at my watch. 'It's only 11.30am.'

She stood up and stretched out her hand. 'I know, so let's go kill eight hours.'

I should have hesitated; said no, thanked her for the coffee and walked out. But it seemed like too much effort, so instead I stood up, took her hand, and said, 'What'd you have in mind?'

She laughed again and gave my hand a squeeze. 'Settle tiger. Despite what I said earlier, I'm not easy.'

My face flushed. 'I didn't mean…'

'Just kidding. Come on, we'll figure something out.'

We spend the rest of the day figuring it out. First rollerblading along the waterfront, followed by lunch at a pub. Afterwards we went to the movies and saw possibly the worst film ever made, an experience made better by the fact we were the only ones in the theatre and spent the entire time yelling at the screen. About halfway through the film she leaned her head on my shoulder and it felt great, and I knew this wasn't real.

After that we went and played pool. I'm a pretty good player but she smoked me in ten consecutive games. It was then she told me she helped pay the rent by hustling pool. I doubt it was real but it sounded awesome.

Somewhere during the day Emily rang – first my cell, which I ignored, and then Cat's. Cat answered and proceeded to tell Emily in graphic detail that she couldn't talk because she was giving me a blowjob. I felt sorry for the two old ladies walking behind us.

Around 7.30 we decided it was time for dinner. At precisely the same time the sky decided to open and it began to pour with rain. As commuters rushed past, kicking up sprays of water with their expensive work shoes, we huddled in the doorway of a closed shop. There we kissed for the first time. One second we were talking and the next her tongue was in my mouth – or mine in hers, it was a bit foggy. But it was great. Eventually I broke away and stared into her eyes.

'What?' she asked. 'Wasn't it good?'

'Yes, it was,' I admitted.

'Then come here.' She pulled me close and we kissed again. The part of me she had already seen naked started to react, and I squirmed a little, then pulled away.

'I can't,' I told her with little conviction.

'I knew it. You're gay, aren't you?'

I shook my head. 'No.'

'Well, you're not in a relationship, so why not? I think you're cute, the bulge in your jeans says you think I'm cute, so what's wrong with two single cute people hooking up?'

'I've been hurt before.'

'Then I'll be gentle with you,' she teased.

'It's complicated,' I replied looking away.

She kissed me again, pushing her whole body against mine. 'Let me uncomplicate things then. I am not looking for a relationship, I'm not interested in happy ever after, and I don't want your life story, or to meet your parents. Emily told me enough about you to make you interesting, I've had fun today, and now I'm horny. It's either your cock or my vibrator, and frankly I'd prefer your cock.'

'That is pretty uncomplicated,' I acknowledged.

We kissed again, and she reached behind me and grabbed my arse.

'Are you turning me down?' she whispered when we broke lips.

I didn't answer. I was tempted, what could it hurt? But I'd been here before, not exactly in this spot, but in this situation, and there's only so much meaningless sex you can have before the meaningless becomes more important than the sex.

Rather than be offended she looked amused at my reluctance. 'Do you know your problem?' she asked, pulling her hair away from her face. 'You take everything at face value. You don't have any faith.'

I looked at her, puzzled. 'You mean religion?'

She laughed, 'No, let's not ruin a good conversation by bringing God into it. Religions might monopolise the meaning of the word, but they don't have sole use of it. Faith is just believing in something you can't see.'

She saw the blank look on my face. 'What we have here is a cute, horny girl standing in front of you, wanting to have sex. Yet you don't believe it, right? You don't think it's real, right?'

I swallowed and looked out into the rain.

'And I'm saying it is. Because this is real.' She reached a hand out into the rain, brought it back into our niche and flicked me in the face with water. 'And this.' She slapped my chest. 'And this.' She grabbed my hand and put it on her breast.

I squirmed with embarrassment, but not enough to take my hand away.

'But if you're saying you can't trust what you see' – she glanced down – 'and feel ...'

I snatched my hand away.

'...then you need to start believing in what you can't see.' She looked around and spied a broken umbrella lying on top of a pile of boxes next to the doorway. The wire frame was mostly there, but the canopy had been reduced to ragged pieces of dark fabric.

'I bet we can step out of this doorway with this umbrella held above us and not get wet.'

My laugh trailed off when I saw she was being serious. 'That's crazy.'

'Of course it is, but sometimes the only way is crazy. So what do you have to lose? You can stand here until the rain stops and never know if I'm right. Or you can take my hand and we step out under this umbrella, and...'

'And?'

'That's the thing, isn't it? Who knows what could happen? We could get soaked – well, more soaked – or we could stay dry because we believe the umbrella will protect us from the rain. But for it to work, to really work, you need to believe in the umbrella, and trust me.'

I looked from her to the umbrella to the pouring rain. 'That's a broken piece of trash, and this morning you attacked me and stole my phone. How am I supposed to trust what you say?'

She held out her hand. 'That's why it's called faith.'

I peered into night for so long my eyes lost focus. Every raindrop a drop of paint on a canvas – meaningless alone but together creating a startling picture of light and shadow.

Turning back to face Cat, I said, 'Okay, but if I get wetter, you're buying dinner.' I took her hand and she smiled at me.

'It'll work, Troy. You simply have to believe.' She raised the broken umbrella over our heads, we took a deep breath, stepped out of the doorway and…

…got much wetter.

She looked at me, rain streaming down her face, and laughed as she tossed the umbrella in the rubbish bin. 'See? Faith,' she shouted over the hissing rain.

'It didn't work, though,' I replied, water flicking off my lips with each word.

'It was never going to work, you idiot. I just wanted you to trust me enough to step out into the rain.'

'You're hands down the strangest person I've ever met,' I informed her. Which was saying a lot, given the number of people I've met.

'Thank you.' She grinned back.

One soggy taxi ride later – the driver making us sit on towels he pulled from his boot before we were allowed inside – we were back at my flat. The place was dark and empty. We were barely through the door before soaking T-shirts hit the floor. Her hands felt like fire against my cold skin, and my lips kissing her breasts through the material of her bra elicited a soft moan. The pants were a bit tricky to remove, wet denim proving an unwelcome distraction, but eventually they too were thrown to the floor. Slowly I kissed my way down her body – her neck, nipples, smooth stomach, all shivering under my ceaseless lips. Pausing below her belly button, I looked up to see her staring at me with a grin on her face. I winked and lowered my head. I heard one moan of pleasure, then blinked...

And I was standing at my front door, Cat in front of me, trying not to peek at the gap in my towel. The sun streamed across her face, filtered through strands of hair that left rippling shadows when she talked.

'Can I...?' she started.

'No.' I slammed the door shut. My groin ached and I looked down, fully expecting to see a hard penis, but it was just a fresh memory. My head swam with the sudden change in environment. I leaned against the door, could almost feel the confusion seeping through the cracks in the door. Slowly footsteps retreated, back into the world, in my memory.

I pulled myself off the door and went back to bed. Despite everything, despite my internal protests that my heart couldn't be hurt any more, a small piece of it broke off and crumbled into dust.

So here's the deal

Everything you just read – the whole day – didn't happen. It was a Possibility, a life that could have been.

That's my curse. I get to live out Possibilities. This is the best way I can explain it. Have you ever thought back on a decision you made and wondered how your life might have been if you'd chosen differently? I don't have to wonder, because I get to live out what the other decision would have been. Yay, you might say, that sounds fun. It's not. I have no control over it, and it's not daydreaming about being rich, or marrying a hot super model.

Sometimes Possibilities can last forty or fifty years. In some of them I'll fall in love, get married, have children, become famous or die horribly, and then they'll end and I'm back to where I am now – which in my real life is twenty-five years old, and thoroughly over it all.

Here's the other important piece of information: it's not time travel. If I live out a Possibility and then bounce back to what I call my real life, I don't have knowledge of what's going to happen next week, or month, or year. I can't get rich off the lottery or sports betting. I've tried. I went to the races after coming back from one Possibility, and bet most of my savings on a 100–1 shot that had already won the race, expecting to be $100,000 richer. Only the horse didn't win – it got caught on the barrier like it had during the Possibility, but this time when a gap presented itself a hundred metres from the finish the jockey failed to take it. You see, everyone makes decisions every day, and every time someone changes a decision – goes left rather than right, takes a risk instead of playing it safe – the world changes. There isn't one future, there's a googolplexian (which is a real number, look it up) of them – in fact more than a googolplexian, because things constantly change.

The first 14 years and 364 days of what I've come to call my real life were relatively normal. I was born, learned to walk, talk, go to the toilet and ride a bike, broke a couple of bones, and most importantly discovered girls. Then I turned 15.

And nothing happened. I woke up, unwrapped my present – a new Walkman from Mum and Dad – ate my eggs on toast with lots of bacon, and went to school like normal. That night I celebrated with three of my closest friends at an all-you-can eat buffet restaurant. It's gone now but it was teenage heaven back then – you could have dessert before, during and after mains. We bet to see who could eat the most chicken wings. Simon won with fifteen. I only managed twelve, but I got my revenge on the soft-serve challenge – he brain-freezed out after two bowls while I squeezed in three. Of course none of us were winners later when it all came up in the toilet. But it was worth it.

Life went on. I started dating Heather Morgan, the most beautiful girl in the world, and it was a pure and eternal love. It lasted three months before she dumped me for my best friend, TJ. This caused a rift in our friendship until she dumped him two months later for a girl from another school. TJ and I made up over a cigarette after school. And half an hour later we threw up together. Neither of us had smoked before – he'd pinched them from his mum. While it was the first of many for him, I never took to it – mostly. This was one of many shared vomit experiences.

I left high school and went to university, doing a degree in marketing because I didn't want to get a real job. During my second year I ran into Heather and, her experimental lesbian phase having run its course, we started dating again. After I graduated and got a job at an advertising company the first thing I bought was an engagement ring. We got married a year later, against her parents' wishes, in a ceremony highlighted by TJ, my best man, shagging a bridesmaid, then getting rollicking drunk and streaking through the reception.

A year later Heather gave birth to our daughter, Rose, named after her maternal grandmother. Heather promptly called her perfect, and although I would eventually share her view, the first time I laid eyes on her Rose was an angry, screaming, red skinned bundle of ugly. The red skin went away, most of the time she didn't scream, and after a while there was more laughing than anger. I loved to watch her sleep – she seemed so peaceful, so innocent.

One night, after Heather had gone to bed, I crept into Rose's bedroom to get one more look before I went to sleep. She lay on her back, one arm above her head and her thumb firmly planted in her mouth. I wanted to kiss her goodnight but was afraid it would wake her. So I kissed my hand, reached it in and gently placed it on her forehead. She stirred a little and I froze. Her skin was warm beneath my fingertips, so smooth and soft. She let out a sigh and stopped moving and I slowly moved my hand away. I remember whispering goodnight to her, then turned toward the door and blinked…

And was standing in my bedroom, the one at my parents' house. It was the most vivid dream I'd ever had. Everything was perfect. Not tidy perfect, but perfect as in exactly as I remembered my fifteen-year-old self's bedroom being. A bed made once a week, when the sheets were changed; a plate encrusted with what used to be pizza poking out from under the mattress; a pile of books currently being read on the bedside table. Even at fifteen I found my tastes in literature changed from night to night so there were always several books on the go. In the corner of the room was a cane washing basket surrounded by dirty clothes, as if the basket hadn't been able to stand the stench of teenage sweat and thrown them up. The air smelt slightly testosteroney, which isn't a word and probably isn't even a smell, but walk into any teenage boy's room and you'll know what I mean. A round mirror hung from the back of the door. The face staring back at me was fifteen years old, still a while away from the regular touch of a razor, an inexperienced face.

I left the room and went into the kitchen. Mum stood at the counter making biscuits, nodding her head in time with a song on the radio, clouds of flour exploding off the counter as she vigorously kneaded dough. It was a scene I'd seen plenty of times – my mum was a big baker, one of the reasons all my friends loved coming to my house. It's also how I subsidised my allowance through the first two years of high school. Every time Mum made a big batch of cookies I'd sneak three quarters of them into my schoolbag and sell them off to my mates. Whenever she made a comment about how fast they went I blamed Dad. The poor guy took a while to figure it out, and by then Mum had forced him into two diets and daily brisk walks around the block. To give him credit, instead of turning me in he simply asked for a ten-percent cut. I think he was secretly happy with the exercise and the money was his way of letting me know how things could have gone if he'd wanted it. As far as I know Mum never found out. Or maybe she did and didn't care.

Mum looked up from her work and smiled at me. 'Morning, dear. You'd better hurry if you expect to get to school on time. And for goodness' sake, Troy, put on some clean pants.'

'What day is it?' I asked in confusion.

'Don't be silly, dear, it's Wednesday – now go.'

'What's the date?'

Every night I cried myself to sleep. Because the longer this went on, the more it seemed real, which meant my other life wasn't. Which meant I would never see my daughter again. Which meant she'd never existed. And at that point of realisation my mind cracked a little. I sank into a deep depression and stayed in bed for two weeks.

My parents went through the full range of emotions – worried, supportive, angry, finally ending with helplessness. They brought in doctors who ruled out physical ailments. They brought in shrinks who told them I suffered from adolescent depression and would work through it given time, and until then here were some drugs to take. The drugs made me worse, but I took them anyway. Partly because I didn't want them to think I was crazy, partly because I was worried I might be, and partly – a tiny part I clung to with all my strength – because I still hoped this was a dream and I would wake up next to Heather, with Rose sleeping in her cot next door.

Eventually I got over it. Okay, that's not true. Eventually I swallowed a bottle of pills. It seemed like the only way back to Heather and our life together. I remember lying on my bed and drifting away, my body turning to dust, a light breeze flicking me into the air. Then I felt nothing.

Then I woke up. For a single elated second I thought my plan had worked, but looking around quickly took away that hope. I was still in my old bedroom. The newspaper I later found on the kitchen table confirmed it was two days after the first time I'd come back to my fifteen-year-old self. Note I say *come back*, because having ruled out dreaming I was leaning towards time travel as a working theory. In fact, given my age and that I loved comics and science fiction movies, it was puzzling why that hadn't been my first theory. It wasn't my last attempt to end it all, but they never seemed to stick.

I never talked to Heather again.

And so it went on, and on, and between then and now I've lived a thousand different lives. Give or take. I stopped counting after a while, because frankly after the first couple it didn't matter how many there'd been. Somewhere along the way I started calling them Possibilities, because it seemed like that's what they were – possible futures, possible lives. I had to call them something, and My Fucked Up Other Lives was too long.

Here's what I know. I've been killed 200 times, died in accidents 350 times, and died of natural causes 280 times. I've been married 60 times, never to the same woman, had 55 children, 40 grandchildren, 30 great grandchildren, 13 great grandchildren, and even one great-great-grandchild. And none of them exist, except in my memories.

Which brings you up to date, more or less. You're probably wondering why I didn't let Cat in the second time. I mean, apart from the pepper spray it was a pretty good day. But here's the problem. What happens to me isn't a *Groundhog Day* situation. It's way worse. If I'd let Cat in the door, everything would be different, every fifty-fifty decision might have changed, even one different decision would alter everything, which means Cat wouldn't be Cat.

Going down the same road twice leads to heartache. Going down the same road a hundred times is masochism. I'd learnt that the hard way, over and over. I haven't given up on life, but when you can't figure out what's real and what's not, you either try hard or you don't try at all.

Home life

When she came home the evening after Cat came to the door for the second time – or the first time for her, it gets a little foggy sometimes – I caught Emily giving me some strange looks.

She was in her travelling gym gear; Thursday night is spin class straight after work. Emily worked hard to maintain her body, and even though I'm her friend, and nothing sexual would ever happen between us, damn she was smoking hot. She would have put a hundred percent into her workout, then showered, reapplied light make up, and put on her travelling gear. There wasn't a lot of difference between her actual workout clothes and those she travelled home in, except one was sweaty and smelly while the other could have been pulled straight off a shop shelf. I'd asked her about it once and she'd replied there was no sense working on the chassis if the paintwork was rubbish – we'd been watching a car show at the time.

In keeping with the workout mode, her long brown hair was loosely held in a ponytail. Coloured, manicured nails sat on the end of ringless fingers. And underneath the well-maintained exterior was a warm, funny, caring woman who loved trashy reality shows. Despite having a job that allowed her to afford better accommodation, with a better class of roommate, she stuck it out with me.

She disappeared into her bedroom while I chopped vegetables for dinner. Emily had many wonderful qualities but she was a shit cook, so I did most of the dinners – and the dishes, and more than my share of the cleaning as well, if we're honest.

By the time she reappeared, wearing her at-home clothes of tracksuit pants, faded T-shirt and fluffy slippers, the vegetables were sautéing.

'Anything exciting happen today?' she asked casually as she snagged a piece of carrot that hadn't made it to the pan.

'Like what?' I responded innocently.

She poured herself a glass of red wine from the bottle that lived on the bench, a 2013 Merlot – apparently a very good year, though since I was a non-wine drinker that meant nothing to me. 'I don't know,' Emily said. 'Did you win Lotto? Meet a new girl? Invent a self-cleaning toilet?'

'Some girl came to the front door this morning.' She tensed and I stifled a smile. I badly wanted to play a bit but decided to let her off the hook. 'I think she was selling something, so I slammed the door in her face. Apart from that, just a normal day. What about you?'

I caught her relieved look reflected in the microwave door. She spent the next twenty minutes telling me how she'd nailed a presentation at work in front of her boss, her boss's boss, and some new guy called Austin.

It was a safe bet we'd never talk about what almost happened. Since I hadn't let Cat into the house I wasn't technically supposed to know about the arrangement, so I couldn't say anything without a lot of difficult questions. You can see how this sort of existence can mess you up.

I figured there would be a few days' grace before she moved on to the next grand scheme to fix me.

Brushing my teeth before bed, I paused to stare at myself in the mirror. I don't know why I told Cat the story about the sun and the moon. It was the first thing to pop into my head.

Only maybe I did know.

In my bedroom I sat on the bed and studied the canvas leaning against the corner wall. It was thirty by forty centimetres – big enough to be visible, not so big it automatically drew your attention when you entered the room. It should be in the closet, or the rubbish, or at the very least turned to face the wall. But I couldn't do any of those things. It was penance for thinking there could be a happy ever after.

The one where I went for a walk

I've always been fascinated by hills. Sometimes I'll look at a hill and get an overwhelming urge to find out what's on the other side. Wellington is surrounded by hills – in fact the whole of New Zealand is never far from a pile of dirt. When I step outside my front door the first thing I see is a hill taunting me with the mystery of the unknown. Or at the very least providing an obstacle between me and a decent hot chocolate.

Most of the time I ignore the taunts, but a few days after Cat's visit I went for a walk. The house down the road was half painted in bright green. Because I'd never left the flat that morning the decision had obviously gone the other way.

When I got over the first hill there was another one, so I kept going. But over that hill was another one, so my feet kept moving. And when I got to where I should have stopped I didn't. And suddenly it was early afternoon and I was thirty kilometres from home with sore feet, and a stomach protesting louder with every step further away from breakfast.

When I stopped, it was on the side of a motorway, traffic hurtling past at bone-crushing speeds, each car seeming to snatch away my discarded thoughts. I was debating whether to turn back or keep going, but ultimately it was more than that. One way represented acceptance of my life, for what it was, the other way the unknown. Of course my whole life is unknown but I could either go looking for it or wait for it to come to me. Every passing car took with it a changed decision.

Whoosh – turn back.

Whoosh – keep going.

Whoosh – turn back.

Whoosh – keep going.

In the end the police officer made up my mind. She spotted me a hundred metres out, flicked on her lights and pulled onto the shoulder of the road. I waited as she got out of the car and approached in that openly friendly but slightly guarded way the police have as they're trying to figure out if you're a lunatic or not. I put on my best I'm-not-crazy smile but she stopped a few feet away.

'Hi, there.'

'Afternoon, officer,' I replied politely.

'Everything okay, sir?'

I appreciated the courtesy but it seemed wrong to be called sir by someone older than me, even if it was only a couple of years.

'Fine, thanks. Just out for a walk.'

A large truck whipped past fast enough to rock her on her feet, and she raised her eyebrows at me. 'Not the best place for a walk, sir,' she offered.

I didn't answer, waiting to see which way this was going to go.

'Can I ask where you're heading?'

I considered the question, and discarded *Fucked if I know*. 'North,' was all I could come up with.

'North is a big place,' she replied.

'It's only a walk, officer.'

She nodded slowly. 'Could I see some ID please?' she asked in a polite way that wasn't really asking.

I pulled out my wallet and handed over my driver's licence. She sized me up against my photo, then asked me to wait. A car shot past, teenagers in school uniforms yelling something out the window that was instantly lost on the wind. I waved anyway.

The officer returned and handed me back the licence. 'It's not safe on this stretch of road, Mr Messer. Can I suggest you think about an alternative route if you're going to continue your journey…north?'

She said the last word with a hint of a smile. It seemed like she was mocking me.

I decided to continue walking. 'Thank you, officer.'

I waited until she'd driven away before pulling out my phone and texting Emily. Otherwise she'd worry even more than normal.

About thirty minutes later I saw two figures in the distance. As the metres between us diminished I could see they were both women. One of them was bent over doing something with her backpack. The other was tall, slightly overweight, with short dark hair and a pretty face that was made less so by her mouth working at a piece of chewing gum. She saw me approaching and said something to her friend who straightened up and turned around.

My stride faltered for a moment. It was Cat.

It wasn't the first time I'd come across people I'd met in a Possibility. I don't know what the statistical probability is, but the real world term for it is 'shit happens'. Still, it seemed strange to come across her again so soon. The look on her face said she recognised me but wasn't sure where from. Even so, I was preparing to walk past when she stopped me.

'Do you know anything about backpack straps?'

'I haven't had any professional training, but I've seen several documentaries on the subject.'

Cat grinned. Her friend obviously didn't share her enthusiasm for my humour.

'Can you take a look at this for us?' she asked. 'There's some' – she dug around in her jacket pocket and pulled out a chocolate bar – 'slightly warm chocolate in it for you.'

I held up my hand. 'As a non-professional I'd have the unions down on me like a ton of bricks if I accepted payment. But I'll take a look for you.'

She gave me the smile I'd spent a whole day admiring. Her backpack was old and worn, and had so many patches I wasn't sure if they were decoration or holding it all together. One of the strap buckles hung by a thin piece of material. There was no way it would support any weight, especially not the stuffed-to-overflowing load the backpack currently contained. I set to work trying to fix it.

'So where are you heading?' her friend asked.

'North.'

'What does that mean?'

'It doesn't mean anything,' I informed her. 'It's a direction.'

Cat laughed. 'Emily warned me about your sense of humour.'

I looked up at her.

Her friend grabbed her arm. 'Wait, you know this guy?'

Cat winked at me. 'Not really, but from what I saw he does have a pretty big penis.'

I winked back at her as her friend choked on her gum. Cat smacked her on the back a couple of times until a small clump launched from her throat, missing my head by millimetres.

'Christ, E, are you trying to kill me?'

'Sorry, Trace. I mean, I didn't see all of it but it looked pretty big.'

'Can you stop talking about the man's penis!'

'Show her, Troy.'

'Please don't show me, Troy.'

'If I had a dollar for every time a woman asked me not to show her my penis…'

'You'd have a dollar?' Cat quipped.

I laughed and continued trying to fix the bag. Eventually I stood up. 'All done.'

'You fixed it?' Cat asked hopefully.

'Nope, I've got no idea how to fix it, but I'm done.'

She nodded. 'Well, at least you met my expectations,' she said.

'I do have two options for you though,' I told her.

She waited.

'Number one, get less stuff.'

She shook her head. 'What's number two?'

'Use the other shoulder.'

'Thanks, you've been a great help.'

'My pleasure, Cat.'

She looked at me quizzically.

'Who the hell is Cat?' her friend piped up.

I looked at her friend, then back to Cat. 'My mistake,' I shrugged.

'Good luck with north,' she said.

I started to tip an imaginary hat, like a mysterious cowboy from the Old West, then realised that would look dicky so instead turned and walked on.

'Freak,' I heard her friend mutter.

You have no idea, I thought.

Cat hadn't reacted when I called her that. I knew she wouldn't, as it was me who'd come up with it in the Possibility, but I still thought there might have been something. I've never met anyone like me. Or maybe I have and didn't know it.

I looked over my shoulder, they were about thirty metres behind me, getting into a beat-up white Ford. An old white guy with a neatly trimmed beard and glasses was driving. Absently I took note of the licence plate number. Cat waved as they drove past. I waved back and watched them until they drove around the corner.

Laughing at myself, I zipped up my jacket, took a step forward and blinked…

And the police officer put my licence into my outstretched hand. 'It's not safe on this stretch of road, Mr Messer. Can I suggest you think about an alternative route if you're going to continue your journey…north?'

I stared at my hand, waiting for memories to click back into place. Then put my licence back into my wallet, and watched as she walked back to her car, indicated and pulled out into traffic. I pulled out my phone and texted Emily. She was used to me disappearing every now and then but I always tried to let her know what I was doing.

About an hour later a beat-up white Ford passed me with Cat in the passenger seat and her friend in the back. Like I said, nothing is ever exactly the same.

Sometime later I side-tracked into a rest stop; my feet, unaccustomed to continuous walking, were starting to make me regret the rash decision of this morning. Every step sent little signals of pain to my brain. The rest stop was empty, so I sat down at the single wooden table and watched the traffic for a while.

A few minutes later a car pulled in and came to a stop a few metres away. Two kids spilled from the back, while a man climbed from the driver's seat and stretched his back. On the other side of the car a woman got out and opened the boot, pulling out what looked like a picnic basket. She looked around her, then over at the table. I flashed her a grin, pulled myself up, and gestured for them to have the table. She gave me a grateful look before going back to wrangling things from the boot.

I wandered over to the wire fence separating the rest stop from a field of cows, leant on a fencepost and thought about the simplicity of being a cow. Where all you needed to be happy was some grass, and occasionally have your teats pulled. I became aware of another presence. She was young, more than six and less than ten. She wore black shorts, a white T-shirt with a horse on it, and a faded blue baseball cap.

'What's your favourite song?' she demanded.

'I don't really have one,' I responded.

She looked less than impressed.

'What's yours then?' I asked.

'"True Colours" by Cyndi Lauper,' she said firmly.

I was surprised. 'Nothing by Beyoncé or Katy Perry?'

She shook her head. 'They're good, but my absolute favourite, the one I love more than any other song in the history of songs, is "True Colours" by Cyndi Lauper.'

'Why?' I found myself curious.

She shrugged. 'It makes me feel good about myself.'

'Good for you,' I replied for lack of anything else to say.

She came up to the fence and looked into the field. 'They're cows.'

'Yes,' I said.

'I thought you were looking at something interesting.'

'I like cows. They know who they are, there're no surprises in life.'

'Until someone shoots them and turns them into McDonalds,' she reasoned.

'I suppose.'

'I mean, someone coming up and shooting you with a gun would be pretty surprising.'

'I expect so.'

She lapsed into silence, having exhausted her opinion on the life and death of cows. 'Do you think it hurts?' she asked.

'What?'

'Dying.'

That's a pretty deep question,' I told her.

'Do you?' she insisted.

I thought about all the times I've died. There was no simple answer. 'I don't know.'

'Of course you don't,' she dismissed me.

'Do you often have these types of conversations with complete strangers?'

'Debbie! Leave the man alone and come and eat your lunch.'

We both looked over to where her mother was waiting at the table, a slightly anxious look on her face. Debbie's father and a boy of about four sat at the table already, faces screwed up in concentration at the food in front of them.

'Am I bothering you?' Debbie asked.

I shook my head.

'What's your name?'

I told her.

'Troy doesn't mind,' she yelled across to her mum.

'I think your mum wants you to stop talking to me.'

'She's okay. If you try anything she'll tell Dad and he'll get his cricket bat from the car and beat you up.'

'Oh,' I said, bemused.

'Only Dad has never been in a fight before so I don't think he'd actually do it.'

'Good to know.'

'I'd be more scared of Mum,' she said matter-of-factly.

'She'll beat me with a cricket bat?'

She laughed. 'No, that'd be silly.'

I pretended to be relieved.

'She's a nationally ranked mixed martial artist.'

I glanced across at Mum, looking properly for the first time. The way she moved was confident, deliberate; I believed the girl. 'So what's with all the questions about death?' I asked.

'I'm nine,' she replied. 'That's what we do – ask questions. How old are you?'

'Twenty-five,' I replied. 'I think.'

She looked at me mockingly. 'You don't know?'

'It gets a little hazy sometimes.'

She looked out into the field of cows. For a moment I thought I'd frightened her off. A soft sound floated out to the world and I realised she was humming. It took me a while to figure out the song, and then I joined in on the chorus, our voices drifting out to our bovine audience.

She stopped singing and I turned to see her smiling. 'Most people your age don't know the words.'

'Most people your age don't know the song,' I pointed out.

'I guess we're not most people,' she grinned.

Kid, you have no idea.

'So why aren't you working?'

'I'm taking the day off,' I replied.

'What do you do?'

'I work in a bank.'

'Do you like it? It doesn't sound very exciting.'

'It's okay.'

She scrunched up her face. 'I'd be bored. I hate maths.'

'What are you going to do when you grow up?'

She looked at me like I was an idiot. 'I don't know, that's tomorrow's problem. Where's your car?'

'Don't have one.'

'Then how will you get where you're going?' she asked, puzzled.

'You ask a lot of questions.'

'I'm nine, remember?'

'Debbie, lunch, now!' her mother called.

She gave a lazy wave of acknowledgement. 'Do you want to have lunch with us?'

Hell, yes, said my stomach. 'No, thanks, I'd better get going.'

Not bothered either way, she skipped back over to the picnic table. I looked at the field but the cows no longer held the same attraction. With a sigh I turned to leave. Debbie was standing right behind me.

'Here,' she said thrusting out a chocolate biscuit. Before I could say thanks she turned and ran back to her family, who were doing their best not to study me intently. I tipped the chocolate biscuit at them by way of thanks, felt like a complete nob, so took a bite and continued on my way north.

I got twenty metres.

Behind me a commotion broke out. For several more steps I ignored it. Then Debbie's mum screamed her name. Spinning around, I captured the scene in one blink; Debbie slumped over the table, mother shaking her, her father rushing around the table with a look of confused terror on his face. Instantly I was on the move, covering the distance in seconds.

'What's wrong?' I asked.

'I don't know. She was talking. Then she let out a cry and slumped over. Oh, God, I don't think she's breathing!' the mum cried.

Instinct kicked in, forgotten knowledge tumbling forward and clicking into place. I snatched Debbie from her mother's arms, swept the picnic table with my arm, scattering food and plates, and dropped her onto the cleared surface. Her breathing came in ragged bursts, her limbs limp, head drooping to one side.

'Debbie!' I called. No response. 'Is she allergic to anything?'

'No, I don't think so,' her mum replied.

I peeled her eyelid back and the pupil contracted; a good sign. I prised her mouth open but it was empty. My eyes scanned her arms – nothing. Her legs – nothing. Wait, there was something on her left leg below the knee. I looked closer; it was a raised bump surrounded by red skin. 'Has she ever been stung before?'

'Stung? You mean by a bee?' her dad asked in confusion.

Not bothering to respond, I peered closer and saw the ragged edge of a stinger protruding from the bump. Using the edge of my fingernail, I scraped the stinger out and wiped it on the side of the table.

'What's going on?' her mum asked fearfully.

'Call an ambulance. When they answer tell them exactly what I say.' In my peripheral I saw her dad fumble a phone from his pocket and push buttons. Meanwhile I bent Debbie's legs to aid her blood pressure, then felt for her pulse. I didn't need to count to know it was way too fast. She needed a shot of adrenalin, which I didn't have, and a way to keep her airway open, which I was lacking.

'What do I say?' Her dad cut into my thoughts.

'Tell them there's a nine-year-old Caucasian female who has been stung by a bee and is presenting with the symptoms of anaphylactic shock.'

'Oh, my God,' her mum cried. Her dad stared at me.

'Tell them, goddamn it!'

He relayed the information.

I looked around. 'Give me your jersey,' I ordered Debbie's mum. She stripped it off and I snatched it from her, wrapping it over and around Debbie as well as I could.

'They said an ambulance is on its way but it'll be at least fifteen minutes,' her dad told me.

Shit. If she didn't get proper treatment in the next thirty minutes she could be dead. It was going to be tight. 'Where are they coming from?'

'I...I don't know. I think they said Paraparaumu.'

My mind raced with options, thoughts coming as quickly as the beats of her overworked heart. 'Call them back. Tell them we'll meet them halfway.'

'Shouldn't we wait?'

'She doesn't have time.'

'How do you know? Are you a doctor? Maybe you're wrong,' her dad argued.

'You look too young to be a doctor,' her mum interjected.

'I used to be older,' I snapped back. Just then the pulse under my fingertips stuttered and stopped. Out of time. Shit. I glanced at my watch, then put my hand on her chest and started compressions.

'What are you doing?' came her mother's voice.

'Her heart has stopped,' I replied without looking up. 'Now shut up, I'm counting.' And focusing. CPR on a child is mostly the same as for an adult, but you need to be careful not to apply too much pressure or you'll snap their ribs. When I got to a hundred I tilted her head back, pinched her nose shut and breathed into her mouth. Her chest barely rose, which meant her throat was constricting. Fuck, where the hell was the ambulance? Start again. Hand on chest, one, two, three. Work up to thirty. Breath. Repeat. Again. Again.

Somewhere outside the scope of my immediate world came the sounds of a vehicle pulling up, and suddenly two people were next to me.

'What have we got?' A firm, professional voice.

'She went into cardiac arrest – ' I looked at my watch with my free hand ' – ten minutes ago. Her airway is restricted. She needs a shot of adrenalin and the AED.'

'Okay, buddy, we've got it.' Someone pushed me to the side and took over, while a second paramedic put an oxygen mask over her face. As they worked on her I took a step back, suddenly aware of the sweat dripping down my back, arms aching, my own breath coming in short gasps.

I took another step back as they continued to work. A voice came out of the throng proclaiming the resumption of a pulse. Without a word I turned and left the rest stop.

Two hours later I stepped into a takeaway shop in a small town. I ordered two cheese burgers, fries, and the biggest milkshake within a hundred kilometres – at least according to the sign above the door. After the first couple of sips I found out why they didn't brag about the quality of the shake. It was so bad I couldn't even think of the words to describe its terribleness. Luckily the burgers redeemed the place. They were huge, packed full of meat, avocado, lettuce, beetroot, onions and cheese. I ate them outside the shop sitting at a rickety metal table with one leg slightly shorter than the others – which was okay because the metal chairs, which seemed solely designed to become unbearably uncomfortable after ten minutes, were also on a lean, so the whole thing worked out.

As I ate, I replayed the rest-stop incident, looking for things I'd done wrong, scratching through Possibility memories to see if there was anything more I could have done. I was pretty sure Debbie was going to be fine. She'd have to take an epinephrine pen everywhere with her for the rest of her life, but that was better than dead. I'm not a doctor, had never been one, but in one of the Possibilities I'd been a paramedic. Sometimes this thing I have pays off, but not often enough to make up for the shitty reality of it.

I ate my unbelievably good burgers and drank my undeniably bad shake and watched life settle for the night. Traffic dwindled as people went home to their families; the only cars belonged to those driving through on their way to somewhere more important. The town they left in their rear-vision mirror had seen better days – the shop fronts were clean but worn, with window frames cracked and faded. The main road stretched fifty metres in each direction, shops bleeding seamlessly into houses with wooden fences in need of painting and short grass. It was early springtime, the evening still and warm. The place felt peaceful, like big cities didn't exist. Like I could spend the rest of my life here, maybe open a small bakery, marry a local girl and raise a family. And then a car whipped past, way too fast, heading south. I glimpsed the licence plate. It was the same one that had given Cat and Trace a lift earlier. I couldn't tell if they were in the car or not. Frowning, I tried to get back the peaceful feeling but it had vanished. With a sigh, I got to my feet, waved to the woman behind the counter, and continued on my way. North.

I walked until it was too dark to keep going, then jumped the fence into a field and made a bed under a clump of trees, out of sight of the road. The only sound was the occasional car. The cloudless sky pricked with pinhole lights and the moon was a slivered hint of its full potential. It wasn't true I didn't care about anything. There was a short list of things that mattered to me. Despite being physically exhausted sleep refused to come. My brain, long considered by my parents to be underutilised, and unreliable at the best of times, flicked through random images like a silent movie. It took me a while to understand they were fragments of Possibilities. The weight of all those deaths, my deaths, pressed down on me like wet mud. The air thickened into treacle and I gasped for breath. My face became wet with tears. A guttural sound escaped from my mouth. In the dark a cow responded and the absurdity of it all saw my tears give way to laughter, and somewhere mid-laugh I drifted to sleep.

I woke up at six, hungry and sore and with a dog licking my face. Accompanying the border collie was a farmer, who politely and with the minimal amount of swearing, suggested I move on. I took a moment to pat the dog, stretch out the kinks in my neck and back, then climbed back over the fence onto the side of the road, with a decision to make. Keep going north, or turn around and head back home? Sometime in the night Emily had sent a text message telling me to call her. I'd do it later. I decided to keep going.

The sun bled around the edges of high clouds and the air was crisp without being cold. Despite the early hour a steady stream of traffic flowed in both directions, evenly spaced like a beating heart. After a while it became hypnotic, step, car, step, car. My brain switched off.

Around two hours later I came to a small town; if there's one thing that's not in short supply in New Zealand it's small towns. Like all towns it had a couple of cafés on the main road. Since I was tired and hungry I picked one at random and went inside. The blackboard menu was surprisingly sophisticated, although experience taught me that food doesn't always match up to the description. I figured it was safe to order eggs on toast, poached, brown bread, with a side of bacon. And coffee. The biggest cup they had. Not fancy stuff –

nothing with a picture of a fern lovingly carved into the surface, or with the words flat or long in the title – just coffee, black and hot.

I sat down at a free table by the front window. I liked to watch the world, especially when it wasn't watching me. Not much was happening so early in the morning. Every now and then a car would stop outside the dairy opposite and a figure would hurry inside, reappearing moments later with milk, or bread, or a newspaper. The sign above the dairy door announced it had been in business since 1957. There were few pedestrians, most lost in their own worlds, focusing on the few feet in front of them.

When my breakfast arrived the portions were generous, but the eggs were too runny and the toast overcooked. Still, I was hungry so I ate it anyway. As the last forkful disappeared into my mouth I spotted a figure out of the corner of my eye. A boy, maybe ten or eleven, carrying a naggingly familiar backpack. The kid disappeared into the dairy. By the time he came out again I was across the road waiting for him. On closer inspection it didn't just look like Cat's. It was Cat's.

'Hey,' I called out softly. His eyes met mine, with a mixture of guilt and defiance. He wore a school uniform, but the untucked shirt and scuffed shoes suggested he wasn't happy about it.

'What?' came the cautious response.

'Where'd you get the bag?'

'It's mine.' He clutched the shoulder strap tighter.

I shook my head. 'No, it's not.'

'Says you.'

'You either tell me, or tell the cops.'

His eyes shifted, weighing up the options, eyeing me to gauge his chances of running for it. Then he relaxed and shrugged, an easy comes easy goes type of thing. 'I didn't nick it. I found it,' he said defiantly.

'Where?'

'In a ditch outside town. I didn't steal it. No one was around.'

'Are you sure?'

He nodded vigorously, suddenly the helpful Samaritan. 'Yeah. I thought someone lost it so picked it up.'

'And you were on your way to hand it in to someone.'

'Yep.'

'Where outside town?'

He told me. I held my hand out for the backpack and he reluctantly handed it over. I shouldered it, then held my hand out again. He stared blankly for a moment, then sighed and pulled a wallet out of his trouser pocket. I recognised it from the Possibility, when Cat bought me coffee.

'Can I go?' the kid asked nervously.

I waved my hand and he took off down the street. Cat's wallet felt warm, probably from his pocket, but it was light. I opened it. The only thing inside was a bank card, the sort that didn't have a name on it. I was pretty sure there should have been more.

I pulled out my phone and called the police. I should have done it because I was worried for her – something major must have happened for the backpack to be in the ditch – but the truth is I did it because my parents had ingrained in me a sense of doing the right thing, and some things don't die.

I didn't give them my name, and I couldn't give them Cat's since I didn't know it. Instead I said I'd seen her hitchhiking yesterday, and explained where it had been found, and on a hunch the licence plate of the white car. I laid it on a bit thick with the car. It might have nothing to do with it, but it made a good story, and got the appropriate response from the police. They promised to send a car straight away and I promised to stay where I was. So I left the backpack with the dairy owner, advising him the police were on their way, and kept going north, barely pausing when I passed the ditch.

That night I stayed in a motel. One night under the stars was enough. When I flicked on the TV the news had just started, the lead story being about the arrest of a fifty-four-year-old male for the murder of two female hitchhikers. I should have cared, but I didn't. So why were there tears on my face? Some days it was harder to fool myself than others. I blinked away the tears.

And stood on the side of the road. Cars whipped past in their steady rhythm. About ten metres ahead Cat and her friend were on the side of the road playing with her backpack. As I watched, the white car pulled over in front of them. I could hear her friend urging her to hurry. I broke into a run and passed them as they got to the car's rear bumper. Pulling the passenger door open I leaned in. The guy gave a startled cry and jerked backwards, banging his head on the window. Cat's friend let out a frustrated yell, thinking I was stealing their ride.

'I know what you are,' I glared at the man. His angry retort stalled on his lips as he looked deep into my eyes. 'And I know where to find you,' I added with menace. Fear flooded his face. I straightened up and barely had time to slam the door before he stepped on the pedal and swerved back into the traffic.

'What the hell! That was our ride,' the friend said – I couldn't remember her name.

'You'll get another one,' I reassured her.

'What's your fucking problem?'

I stayed silent.

'Do you know how far we have to go? He was the first car to stop for us. Fuck.'

'Relax, Trace,' Cat said.

'Relax!' her friend spluttered.

Cat stared at me, then she winked and smiled. 'If you're trying to pick us up you're not off to a good start.'

'Nope,' I replied.

'Pick us up? He's a fucking jerk.'

'Yeah, but he has a big dick.'

Trace's face turned purple.

'Sorry, Trace. I mean, it's not the biggest I've seen, but overall it's pretty big.'

'Can you stop talking about the man's penis!' Tracey begged.

'Show her, Troy.'

'Please don't show me, Troy. Wait, you know this guy?'

'If I had a dollar for every time a woman asked me not to show her my penis…' I offered.

'You'd have a dollar?' Cat quipped.

'Actually two,' I replied.

She smiled that smile I remembered, and I wished for the millionth time that my existence was anywhere close to normal.

'Hitchhiking is dangerous. Take care, Cat.'

'Cat? Who the hell is Cat?' her friend interrupted.

Cat held my gaze and nodded slightly. 'Cat. I like it. See you around, Troy. Come on, Trace.' She grabbed her friend's arm and they moved off. Her friend almost fell over with shock when I rushed past them.

The trouble with rest stops is they all look alike, but I was pretty sure I found the right one. Then I settled down to wait, patiently at first, then more anxiously as time crept past. I paced back and forth, glancing at the road expectantly with the sound of every car engine. Time approached, then receded into the past. No car, no Debbie with her family.

Maybe they left home five minutes later, maybe they stopped earlier, or decided to keep going. All those decisions changed. I didn't even know her full name – no way to track the family down and warn them of her condition. This is my reality.

I turned and headed home. Running away wasn't working, it never did.

I never found out if she was okay.

The one where I went to a show

A few weeks later Emily dragged me to the theatre. Not the good sort of theatre, with popcorn and ice-cream, and previews of upcoming attractions. The boring sort where you got to watch people with day jobs feed their secret desires for fame and fortune.

Unfortunately, Emily shot down all my protests, demanded I get dressed up, and triumphantly shepherded me out the front door. I didn't even know where we were going or what the show was until we arrived. Its name, *The Hard Way*, meant nothing to me, and neither did any of the names in the programme. The place was packed – mostly with friends and family, I thought vindictively, then wondered which one Emily was. I scanned the programme again, but before I could ask her the lights went down and murmured conversation gave way to expectant silence.

It turned out the play was about some guy packing up the house of his dead father. Over the course of the morning all these people arrive who know the father better than the son did. I don't remember much about who they were, or how the story ended, because about ten minutes in I stopped paying attention. That's when the character of Jasmine came onto the stage. There was something familiar about her, but I couldn't pick it. Before she could say her first line she turned to face the audience, and her face fell into shadow, light filtering through strands of hair. It seemed like she was looking straight at me, into me. It was Cat. I stole a sideways look at Emily, but her focus remained on the stage. Was this a set-up or a coincidence? Experience made me more inclined to believe it was the former.

Cat was good, really good. She commanded attention.

'I work in a library. There are literally thousands of books sitting on those shelves. And a huge number of them never leave. They're forgotten stories, waiting for an audience that in some cases never comes. They sit day after day, gathering dust, and once a year I have to take those books down from the shelves and give them one more chance to live, one more chance to fulfil their purpose, to be read by someone, to be loved by someone. And if no one wants them, they get destroyed, forgotten…' When she broke down in tears, a lump formed in my throat.

At the interval I checked the programme. Jasmine was played by Elissa Sanders.

'The girl who plays Jasmine – I think she's the one who came to our door the other morning.'

Emily attempted innocence. 'Oh?'

'Do you know her?'

'Sure – we work at the SPCA together. She told me she was in a play so I said I'd come and watch.'

'Did you also tell her you were dragging your flatmate along under duress?'

'Are you saying you're not enjoying it?'

I clamped my mouth shut and turned away.

She laughed. 'Exactly.'

'Shut up,' I sulked.

'She's cute,' Emily observed, and when I didn't answer she prodded. 'Don't you think?'

'She's all right – for a crazy woman.'

Emily turned to study me. 'What makes you think she's crazy?'

'She's friends with you, isn't she?'

'So are you,' she pointed out.

'I've never said I wasn't crazy.'

'So you'll have things to talk about later.'

'Later?' I asked with a sinking feeling.

'When we meet her at the pub,' Emily replied smugly, further conversation cut off by the lights dimming.

'Bitch,' I muttered. She patted my arm in silent victory.

The rest of the play was pretty good, I think, but I was still fuming over Emily's upcoming attempt to set me up with her friend.

After the applause died down we shuffled outside and stood amongst the mingling crowd. As it began to thin out, a side door burst open and Cat spilled out into the foyer. Despite knowing her real name now, the rebellious child inside me refused to use it, preferring to think of her as someone from a Possibility rather than the real person standing in front of me.

'What did you think?' she demanded of Emily, full of adrenalin from the performance.

'Magic.'

They hugged, then she turned to me. 'Come here.' She grabbed my hand and led me across to the exit she'd come out of, where she positioned me on one side and told me to knock on the door. Then she went through and closed it. Confused, I knocked on the door. It immediately opened.

'No,' Cat said, then slammed the door shut again. I guess I deserved that.

It instantly opened again and she grinned at me. 'Now that's out of the way, let's get a drink.'

Emily looked bewildered. I said I'd explain later.

The nearest pub was a five-minute walk. Cat walked between us, talking non-stop about the performance, relating how the director had panicked due to one of the actors being five minutes late, and how the prop doorbell had malfunctioned. None of which had been apparent to the audience.

The bar was half full, not bad for 9.30 on a Thursday night. The girls found a table while I ordered the drinks – vodka for me, gin for Emily, red wine for Cat. For the next half-hour conversation and alcohol flowed in equal parts. Cat was as intriguing as I remembered, but of course I wasn't supposed to know that so I pretended we were meeting properly for the first time.

Despatched back to the bar for the last refill before home time, I sensed someone step up beside me.

'Hi, Troy.'

I looked around and internally cringed. Standing next to me was a tall brunette. Jennifer was one of the girls Emily tried setting me up with. It wasn't until after we slept together that I realised she was completely bat-shit crazy. The morning after she'd started talking about love at first sight, and meeting her parents. It had taken some fast talking, and changing my cell phone number, to extract myself from the situation. It'd been eight months, and she didn't look happy to see me.

'Hi, Jennifer.' I flicked a desperate look over to our table, but the girls were deep in conversation.

'How've you been?'

I offered a non-committal response, hoping to end it before we got in too deep.

'You know I loved you, Troy.'

Too late. 'You didn't really know me Jennifer.'

'I knew enough. Sometimes the connection between two people is instant.' She reached over and placed her hand on top of mine.

I gently pulled it away.

'You can't deny there was something between us. The sex was amazing,' she argued.

Actually the one time we had sex was pretty great, but any future attempts were stalled by her already picking out her wedding dress. I hadn't needed a Possible future to tell me it was going to end badly. 'Look, Jennifer, it's nice seeing you, but I have to get back to my friends.'

She grabbed my hand again. It was like having an eagle land on you, talons digging into flesh like a dead rabbit.

'Don't deny you loved me. I saw it in your eyes.'

Surely all she saw in my eyes was panic. Suddenly I felt a hand on my shoulder and I was spun around. There was a sharp crack and my head snapped sideways.

'You bastard,' Cat said. 'You think you can get me pregnant and then go and chat up any slut you meet?'

'I…I…um…'

'Save your smooth talk. I can't believe I fell for all your lines.'

'Who are you calling a slut?' Jennifer demanded.

'Save it, lady. This guy promised to marry me, got me pregnant, and is now trying to weasel out of it.' Her nostrils flared, eyes glared at me, and for a second I thought maybe we had slept together. Over her shoulder I could see Emily staring in shock.

'Is that true, Troy?'

I looked between the two of them, matched expressions of outrage burning holes into my face. 'It must be,' I finally got out.

Cat turned her attention to Jennifer and offered a rueful smile. 'I'm sorry I called you a slut. It must be all the hormones inside me.' Damn if she didn't actually put her hand on her stomach. A bit overkill in my opinion.

'Of course. I didn't realise. I'm so sorry. I hope things work out for you two. I…' Jennifer stopped, clearly embarrassed. 'I think I should go.'

We watched as she scurried out the front door as quickly as she could.

Cat turned to me. 'Well?'

'Thanks,' I replied.

She snorted and shook her head slightly. 'Whatever. How was the acting?'

I rubbed the side of my face. 'Believable.'

She shifted uncomfortably, then reached up and kissed me on the cheek. 'Sorry about that,' she whispered, her warm breath caressing my skin.

'I'll forgive you.'

She stepped back and grinned.

'If you pay for this round,' I finished.

She took another step back and laughed. 'I'm a poor actor.'

'Just my luck,' I muttered, pulling my wallet out. The bartender winked at me as I shook my head.

'You know, you're pretty strong,' I told Cat as I set down the glasses.

'Damn straight. You probably could have handled it without me though.'

I shook my head. 'Nah, I'd rather run than fight.'

'Doesn't that get tiring? How do you know when to stop?'

I shrugged. 'I don't know.'

'How long have you been running?'

'About ten years,' I replied softly, drawing a sharp look from Emily.

Cat peered under the table.

'What're you doing?' Emily asked.

Cat winked at her. 'All that running –, he must have calves of steel. I look forward to seeing them.'

My face exploded with heat as I shifted my legs self-consciously. Cat just laughed.

We said our goodbyes on the footpath. Emily got a firm hug, I received a sketchy wave, before we climbed into cabs and went back to respective houses.

Along the way Emily turned to look at me. 'What do you think?'

'About?'

'The current economy, you moron. Elissa, of course.'

'She seems nice.'

Emily leaned back in the seat, eyes closed, a satisfied look on her face.

'But, Ems, nothing's going to happen.'

'We'll see,' she replied smugly.

'Ems! I'm telling you, nothing is going to happen. Yeah, she seems nice, but she's not interested and I'm not interested so nothing is going to come of you playing matchmaker.

'We'll see,' she repeated, and despite my continued protests she refused to talk about it any more.

That night I lay in my room thinking about Cat. I recalled her lying next to me, under me, the smell of her skin, the taste, and the warmth. My body reacted accordingly, but instead of giving in to basic urges I restlessly kicked the covers off, flicked on the light and paced the room. Something about this girl was getting under my skin.

My left hand itched. I glanced down in surprise. The last time it had done that I was fifteen years old and…I turned my attention to the canvas in the corner.

'Fuck that,' I said bitterly and drank myself to sleep.

The next weekend was my birthday. It's difficult to get truly excited about turning twenty-six when you've done it a few times, but for my parents it was a one-off so they insisted on celebrating.

Celebrating for Mum and Dad is dinner at their house, so luckily my birthday fell in February, and the weather was warm enough to barbecue. My mum is a brilliant baker, but her cooking lacked any imagination. Instead Dad would be let loose on the grill, where he would make my favourite – prawns in garlic sauce. This had stopped being my favourite dish about a hundred Possibilities ago, but Dad didn't know it, and never would.

Emily let me borrow her car, and as I was walking to it I came across the couple from down the road. They were standing outside their bright-green house having an argument about the letterbox.

The woman snagged me by the arm. 'You, help us out. This one or this one?' She held up two pictures of letterboxes. 'This one is guaranteed to last ten years, and this one is likely to fall apart in two.' No prizes for guessing which one was her preference.

'That one,' I pointed to her option and she gave her husband a triumphant look.

Mum had ordered me to come around at 3pm on the Sunday to help in the garden before dinner. She was in the kitchen when I arrived, icing some homemade biscuit fudge – still my favourite despite all the Possibilities. I watched her for a moment. Mum was forty-nine years old, a tall, proud woman, slightly overweight, hair coloured brown to hide the greys. As always she wore a blouse, slacks and slippers. The slippers were black, paper thin, and older than me, well me in real life anyway.

'Hey, Mum.' I dutifully kissed her on the cheek.

'Your father is out the back. Can you go make sure he doesn't pull up too many flowers?' she replied absently.

'Sure.' I went out the back door, feeling her eyes on my back. It was a standard exchange between parent and child, repeated in countless homes across the world, but I knew it hurt her every time we did it. We'd been close, all three of us, and then one day things changed and she didn't know why.

'Hey, Dad.' I spotted him in the process of pulling up one of Mum's prize petunias.

He paused and wiped his face with the handkerchief that always sat in his left trouser pocket. He was overweight, a mirror image of Mum, with thinning hair cropped short, and thick-rimmed glasses. 'Hi, Troy. No Emily?'

'She's in Christchurch for work. You know you're pulling up Mum's pride and joy, right?'

He looked down at the half-manged bush in horror. 'Bugger. Help me put it back in.'

Dad hated gardening – to him it was a necessary chore – but he knew the consequences of pulling up the wrong thing. Between us we managed to repair it, although its chances of living were marginal. We spent the next two hours destroying weeds and by the time Dad called it quits I was sweaty and tired.

'Fire up the beast, Troy. I'll get the meat.' Dad disappeared through the back door while I uncovered the four-burner gas barbecue, nicknamed The Beast. It was immaculate, the grill lovingly cleaned after every use and the outside rubbed down with a damp cloth every day, even when it wasn't used. Some men going through midlife crises bought sports cars. My dad bought a barbecue.

I studied the backyard. This was the house I'd grown up in, spending lazy summer days playing cricket, or inventing games that I always won – my games, my rules. The house hadn't changed in twenty-five years, apart from a new paint job, but the backyard had tried out several looks during that time. My earliest memory was of a small vegetable patch in the back corner, a washing line, great for spinning around on, and grass covering everything else. As the years went by the vegetable patch got bigger, the clothes line was replaced by a retractable one, and the grass became patchier. Then one day, when I was eleven, I came home from school to find my mother ripping out all the vegetables and planting flowers. When I asked her why, she said she needed more beauty in her life. We ate mainly vegetables for a week. And I didn't really understand why, but there was a strained silence at dinner for a while.

In the past ten years of my real life the flower garden had gotten bigger, to the point it had taken over the entire backyard. I'm not a flower guy, but even I had to admit it's impressive – every summer an explosion of colour moving gently in the breeze. If you sat in the middle of the garden it was like all the world smelled sweet, the only sound an occasional bee lazily floating from flower to flower. I felt at peace here and would have come every day, except that would have meant seeing my parents. I've tried recreating the feeling in the backyard at our flat, but it's not the same.

Dad came back outside with the plate of prawns and as I watched him cook we went through the normal dance:

How's work? Fine.

And Emily? Good.

Did I have a girlfriend? No.

Did I have a boyfriend? I'm not gay, Dad.

You should call your mother more. I will.

He sought the answers my Mum wanted but without asking direct questions, because they wanted to know I was okay yet were afraid I wasn't.

Are you okay? Not really.

What's wrong? I think I'm crazy, but if I'm not then I have the ability to live multiple lives

Why are you so distant to your mother? Because I love her.

That's not an answer. It's just a phase, I don't mean it.

Because even if they asked the right questions there are some things I can't tell them. Which isolates me from the rest of the world. Because what I can't tell them – what they wouldn't understand – is that I love them more than anything. But with this thing I have that curses me to live Possibilities, in all those lives I've watched my mum and dad die over and over. After a long and fulfilled life, or brutally early, or losing the battle with illness – the how doesn't matter as much as the what.

I remembered the devastation of the first time. I was thirty-five when Mum succumbed to cancer. Standing next to Dad, hand on his shoulder, listening to friends, family, strangers talk about the wonderful person she was. Dealing with the aftermath, the kind words, the shaking heads, 'taken too soon,' comforting a grieving widower while dealing with my own emotions. The days that followed were filled with anger, and loss, and disbelief that one of the two constants in my life was gone.

Snapping back to my real life, seeing her for the first time again, alive, standing in her kitchen making biscuits, flour on her hands, a little smudge on her face. Looking at me with concern as I burst into tears. Then it happened again, and again. As a child you expect to outlive your parents, but when they die it leaves a hole. When they die repeatedly the hole stretches into a bottomless void that sucks your emotions in and leaves you with … this.

That's why I don't call Mum as much as I should – the pain of losing her all those times was too much.

The one with the birthday present

Emily's birthday is two weeks after mine, a fact that had been the source of many joint flat parties. Thanks to my meticulous planning and organisational skills, I left it up until 4pm on the day of her birthday before panicking about her present. With my birthday being first I had the benefit of gauging effort and cost from her before having to reciprocate. Unfortunately both were usually high. I think she did it on purpose, laying down the challenge. Thankfully I was usually up for it, but not without considerable angst. Every year I vowed to allow plenty of time, and every year I don't.

This year she bought me the latest book by Oliver Atkinson, my favourite author. And she'd had it signed by him, with a personal inscription. Bitch. How could a pair of gloves or some nail polish compare with that? To make it worse, this year was her thirtieth, so the stakes were even higher. Nothing good came from a birthday with a zero on the end, especially when you're the one who has to buy the present.

Adding more fuel to the train wreck that was my present-buying ability, Emily was back with her on-again off-boyfriend, so there was the minefield of buying something not too intimate, yet reflecting our friendship. In other words, I had no idea.

Which is why I was standing like a statue on the ground floor of the biggest department store in Wellington, debating whether to turn left to women's clothing, go straight to make up, right to household goods, or up the escalator to electronics. The choices were almost non-existent. Right would have gotten me slapped, up was too impersonal, straight was a road I didn't want to go down, so left it was.

I knew the sort of things she wore, so I wasn't starting completely from scratch. Yet it was still fraught with dangers.

'Can I help you?' The smartly dressed shop assistant in her early twenties made me feel old.

I told her I was looking for a birthday present and she nodded, like it was the only reason people came into the store. 'Girlfriend?'

'Friend.'

'Girl?'

I looked around me and she smiled. 'We're told never to make assumptions.'

'Yes, girl.'

'Are you close?'

'Yes.'

'What's your budget?'

'Enough to stop me seeming cheap, but less than an amount that makes me seem rich.'

She looked at me with renewed interest. 'Are you rich?'

'Is that relevant to buying a present?' I asked.

'It might be,' she flirted.

'I'm not rich, or in the market for anything more than a gift.'

I flattered myself she looked disappointed, but she continued to ask questions and we slowly narrowed the selections down to a black blouse that had faded patterns on the lapels. The price tag of $75 was smack bang in the middle of an appropriate price range.

'Come again,' the sales assistant said cheerfully.

I fully expected to, in exactly one year's time.

Emily took the package off me at her front door, smiling at the professional wrapping. She ushered me into the kitchen where her boyfriend Ben poured the wine. He gave me a guarded smile, untrusting of the single male constantly sniffing around his woman. Those were pretty much the exact words he'd said to me when he and Emily started dating. After rejecting several responses, including punching him in the face, I simply replied Emily was her own woman, not anybody else's. There'd been an uneasy truce since then. Every time they broke up he held me responsible, and every time they got back together he considered it a triumph over the evil friend secretly in love with her and trying to steal her away from him. In short, he was a dickhead. But Emily liked him, so I remained mostly supportive.

They'd moved in together six months ago, a move I was totally against because they'd only recently renewed their relationship – and because it meant I needed to get a new flatmate, which I'd failed so far to do. I think part of me was waiting for this thing to fail and for her to move back in.

'It's beautiful,' she declared, earning me a scowl from Ben. 'Very corporate.'

Dammit, I'd gone too conservative.

Ben handed me a wine, his smile warmer now. 'I bought her a necklace. Show him, babe.'

The thing I now noticed wrapped around her neck must have cost a fortune. When he looked away she gave me a wry look, and I rolled my eyes.

Dinner was pleasant enough – Italian food ordered in, which went well with the wine. As we were clearing the table after dessert Ben's cell phone went off. There was a brief unhappy conversation, the gist of it being that he had to go to work. He looked between Emily and me, torn between duty and insecurity. Duty won, but not without a fight.

'I'll drop you home, Troy,' he suggested brightly.

Emily slipped her arm through mine. 'No, you won't. We have to catch up. I'll see you later, Ben.'

He disappeared out the front door in a cloud of muttered protests and apologies.

'He means well,' she said once the front door closed.

'They always do, right up to the point where they cut you up and make a paperweight out of your skull.'

She punched me on the arm. 'My boyfriend is not a psychopath.' She gathered plates and started filling the sink.

'Seriously, what are you doing here, Ems?'

'I'm doing the dishes.'

'You don't do dishes,' I retorted.

'Things change. I'm a domestic goddess now.' She raised her yellow rubber gloves as proof.

I picked up the tea towel and waited expectantly. She looked down at the sink full of dishes and bubbles and sighed, then picked up the brush and began cleaning. 'Have you found a new flatmate?'

I took a plate from her and wiped it dry without answering.

'I'm not coming back, Troy. This thing with Ben is going to work out.'

Moodily I continued drying. 'What makes this time different?'

She paused and looked across at me. 'He loves me.'

'But do you love him?'

'He makes me feel good.'

'That's what I thought,' I said.

'Shut up,' she snapped.

So I did. It wasn't until the dishes were all done she spoke again. 'Do you remember when he first asked me out? I thought he was cute, but…'

'But what?' I prompted.

She gave me a thoughtful look. 'Sometimes I'm not sure whether I said yes because I liked him, or because I was pissed off at you.'

I stared at her in amazement.

'Oh, it wasn't anything you'd done in particular. But we'd been flatting together for years and I kept waiting for you to start living. To start showing me you would change. Do you remember what you got me for my birthday that year? A scarf.'

'I thought you liked the scarf.'

'I loved the scarf, but it was a scarf. It's one step up from socks or underwear. I wanted you to put some thought into it. I wanted you to show you cared about me. Cared about anything. And a scarf didn't cut it. So when Ben asked me out I figured, *What the hell, at least he cares about me.*'

'I do care about you,' I protested.

'With a scarf?'

'It was a nice scarf.'

'It was the sort of thing my mother would buy for me. I wanted you to get me something that showed you knew me.' She started pacing the floor.

'Why didn't you say anything?'

She laughed bitterly. 'I'd been trying to tell you for months. You obviously weren't listening.'

'Why haven't you said anything before now?' I asked defensively. 'I thought we were friends.'

'We are friends, Troy. You didn't piss me off – you disappointed me.'

I didn't want to hear any more, almost reached up to cover my ears. 'Sorry to disappoint you,' I said sullenly. 'I should go, before the guy you don't love comes home to the house you don't want to live in and makes you do more domestic things you hate.' It was petty, but I was hurting and embarrassed and pissed off. I ignored her calls and slammed the front door, not calming down until I came through my own front door and threw my shoes across the bedroom. A few swear words later I'd settled enough to realise I never felt angry in the first place, just guilty. Out of habit I looked at the corner of the room where the canvas used to be. I'd thrown it out a couple of years ago, but still found myself looking for it in moments of stress, or stupidity. Reaching for my phone, I thought about what to say as an apology. *I'm a dickhead* seemed to be a good start. I typed it in, and blinked...

And stood on the ground floor of the department store. My eyes, having come from bedroom light at night-time, strained against the sunlight pouring in through tall windows. I blinked a few times and they slowly adjusted.

The displays looked different; the clothes weren't the same. I pulled my phone out and saw I was back four years, it was 2016 – 4pm on Emily's birthday. Some things don't change. I had a do-over, but apart from knowing that she was reaching the end of her tether and about to start dating Mr Bland, and that I mustn't buy her a scarf, I didn't know much. Well, actually I knew a lot, but not the most important thing. What the hell to get her for a present?

I wracked my brain for ideas, trying to think of what I'd bought her in the past, both in real life and Possibilities. Inspiration remained elusive. I closed my eyes and tried to think of everything I knew about her. Frustratingly nothing leapt out with a big sign saying *Buy this for her*.

'If you're pretending to be a statue you're doing a great job.'

I opened my eyes to find Cat standing in front of me. Her hair was tied up and she wore a grey T-shirt and jeans.

'On the other hand, if you're trying to hide by being a statue then I'm sorry to tell you it isn't working.' She grinned and I felt my mouth respond.

'I'm looking for a birthday present for Emily.'

'Oh, what are you going to get her?'

'If I knew that I wouldn't be standing here,' I replied.

'Where would you be standing?'

'I wouldn't. I'd be walking.'

'Technically you have to stand to walk,' she pointed out.

'Why is it every time I talk to you I get a headache?'

She grinned again and I noticed the way her eyes sparked. Dammit, stop it.

I asked, 'What are you doing here anyway? Are you stalking me?'

She casually looked around then leaned in closer. 'You wish,' she whispered.

I didn't know how to respond so I just gaped at her.

'Take a picture,' she advised me. 'It'll last longer.'

Something tickled the back of my brain and I tried to tease it out, but it remained elusive. Something to do with Emily – something she said, or did, back in school.

An idea came to me. 'I need a computer.'

'Wow, that's an expensive present.'

I kissed her on the forehead. 'Thanks, Cat.' Spinning around, I headed back to work. Hopefully there was enough time to get everything sorted.

Later, after we'd eaten large servings of Emily's favourite meal of homemade cheesecake with red wine – it was the one time a year she didn't give a shit about diet – I handed her a plain white envelope. She looked at me questioningly, obviously wondering where the real present was, and I gestured for her to open it.

Inside was the obligatory funny birthday card, and inside that a single sheet of A4 paper, folded into thirds. She smoothed it out and read it, then reread it, before looking at me with curiosity. 'What made you think of this?'

'I remembered that you were into photography at school. I thought it might be something you could get back into.'

She looked back down at the paper, momentarily lost for words.

'And I wanted to let you know that I know,' I said, and when she gave me a puzzled look added, 'That sometimes it's not easy living with me. I wanted to give you something that showed…'

She nodded in understanding. 'It's lovely,' she said softly.

'Promise me you won't turn into some artist type who's always talking about light and composition,' I said to lighten the mood.

'We could become a bohemian flat. I'll turn your bedroom into a darkroom.'

'Where am I going to sleep?' I protested.

'No time for sleep – you'll be outside painting the stars and leaving stained clothes in the bath.'

'You've given this way too much thought. And no one uses a darkroom any more – it's all digital.'

'Hush, don't ruin my fantasy. So will you join me? Start painting again?' she asked casually.

'One step at a time,' I lied.

She sipped her wine instead of replying. Maybe she didn't believe me. I wouldn't have.

'This is a lousy present,' she stated. 'Now I have to go out and buy a camera. There's no sense in doing lessons without one.' She waved the paper.

'It's the gift that keeps on giving,' I replied smugly.

'Shut up and get me more cheesecake.'

Ben's name was never mentioned.

Later I sat on the edge of my bed and gazed at the canvas – mostly finished except for a blank piece in the top left-hand corner. Where something would naturally be painted, given the rest of the picture.

It was a reminder of a time before the Possibilities. Finishing it would be an acceptance.

I would never do it.

The one at the beach

A week after her birthday Emily and I hit the beach. She said the sea air would be good for me, Emily-speak for she had a new bikini and wanted to test it out, which is Troy-speak for she wanted to show off her body and be admired by all the boys and called a bitch by all the girls. Emily isn't vain, but she worked hard to stay in shape and sometimes liked validation with admiration from others. At five foot six, slim and toned, with long brown hair, admiration wasn't in short supply.

We live a five-minute walk from a beach. So of course we hopped into the car and drove thirty minutes up the coast. To be fair our local beach is usually buffeted by a cool southerly, so there was a certain logic about making the trek, but it was still a pain in the arse.

The day was bright and warm, the beach packed with families and couples and groups of friends. The heat forced some people under beach umbrellas, while others revelled in it. Children darted between the water and family blankets, pausing to get a drink or reluctantly be re-sunscreened. A group of teenagers were throwing a ball around, and overhead seagulls circled like vultures, waiting to swoop on discarded morsels of food. The waves were steady but not high, and heads were dotted on the surface, calling for reluctant friends to join them.

Emily staked out a spot that didn't meet her precise requirements but was the best available. She liked to be halfway between the road and the water to ensure maximum foot-traffic exposure.

'Put some sunscreen on me,' she ordered.

I took the sunscreen and rubbed it on her back. Once done, I haphazardly applied some to my arms and legs. Skin cancer was the least of my worries. Emily set the alarm on her watch – fifteen minutes on her back then time to turn, like a rotisserie chicken. I laughed at the sudden image of a chicken on a stake wearing Emily's bikini, and she raised her sunglasses.

'What's so funny?'

'Just remembered something I read earlier.'

She studied my face for a moment, then settled back, covering her eyes once more. 'You don't do enough of that.'

'Reading?'

'Laughing, you dick. You're such a grump all the time. Honestly, I don't know why I put up with you.'

I didn't know the answer. She was my best friend, but I knew it was hard work for her. 'Why do you?'

'Why do I what?'

'Why do you put up with me? Why aren't you off living with some fabulous man, shagging your brains out every night and having fun?'

'Are you asking me why we're friends?'

I gazed at the water. 'I guess.'

She was quiet for an eternity. Suddenly she sat up, took off her sunglasses and punched me in the arm. 'God, you're such a dickhead. Why does there have to be a reason? You need to stop looking for meaning behind things and accept them for what they are. We're friends because we are. Now shut up, you're ruining my rays.'

She lay back down and closed her eyes. Our friendship had been born at school, after all the shit with Heather. Everyone else looked at me strangely. Emily walked up to me and said, 'Tough break.' By the end of that year, she and I were firmly and permanently planted in the friend zone.

I lifted handfuls of sand, letting it fall through my fingers, and thought about the story I'd told Cat – how the beach used to be a mirror before it was shattered by a moon who hated its reflection. I smoothed the surface, and wondered what I'd see if the sand was still glass. Quickly I scuffed it up, already knowing the answer.

At fifteen minutes Emily's watch beeped and she turned over. I became officially bored, so wandered a few feet away, knelt in the sand and began to dig. The sand here was firmer, better for what I was doing, which was … I don't know really, creating something from nothing, attempting to exert control over a malleable substance, bring order to chaos. Or maybe it felt good to take a handful of wet sand and mould it into something.

Suddenly Emily stood over me. I glanced at my watch, surprised to see an hour had passed.

'What are you doing?' she asked curiously.

'Just playing around,' I replied, carrying on with the work.

'Boys!' she retorted. 'Always playing with things. I'm getting some lunch. You want anything?'

I shook my head and she left in search of something healthy to eat. A little while later I heard loud voices. The group of teenagers who'd earlier been playing with a ball were arguing. I didn't catch what they were saying, and didn't care, so went back to my task.

Suddenly a shadow blocked the sun. I looked up, expecting to see Emily; instead it was one of the teenagers. I glanced past him to see the rest of the group heading off down the beach. One of the girls gave a couple of backwards glances before being dragged away by her friend.

'What are you building?' he asked.

'How do you know I'm building anything?'

'Otherwise you're just a sad guy playing in the sand by himself,' he retorted.

I ignored him.

He looked up the beach at his friends, then back at me. 'Can I help?'

No, you can fuck off, I thought. Leaning back, I stretched out sore muscles. 'Sure. Do what I say when I say it.'

Close up he looked around sixteen, with shaggy brown hair and a solid build. He wore black board shorts, baggy grey singlet and bare feet. He saw me looking at him and glared back defiantly. I pointed at a pile of sand. 'Put that over there.'

He was pretty good at following directions and seemed in no mood to talk so we worked quietly.

Finally I said, 'You seem pretty pissed off at the sand.' He looked at me in confusion. 'The way you're slamming it down I figure you and sand have some history and this is payback.'

He looked down at his hands, then laughed ruefully. 'Well, sand is always getting up my ass, but I guess I could cut it a break.'

There was more silence.

'I'm Steven,' he said.

'Troy.'

'So it'd be easier to do this if I knew what we were building.'

I sat back on my haunches and wiped sweat off my forehead, replacing it with a fine layer of sand from my hand.

'We're making the moon,' I said.

He looked confused for a second, then shrugged. 'Okay.'

'Okay? No follow-up questions?'

'Look, dude, I don't really care what it is. I'm just filling in time until my friends stop being dicks.'

I laughed. 'Fair enough.'

More silence.

'Don't you want to know why my friends were being dicks?'

'Nope.'

'Man, I thought that's what all grown-ups want to do – talk about feelings.'

'For a start I'm only about ten years older than you. And secondly I'm not like other grown-ups. If you want to talk I'm not going to stop you, but let me be up front – I don't care what your problems are. That's between you and your dickhead friends.'

'Don't call my friends dickheads.'

'You did,' I reminded him.

'So? They're my friends, I'm allowed to.'

I remembered teenage logic.

'Besides, they're not usually dicks, just right now.'

I didn't reply, but somehow he took it as encouragement to keep going.

'And not all of them are anyway, only Harris, and he's jealous.'

I scraped away some sand and used one hand to scoop a hole out of the surface.

'I should never have told him I like Jessica.'

There it was, the source of teenage angst the world over – girls.

'And he told her and now she hates me and I can't hang around with them any more because Harris will act like a fuckwit. Sorry.'

'For what?'

'Swearing.'

'I don't give a fuck if you swear or not. If Harris is a fuckwit, then he's a fuckwit.'

He grinned, then sighed and looked serious again.

'Put a pile of sand there. No, not like that – like this.' I showed him what I wanted.

'This sucks, man.'

I figured he wasn't talking about the sand sculpture. 'Did she say she hates you?'

'Huh? No, not exactly, but she didn't say anything when Harris started ragging on me. If she'd liked me she would have said something – right?'

I thought about being fifteen and Heather Wilson and I laughed bitterly. 'Hell, no. Boys, girls, doesn't matter – when you're with a bunch of other kids and the pressure is on you clam up.'

'That sucks.'

'Of course it does,' I agreed.

'So what do I do?'

He wasn't going to let it go. I sighed. 'Do you like her?'

He looked away, his face flushing red. 'I guess.'

'Mate, it's not some test you haven't studied for. Either you do or you don't.'

'Okay. Yeah, I do,' he admitted.

'Then get her on her own and talk to her.'

'And say what? *I like you*?'

'There are worse ways to start a conversation,' I said.

'And what if she doesn't like me back?'

'Then you'll feel like shit for a while.'

'That doesn't sound like fun.'

'Who said love was fun?' I asked.

'Hey, who said anything about love? I just like her,' he argued.

'Same principle.'

'You should meet my sister.'

'Why?'

'She's fucking weird too. And she's old like you.'

'Fuck off.' I threw a handful of sand at him and he ducked, laughing.

'Seriously, I can introduce you. I think you'd like her.'

I shook my head. 'You always try and set your sister up with weirdos you've just met?'

He laughed again. 'Okay, maybe I'll tell her tomorrow.'

My fingers squeezed sand. I hate that word.

We worked for another hour, mostly in silence, occasionally talking about sports or movies. He seemed like a good kid, and he reminded me a lot of myself at that age, only not completely fucked. At one point he happened to glance up and froze. I turned to see a girl approaching along the beach. She was alone and hesitant. Steven furiously moved sand around with his hands, mostly undoing all the work he'd spent thirty minutes doing.

I told him, 'Okay, we're done.'

He looked up, startled.

'Go talk to her, numbnuts.'

'Numbnuts?' he replied.

'Fuck off. You're annoying me.'

He looked over at Jessica, then grinned at me. 'You're a dick,' he announced, then jumped to his feet and walked over to the girl. I didn't watch him. Whatever happened, it was his life, not mine. But when I looked over a while later they were gone.

Sometime later Emily came back. She opened her mouth to ask, then closed it again. She was used to me doing odd things. She'd bumped into a friend and was it a problem if we didn't go home until later? I asked her to clarify later – always an important question when dealing with Emily. She mentioned a vague time range and I said sure, it didn't bother me. She promised not to forget me and left again to find her friend. Despite her insecurities, or maybe because of them, Emily had a lot of friends and always seemed to bump into them when we went out. She hardly ever forgot me.

I spent the rest of the afternoon working on the sculpture. Occasionally someone would stop and admire it, and ask questions, but mostly I was left alone. A madman playing in the sand. The day wore on and the beach began to clear as people went in search of food, or homes, or the rest of their lives. Every now and then someone would walk past, their dog bounding back and forward, joyful at being off the leash. Some dogs would trot up, then veer off to chase a seagull. Still I worked on. Eventually the quiet fell to nature, the heartbeat of the water the only sound as it stole up the sand, then skittered back to the safety of the ocean.

Finally I was done. The end result was about three metres round, half a metre raised – the full moon, complete with craters, imperfections and shadows. I sat next to it, muscles aching, suddenly aware of hunger and thirst, and the heat on my skin despite the sinking sun. I vaguely remembered putting sunscreen on but it seemed a long time ago.

When I started this morning I was killing time until we went home. But over the course of the day spent creating this thing a purpose had evolved as a shape emerged. For some reason the story was stuck in my brain. I am the moon, despising my reflection, wanting to punish something – anything – like the moon punishes the beach, smashing it, relentlessly tormenting it and never ceasing. But I had nothing to punish, no tangible reason or cause for why I was this way. I was a victim without an offender.

This sculpture was a stupid desperate attempt to show the moon its beauty. Maybe then it would stop punishing the sand, and there might be hope for me. Hope that there was an end to this existence I led.

The sun sunk lower and the moon muscled its way skyward, drawing the water with it, threatening the sculpture before the moon could reach high enough to see it. Scrambling up, I desperately began digging a trench, a futile attempt to hold back nature for the briefest of moments.

'No!' I cried out, tears streaming down my face, dropping to the sand to mingle with the seawater, as if my own body was working against me to hasten the moon's death. 'A little higher,' I urged the silver ball.

Water reached the trench, teasing me for a moment before retreating, giving and taking hope with each rhythm. My hands were coated in wet sand as I furiously bailed the trench, but every beat brought more. As the sun disappeared beneath the horizon, the ocean nibbled hungrily at the edge of the sculpture. I collapsed panting into the sand next to my offering, staring at the real one, and darkness settled over the world, crushing me by its expanse.

At the next wave my legs were wet up to my knees.

'FUCK,' I shouted.

The next wave brought water to my thighs. My sculpture was lost, my offering to the universe rejected as inadequate. I wanted to lie there and let the water carry me out to the depths. Death had never taken before, but maybe this time it would and I could finally be at peace.

No, I couldn't do it – not to my parents, or Emily.

Yet the next wave brought water to my waist and I felt its tug as it retreated, the lure becoming stronger. *Come with us,* it said. *Soon*, I whispered back.

The next one reached my stomach. *Come play*, it hummed insistently. *Patience*, I replied.

The next came up to my chest, the pull more powerful now. *Help*, it said.

Wait, that wasn't the water. I shook my head. There it was again – a voice: 'Help!' There was something vaguely familiar about it, but the water was comfortable, soothing. Now it was up to my armpits, and as it left again I moved with it, just an inch. It wouldn't be long.

'Help!' cried my sand sculpture. 'Someone help!'

No, not the sand.

My eyes snapped open. Emily! I leapt up, trying to get my bearings, to pinpoint the sound. The cry came again, this time more muffled, it was about twenty metres up the beach. I sprinted, kicking tufts of sand behind me. Another sound came and I corrected my course.

'Shut up,' grunted a male voice.

Before me lay a series of undulating sand dunes. I knew from previous visits to the beach that there were pockets in the dunes, places where you can't be seen from the beach or the road. I could hear the sounds of struggling, then thud, and someone crying. My mind raced, telling me to be cautious, to find out more information, but a white-hot rage flooded my body and I charged to the top of the dune, feet slipping, catching, stumbling, pausing at the top for a split second, taking in everything, before sliding down the other side.

In the pale moonlight I saw a jumble of shapes – two bodies on the ground, writhing, struggling, and two others on top. A terrified face turned its unfocused eyes in my direction. It was Emily. One of the men had her pinned to the ground, his pants around his knees.

She ripped a hand free and tore at his cheek with her nails. He jerked back, raised a fist and punched her in the face, all in the time it took me to slide down the sand. He placed his hand on her bikini top, maybe to rip it off, but he never got a chance.

I hit the base of the dune and used my momentum to launch a front kick, weakened by the lack of traction in the sand. I connected with his shoulder, his head snapped sideways and he fell off. I moved forward with the kick, his friend looking up from his own victim in time for my fist in his face. It was perfectly weighted; I felt his nose collapse beneath my knuckles, heard a loud crunch as the cartilage shattered. He flew backwards, tumbling into his friend, a tangle of limbs.

For an instant everything froze, then time started again, and the man whose nose I'd broken freed himself and climbed to his feet. Blood ran down his face, his nose pointed sideways, and his eyes blazed in anger. He stepped forward, hauling his shorts up as he came. Suddenly his eyes went blank and all the air exploded from his lungs.

I looked down in time to see his victim withdraw her foot from his groin. Before I could move she jumped up, grabbed his T-shirt and kneed him in the balls. He fell to his knees, dragging her down with him. He reached out and lurched his head back, but before he could complete the head butt I pushed past the girl and punched him twice – left eye, right eye. She released her grip and he fell backwards. This time he didn't get up.

Emily's would-be rapist struggled to his knees and I snapped my leg forward, driving my entire weight into his stomach. He let out an explosive sound and pitched sideways, his head clattering against his friend, and they both lay still. I heard panting and whirled around ready for another attack, then realised it was me.

I turned back to Emily, who lay shivering on the ground. I knelt beside her and she threw her arms around my neck and tried her best to squeeze the life out of me.

'It's okay, Ems.'

'Jesus, Troy,' she sobbed into my chest. 'They were going to…'

'But they didn't,' I soothed, and turned to her friend, who was kneeling on the sand about half a metre away. 'Are you okay?' She raised her head and her face mirrored Emily's fear. My heart froze. It was Cat.

'I think so.'

Her hair was a mess, there was sand all over her, and she had a small cut on her left cheek. I could actually see the light in her eyes disappearing into horror.

One of the guys moaned and rolled over. At the same time a voice called out from the road. I wasn't paying attention but Cat responded.

A couple of seconds later a head popped over the sand dune. 'Elissa!'

I looked up. It was Steven. He stared, dumbfounded.

'Steven, call the cops, will you?'

'What the fuck is going on?'

'Language, Steven,' Cat said automatically.

'Jesus, what happened here?'

'Just call the cops, Steven. Tell them two girls were attacked,' I repeated.

Steven looked down at the groaning, bleeding men. 'Did they…?'

'I'm okay. Troy stopped them before anything happened. Now please call them.'

Steven looked, seeing me properly for the first time, shocked by recognition. He looked down at the men again, his fists clenched tight, then he turned and disappeared from view.

As I watched, the Cat I'd come to know disappeared from view, leaving in her place a scared, hurt girl in shock. I glanced down at

Emily, my best friend, and back across at Elissa, the woman I could love, and the rage I'd previously felt reignited. I looked at the men, vision narrowed by blood boiling in my veins, and suddenly the pain inflicted on them wasn't enough. They needed to suffer more. I made to move and Emily clutched me tightly.

'Where are you going?' she asked in a panicked voice.

For a second I thought about tearing myself free and rushing over to their prone bodies, pounding them again and again, smashing them into pieces. Then I looked into Emily's eyes and saw the fear, and all thoughts of retribution vanished. 'Nowhere, Ems, I'm right here. But she needs us too, so can we shuffle a little that way?'

All the strength had gone from Emily's limbs so I did most of the work, but we managed to bridge the gap between us and Cat. I wrapped my free arm around her and she leaned into my shoulder and began crying.

'You know, you guys are going to owe me a new T-shirt after this. Tears and snot are extremely hard to get out.'

Neither of them reacted to my poor attempt at humour, but I swear Cat wiped her nose on my sleeve. My hand hurt like hell. I flexed it slightly and pain shot through my arm. Probably a broken bone. Not the first; unlikely to be the last.

'Jesus, Troy,' came Emily's muffled voice. 'Where did you learn to fight like that?'

Which wasn't an easy answer. In one Possibility I'd studied mixed martial arts and got pretty good at it. In another I'd taken up boxing, and sucked at that, but still got taught how to throw a punch. The thing is, I remember all those other lives. Not every single memory, but enough to know what to do in a situation like this. 'You're my best friend, Ems. Nobody messes with my friends.'

'Karate Kid.' Cat let out a ragged laugh. 'I'm glad he's your friend, Ems.'

'I think there's a story in there, but I'm too tired to hear it,' Emily said sleepily.

'Don't fall asleep, Ems.' I shook her a little, worried shock was setting in. Where the hell were the police? Cat started shaking, and like an infection Emily joined her. I had nothing to keep them warm, other than my rage, which bubbled under the surface, and part of me hoped one of the men would move, giving me a reason to release the anger.

That's how they found us. The police, Steven, their parents, a blur of people asking questions. I started shivering and someone brought me a blanket, but it wasn't shock – my clothes were wet. A paramedic confirmed my knuckle was probably broken and I should go to the hospital for an X-ray. I said I'd go tomorrow. At some point one of the police officers called me a hero which meant nothing to me. A little while later I overheard one of the ambulance crew say they thought the guy with the broken nose would need emergency cosmetic surgery, and that made me feel warm inside.

The police took my statement, asking the same questions a few times, checking the answers were the same. They tried the same with Emily, but her responses were devoid of life, and I saw them talking to Cat as well.

As the crowd started to thin Steven sidled up to me. He looked like he wanted to say something but didn't know how. He kept looking over to where Cat was being comforted by their parents.

'Go talk to her,' I said.

'Huh?'

'Your sister needs your support. Go on, numbnuts.'

He grinned at me and took a couple of steps towards his family, then looked over his shoulder. 'Thanks.'

'No problem.'

'Dick,' he added.

I went to throw something at him and winced at the sudden movement in my hand. He laughed and took off.

One of the police officers brought Emily over to me and said I could take her home. She was wrapped in a blanket, clutching it around her like a protective shield, and looked completely vulnerable. I wished I had some control over the whole life thing, that I could blink back to earlier today to save her from this. But it doesn't work that way.

We didn't speak to Cat again before we left. I looked over as she was being bundled into a car by her parents, Steven glanced back and gave me a nod before disappearing. Emily and I climbed into her car and set off for home. Five minutes into the journey I pulled over so she could throw up. After that she dozed the rest of the way home.

I half-carried her into the house, and before she went to bed I made her drink a double shot of gin, her alcohol of choice. After she'd settled I sat at the kitchen table icing my knuckle and drinking straight vodka. The alcohol burned my throat but did nothing to drown the sound of bone breaking, the man's nose beneath my fist replaying in a constant loop. I didn't regret it, considering what he was in the process of doing, but it still made me feel sick.

Two hours later I was still sitting there, lights off, third drink half-empty in front of me. I've tried alcohol before as a memory suppressant and it works for a while, but never for long enough. Tonight wasn't the first fight I'd been in, and now every single one of them replayed over and over like a highlights reel, bringing with them unwanted memories of those lives. Times I wanted to forget, but my punishment is to remember.

One in particular stood out. Then I'd been in a similar situation – not with Emily, but another girl I'd known in that Possibility. She'd been attacked, and I'd been too late to stop it because I'd made the decision to stop for ice cream before meeting her on the beach. I hadn't even wanted the ice cream, it was just there and I thought what the hell. By the time I got to her she had been raped by two men and left with physical and emotional scars, and two months later she committed suicide. Because I stopped for ice cream.

I thought about fifty-fifty decisions and the consequences – intended or not – that come with them. I wished I could go back in time and stop those guys before they touched Emily and Cat, but if I went back in time they might not have touched the girls anyway. Fifty-fifty, they might not even be there. Fifty-fifty, Cat might have decided not to go to the beach that day. Fifty-fifty, Steven might not have fought with his friends. Fifty-fifty, Emily might not have got hungry at the time she did so she could go to the café at the exact time to meet Cat. The number of decisions made to get to that point might have all changed. Time travel doesn't work; it's nice to see in a TV programme but it isn't reality.

A while later Emily woke screaming. When I went into her room she was sitting bolt upright in bed, hyperventilating. It took me a full five minutes to coax her into lying down again. As I sat next to her, stroking her hand soothingly, she haltingly told me what had happened. How she met up with Cat, and they had eaten at a place on the foreshore. The two guys had offered to buy them drinks, but Cat said no since she'd got a bad vibe from them. When the girls left the men followed them, and grabbed them and dragged them into the sand dunes.

I could hear the terror in Emily's voice as she replayed the night. In one of my lives I'd volunteered at a suicide hotline – ironic, given how many times I'd thought about or tried suicide – and I recognised the feeling of helplessness she felt, the victimisation, the loss of hope. I was pretty sure Emily was strong enough to come back from this, but I couldn't take the chance – not with Emily, one of the few constants in my life. My real life.

'Talk to me, Troy,' she begged. 'Anything to get his voice out of my mind.'

So I did. I started with general stuff, things I'd read online, anecdotes from my life. At some point when she had drifted away I told her about the girl, the one I didn't save – my twelve-year-old daughter Victoria. When my voice faltered I sat for the rest of the night, rubbing Emily's back every time she cried out, soothing words the only comfort I could offer.

Sleep eluded me, thoughts of all the pain and loss I'd experienced too real and raw to allow rest. At the start I'd wondered how I could cope with it all without going crazy. Maybe it was already too late.

The one with the brother

Life went on. I heard from Emily that Cat was coping by ignoring what happened and throwing herself into work. She no longer worked at the café, but had a job at a clothes shop. Emily gently suggested Cat might like to see me, then not so gently told me to get off my arse and go talk to her.

I said I would but I didn't mean it. I had broken my knuckle, two of them actually, so my hand was bandaged and splinted and hurt like fuck.

Emily slowly recovered. She had the occasional nightmare, although that was helped by the sleeping pills her doctor prescribed. She didn't realise it, but I kept a close eye on how many of them she had.

I've said the list of things I care about is short, and it is. But Emily is near the top. There would never be anything more than friendship between us, but she has stuck by me all this time, and she may be slightly crazy, but she's my kind of crazy. I would do anything to protect her; she would say I saved her from a far worse attack, but all I thought about was how I could have prevented the whole thing. If I hadn't been obsessing over that stupid fucking sand sculpture I would have heard her calling out earlier, and then she might not be a shell of who she truly is.

Steven showed up at the front door one night. 'Hey,' he said, shuffling nervously on the doorstep.

'Hey,' I replied.

'Can I come in?'

I opened the door wider. We sat at the kitchen table. He refused to meet my eyes and I wondered what was going on. It didn't seem like he was going to tell me anytime soon, so I got the vodka down from the top shelf and poured us both a glass.

His eyes widened when I put one in front of him. 'But I'm only sixteen.'

'Okay, but I don't have all night for you to tell me what you want, so drink the vodka and talk, or drink the vodka and fuck off. Either way, just drink the damn vodka.'

He looked at the glass for so long I wondered if it was his first drink, then he lifted it to his lips and drained the whole lot in one go. Immediately he had a coughing fit and his eyes watered. 'I'm more of a beer guy,' he said when he could speak again. I rolled my eyes and he grinned, then looked serious again. 'I want to know if you can teach me.'

'Teach you what?'

'Jess and I are going out.'

'Congratulations,' I said.

'Only I've been thinking about that night, about what Elissa said you did to those guys.' He paused and I waited. 'Look, man, I'm not a fighter. If I'd come across those guys raping my sister I would have shit myself. I couldn't have helped her.'

'Maybe, maybe not,' I said.

'I would have tried, but I've never been in a fight.'

'What does it matter? It's over.'

He looked at his hands nervously. They were shaking slightly. 'Like I said, Jess and I are going out.'

I suddenly got it. 'To be honest, most of what happened was adrenalin.'

'But you saw what was happening – there were two of them and you didn't hesitate.'

'Yeah,' I admitted. 'But if I'd stopped to think about it I probably wouldn't have.'

'That's bullshit.'

'So you want me to teach you how to fight?'

He looked at me eagerly. 'Yeah.'

I poured myself another drink. He pushed his glass over the table hopefully but I shook my head. 'Make a fist,' I ordered.

He looked confused, then clenched his right hand into a fist.

'Congratulations. You know how to fight.'

He looked down at his fist then over at me, clearly disappointed.

'Look,' I went on, 'I know enough to get by but I'm not a teacher.'

'Fine.' He stood up abruptly. 'Thanks for nothing.' He strode to the door.

Fucking teenagers. 'Wait.' He stopped. I got up from the table and went over to him. 'Why don't you ask me what you really want to know?'

He looked away, at his shoes, the wall, the fridge, anywhere but at me. Then he met my eyes. 'I don't want to be a coward,' he said, and there was something vulnerable about the way he said it.

'Then don't be.'

'Okay, cool, thanks,' he said sarcastically.

'Being afraid of a fight doesn't make you a coward. In fact, it makes you smart. I was scared when I got to the top of that sand dune.'

'But you kept going,' he insisted.

'Because it mattered, because it was my friend.'

'But what if I can't do that? What if someone attacks Jess and I'm too afraid to do anything about it?'

'Close your eyes,' I told him. After a few seconds he did. 'Picture Jess in your mind. Can you see her?' A smile played across his face. 'Okay, imagine a man grabbing her, shoving her to the ground, tearing at her clothes.' He shifted uncomfortably. 'Imagine he pins her hands above her head and pulls down his pants. He's about to fuck her, he's about to hurt – '

'Stop it!' His eyes blazed and he raised his fist.

I waited for the light to go out of his eyes and his hand to relax. 'I think you just answered your question.'

'Fucker.'

'Sometimes,' I agreed.

He wiped his brow. 'But I still don't know how to fight.'

I sighed, suddenly over this conversation. 'Look, I can give you some pointers on which martial arts or boxing classes are the best, but there're only three things you need to know about fighting so listen up. If he can't see, breathe or walk then the fight is over, so aim for his nose, his stomach, or his balls.'

He looked stunned, but there was a look in his eyes like he'd burned the words into his brain.

'Okay, I'm a busy man so get out.' I pushed him into the hallway and we walked to the front door.

'Mum and Dad want to come around and see you, to say thank you.'

'Tell them there's no need.'

'They won't listen to me.'

'Make them listen,' I said bluntly.

'I don't understand why you're being so shy about this. I'd be milking it for everything.'

The media had been around but I'd told them that because the matter was before the courts I couldn't comment, which was partially true. In reality I didn't deserve the attention.

Steven paused on the front step. 'Elissa's back living at home. She's pretending she's okay but she's not. I thought maybe you could talk to her.'

'She's strong. She'll get through this.'

He looked at me, puzzled. 'How do you know what she's like?'

'She has to put up with you, so she must be strong.'

'Wanker,' he said and went out the door.

I thought of calling something out, to get the last word in, but closed the door instead.

Back down the hallway I went into the bathroom and looked at myself in the mirror. The reflected face was covered in broken lines, the shadowed eyes with faded colour. I stayed in front of the mirror for a long time, hoping each blink of the eyes would change the perspective, bring hope or acceptance, but nothing ever changed.

Yet Steven's visit had given me an idea. When Emily got home later I suggested something. She seemed hesitant, but the following Sunday I woke up to find her standing at the end of my bed dressed in tracksuit pants, a running singlet and running shoes.

Over the next two weeks I taught her how to fight. Not the Hollywood montage type where you wash cars or do 1,000 push ups a day. The real-life version where I showed her the dirtiest, most effective ways to inflict pain on a man, how to break fingers, gouge eyes and break kneecaps with the minimal amount of force. At the end of the two weeks she threw away her sleeping pills and slept well for the first time since the attack, albeit with a couple of drinks to help. I still watched her like a hawk.

The one with the revelation

'What the fuck are we doing here?'

Emily ignored me and kept pushing. I grabbed the wheels and hauled backwards, and our progress shuddered to a halt.

'Troy, let go!'

'No. This is stupid. I want to go home.'

She gave up and came around to the front of the chair. Her face glistened with sweat and she panted from the effort of pushing a dead weight uphill. Her normally groomed hair was tangled and damp, and the singlet top she wore clung to her stomach.

'No,' she said calmly. 'It took me weeks to get you to agree to this. We're not stopping now.'

'Why don't you leave me alone!'

She leaned forward and grabbed me by the shoulders. 'Because, you moron, I'm all you've got left. Your parents died at the same time your legs did, and you've driven away everyone else. If I go you have nothing.'

I looked down at my wasted legs and felt the world darken around me. 'I already have nothing,' I said thickly.

She released one shoulder and the next instant my cheek exploded as she slapped me. I looked at her in amazement. 'Are we clear?'

Taking my silence as consent, she walked around the back of the wheelchair and began pushing. This time I didn't stop her.

It took a further five minutes of manoeuvring before we reached the lookout. The warm breeze did little to cool us down, but the lookout had a roof which protected us from the sun. To the south was the ocean, and in the distance the tip of the South Island. To the north was the harbour, dotted with white sails and surrounded by hills. I couldn't see much of it from my sitting position, but I'd been here plenty of times.

'Okay, we're here. Now what?' Bitterness had wormed its way into my voice a year ago and now was such an integral part of me I couldn't remember how I sounded without it.

'I don't know,' Emily admitted. 'I actually didn't think I'd get you this far.'

'You hit me.'

'It's been a long time coming,' she replied.

'Did you enjoy hitting a cripple?'

'I don't enjoy any of this, you bitter, nasty, foul-mouthed son of a bitch.'

'Then why don't you join the long list of people who fucked off?' I shouted.

Before she could reply a bunch of runners came up the steps and leaned on their knees, panting like dogs. Even though I was never a runner, it served as another reminder of what I couldn't do. One of them asked Emily to take a group photo of them and she obliged, directing them into the best set-up, then clicking a few pictures on a phone. They thanked her then set off again. I was still seething.

'I am going to fuck off.' She rounded on me. 'Right after I say this.'

My mouth opened, then shut straight away. Of course she was

going to leave. Everyone else had. A tiny part of my brain told me it was my fault and I told it to shut the hell up.

Emily took a deep breath and continued in a calmer tone. 'You have every right to be angry – what happened was terrible – but you're still alive. So stop feeling sorry for yourself. Just fucking *stop* it. Because this is your last chance. When I'm gone, I'm gone. That's it – I'm not going to spend the rest of your life watching this.' She gestured at me. 'You have a choice, right now! That way is self-pity.' She pointed south, where white caps rode to the beach in ceaseless churning. 'That way is life.' She pointed north, where civilisation crept up hills, nestled amongst green. 'If you choose north then come and find me. Otherwise enjoy what's left of you.' She stormed off.

'Wait! How am I going to get home?' I shouted after her.

'Your arms work,' she called over her shoulder.

'You can't leave me here!' I screamed, slamming my hands on the arms of the chair.

She kept walking.

I waited for her to come back, but as the seconds dragged into minutes it became clear she was gone. I clenched my hands, looking for something to throw or hit. Anger reduced my vision to pinpricks. I sat there, perfectly situated between north and south, life and not. I'd wished many times that I had died in the accident rather than ending up in this chair. I had full mobility from the waist up, but the crash might as well have paralysed my brain. It's lives like this that are the worst. Waking up every day expecting to be okay again, waiting for the next blink to take me out of this Possibility, and with every passing day hope draining away, and acceptance growing that this was my real life.

I looked south for a long time. To the left of the mass of land in the distance was the horizon, endless flat space where sky met world, but its beauty was wasted on my darkness. Reluctantly I dragged my eyesight to the north. It was closer, broken by structures and hills, but it seemed more out of reach. Emily was right. I'd been so consumed by bitterness I'd driven away all the people I cared about, or who cared about me. She was all I had left. My last link to finding a way back, but I wasn't sure I wanted to take it. I don't know why she'd stuck around for so long. Probably pity. Even before the accident it seemed strange that we were friends. I didn't deserve her, but she was going so that was okay. I'd be alone and that's the way it should be. Maybe this was a Possibility, maybe real life. Either way it didn't matter – I still woke up every day knowing that the death of my parents was on me. I was the driver, distracted by my phone, failing to see the red light. The chair was punishment, a 24/7 reminder of my stupidity.

The view exploded at me, and I flinched. When I looked back a cat crouched on the wall staring at me. It was a tabby, with a streak of white from its neck down to its tail.

'Fuck off!'

She sat down and licked a paw.

'I don't believe in symbolism,' I told it in a calmer voice.

She yawned at me.

'You're just a cat.'

Apparently she took offence, turning her back and licking herself.

'A stupid coincidence.'

She paused mid-wash, her tongue poking out towards me.

'You're probably not even real,' I said pettily.

She crouched, and leapt from the wall onto my lap, the motion pushing my chair back a little.

'Jesus!'

She sniffed at my legs, then my t-shirt. I picked her up and dropped her on the ground, but she wasn't having a bar of that, immediately jumping back up. I tried once more, this time throwing her halfway across the lookout. She landed on all four paws, trotted back across and for a third time landed on my lap.

'What the fuck do you want?'

She had a collar with a nametag. On one side was a phone number, the other her name: Maddy. 'Leave me alone,' I told her. 'Maddy.'

She ignored her name and kept sniffing me. Apparently, paraplegics are catnip to cats.

'Fucking hell, cat.'

She stopped what she was doing and looked up at me expectantly, staring in the unblinking way that cats do. Suddenly she hissed at me, leapt onto the north-facing wall and disappeared over it.

The timing of the cat's visit was troubling. I don't believe in a higher power, or supernatural shit, but given what I'd gone through it was hard to dismiss the thought that some things aren't mere coincidences. A soft breeze blew thoughts across my mind. My stomach clenched at the thought of Emily out of my life. My only – my last – friend. I suddenly realised I did have more to lose. Also, out there somewhere was the real Cat. She'd come around soon after the accident, and I'd been cruel to her. My face flushed with the memory of nasty words I'd said.

I gripped the chair firmly, wheeled around and pushed myself down off the lookout. I hadn't gone more than twenty metres before I saw her leaning against a fence, triumph written all over her face.

'I thought you were going,' I said.

'Like I would,' she replied smugly.

'I fucking hate you.'

'No, you don't,' Emily replied. 'You love me.'

I shook my head and blinked…

And stood in the middle of a clearing, surrounded by trees, the only sound the wind moving branches and leaves. The sun was high in the cloudless sky and sweat trickled down my shirtless back. Did I remember to put sunscreen on this morning?

I was still shaking my head and my knees felt weak. I plonked down before they gave away. Slowly the wind in my head died and thoughts settled. Lacking a mirror, I looked down at my hands – young, firm, left hand slightly malformed and healing. Some rustling drew my attention to the edge of the clearing.

Emily appeared from behind a tree, buttoning up her shorts. As she approached she pulled a handy wipe from her pocket and cleaned her hands. 'What are you doing down there?'

'Got tired waiting for you,' I shot back, feeling better.

'You know, you need some guy friends so you don't feel the need to drag me into the wilderness.'

Everything clicked into place. It was October 2016, and this morning I had convinced Emily to come on a hike with me. I pointed. 'The carpark is a five-minute walk, Ems – we're hardly in the wilderness.'

She stuck a finger in my face. 'All I know is I just squatted behind a tree. That's not something you do in civilisation.'

I grinned. 'Thanks for taking one for the team.'

She gave me a disgusted look. 'I'm thinking of changing teams.'

'You'd make a lot of men very unhappy,' I quipped.

'And a lot of women ecstatic,' she retorted with a flick of her hair.

We broke out laughing.

'Seriously, Troy, what the hell are we doing up here?'

'Hey, you didn't need to come. All I said this morning was that I planned on walking up the hill – you're the one who said you wanted to come.'

'I was bored. Now I'm bored and sweaty. Why didn't you insist on going alone?'

I laughed again, and promptly swallowed a bug.

Emily watched with amusement as I coughed it back up. 'See, even nature doesn't want you here.'

'This way. It's not far, I promise.'

'Okay, but remember you taught me how to fight so if you're lying to me I'll kick your ass.'

I didn't reply, and was glad when Emily put earphones in and switched on her iPod. We made our way across the clearing and onto a path littered with tree roots. Out of the sun the temperature cooled to pleasant though some rays pierced the foliage, casting shafts of light and shadows. Birds rustled in the trees, occasionally darting across our path, or exploding from tree branches at a perceived threat.

What scared me most was the thought always bubbling under the surface when I return from a Possibility. Am I crazy? Is everything in my mind? Sometimes I cling onto that thought, because being crazy is easier to deal with. Crazy can be cured, or at the very least medicated. The alternative – that this thing is real, that I really am living all these Possible lives – there's no obvious way out of that. Even now my legs were wobbly, like they remembered they weren't supposed to work. I glanced at my hands, expecting to see calluses from using the chair.

But what disturbed me more than anything was meeting Cat again. Okay, this time it was an actual cat, but the symbolism seemed pretty clear.

She kept popping up, which was weird. Sure, I'd met the same people in different lives – I live in a city with 400,000 people, so the laws of probability virtually guarantee I'm going to run into the same people. But this felt different. In each of the lives she was central, an important character in the story. That had never happened before, ever. I didn't know what to make of it. I didn't know if there was anything *to* make of it. Maybe it was simply a huge coincidence. What made it worse was I found myself liking her. That couldn't happen. That way lay heartbreak. Liking someone, falling in love with someone, never ended well, and it always ended.

We broke out of the trees onto a road, and followed it a short way up to the lookout. We were the only ones there. To the south we could see the ocean, sun glittering off the still water like diamonds. North we could see the harbour, small white sails lazily gliding along on the light breeze. Even Emily seemed impressed, at least enough to take her earphones out. It felt strange to walk onto a platform that minutes before I'd been wheeled onto.

'Shit, I've lived in this city for twenty-five years. Why have I never come up here?'

'You hate exercise,' I reminded her.

She looked down. 'Does this look like the body of someone who hates exercise? I love exercise – I hate walking.'

'You know I'm not going to comment on your body.' I grinned.

'Wise man.' She pulled her camera out and spent a few minutes taking pictures – checking, deleting and repositioning until she had the results she wanted. Satisfied, she leaned on the guard rail and drank in the view. 'Is this why you climb hills?'

'Why did the chicken cross the road?'

She turned to look at me. 'Huh?'

'Because it wanted to see what was on the other side.'

She thought about it for a moment. 'So you're the chicken.'

'I've been called worse.'

'But why?' she persisted. 'What's so important about the other side of the hill?'

I paused before replying, wondering how much to say. She deserved something, but not the truth. 'I'm not happy, Ems.'

'No shit,' she snorted. 'Sorry,' she added when seeing my expression.

'I know I'm not always the easiest to live with.'

'No, you're not, but you saved me from a vicious attack so I think we're even.'

Not even close, I thought.

'So why aren't you happy?'

We were on dangerous ground. 'I'm struggling to find where I fit in the world. I guess I'm hoping there's something better on the other side of the hill, something that makes more sense.'

'Is this to do with your depression?' she asked in a voice filled with forced calmness.

I looked at her sharply. We'd never broached the subject before; fear kept us dancing around the issue – her afraid of the answer, me afraid of what the answer will do. I'm not sure I've ever been depressed, not in a medical way. Or maybe I have, maybe this life is one big depressive denial. 'See, this is why I don't say anything,' I said.

'Why?'

'Because it gets you all worried.'

'I'm already worried, Troy. I remember you in school – you were fun, you had friends and you were optimistic about the future. You had a spark. Now you don't. I get what happened with you and Heather, but it was a long time ago. So of course I'm worried.' It came out in a rush. She looked away in frustration.

'I'm sorry. I don't want you to worry about me.' I wanted to give her a hug, tell her everything was going to be fine, but I stayed still, hands gripping the lookout railing.

'That's what best friends do,' she snapped. 'Who sat by me all those nights I had nightmares?'

'Gin and sleeping pills?'

'Don't be a fucking arsehole.'

'Can't help it,' I grinned.

She punched me in the arm, hard. Maybe teaching her to fight wasn't the best idea after all. 'Don't you worry about me?' she demanded.

'Not as much as I used to,' I admitted.

'I still get nightmares,' she said.

'I know.'

'But I'm going to be okay.'

'Because you're strong,' I told her.

'You're only as strong as the people around you.'

I looked away in embarrassment.

'Do you seriously think you're the only one who's struggling to find their place in the world? Everyone at some time or another has struggled to figure out their way forward. You're not special, Troy.'

'Gee, thanks, Ems.'

'Do you know the difference between those who succeed in life and those who don't?'

A sarcastic response lived and died on my lips. I shook my head.

'The people around them.'

I nodded slowly. She meant well, but it was different for me. I was different.

'Elissa isn't doing great.'

'She has her family and friends for support. She'll be okay,' I said.

'Yes, she does,' Emily replied as she prowled restlessly across the concrete, 'but she doesn't have you.'

'She doesn't need me,' I protested.

Emily stopped and jabbed me with her finger. 'I don't know if she does or doesn't. But she needs something, and you can help.'

'I barely know her!'

Emily locked eyes with me, her gaze boring inside my brain, instantly turning protests to vapour. 'You can help,' she said, emphasising every word.

I wanted the conversation to end.

Her gaze dropped, with a sigh she said. 'I love you, Troy.'

'I love you too, Ems.'

She leaned in for a hug. 'Sometimes I think life would be easier if I was in love with you.'

'I've thought about it,' I admitted as we turned back to the view.

'And?' she asked.

'I think it would be bad for you.'

She looked away and used a tissue to wipe a tear from her cheek. 'It'd never work anyway.'

'Why's that?'

'I like to lie on beaches, you like to climb hills. Polar opposites,' she pointed out.

'You like gin, I like vodka.'

'You watch those awful horror movies, I prefer romantic comedies.'

'I like pizza, you like oysters,' I said.

'Why are we friends again?' she asked with a laugh. 'Are you going to be okay?'

I didn't want to lie, but I needed to say something. 'Sure, Ems. I'll be fine.'

'Is there anything I can do to help?'

I put my arm around her shoulder. 'Just keep being annoying.'

'Good, because I'm really not looking for any extra work.'

'Bitch,' I told her.

We were stopped from further banter by the arrival of a busload of tourists. We graciously took a few group photos for them, then made our escape.

'Troy.'

'Yeah?'

'There was a road up here? And you made me walk through the woods? I hate you.'

A couple of days later I went to see Kelvin. He was finishing his Wednesday morning guilt session, otherwise known as prayer service. Kelvin had been the priest at the church for thirty-five years. He knew all his parishioners by name, he'd done the wedding services for most of them, baptised others, and in some cases done both. I hadn't seen him for a while, mainly because he knew my parents, so it was like an extension of guilt every time I talked to him. He never failed to ask why I didn't talk to my mother. But I confided in Kelvin, partly because I liked him, and partly because he is a priest and I figured anyone who believes in an invisible omnipotent being should be sympathetic to my situation. Having said that I don't want him to think I'm bat-shit crazy so he only gets the highlights.

He was in his early seventies, a big man with bushy white eyebrows, an out-of-control beard that had streaks of dark amongst the grey, and little other hair. Large, thick-lensed glasses constantly slipped down his nose. He had baptised me, something he liked to remind me of every time we met. My parents loved him. He'd been around the house for dinner a lot while I was growing up, and he was pretty cool for a priest. He rarely talked about God outside of church, unless he felt like someone was straying too far from the strictures of the *Bible*. Then he pulled out a quote or two, a gentle reminder that they were wrong and God was right.

'Troy,' he boomed in a voice as wild as his beard. 'It's been a while.'

'Yeah, I've been busy.'

'You didn't let me finish. It's been a while since you called your mother.'

I cringed and he laughed at my reaction.

'She asks me to pray for you every Sunday.'

'Sorry.'

'I'll let you in on a secret, Troy. I'd pray for you anyway.'

I raised my eyebrows.

'People worry about you, I worry about you, so I ask God to keep an eye on you.'

'God and I aren't exactly on speaking terms,' I replied.

He gestured around the quiet church. 'And yet here you are.'

'To see you, not God.'

'For all intents and purposes it's the same thing,' he said.

'Got a god complex, Kelvin?'

He laughed long and hard. 'No, of course not, but I am his representative.'

I looked around. Nothing had changed since I was little. The same hard seats, the same worn prayer books, the same stained-glass windows infusing the dust-filled air with radiant light. The same priest wearing the same robes. The same open friendly look on his face. I fought an urge to confess to eating lollies during the service when I was six.

'So what can I do for you, Troy?'

I wasn't sure where to start. It's hard to know how much to tell people. 'There's this girl,' I began.

He smiled, took off his glasses and rubbed them on his robes. 'Of course there is.'

'This girl is different.'

His smile widened. 'Oh, so you're in love? Well, it was going to happen eventually.'

Kelvin had married me, in this church, thirteen times – all in Possibilities he never lived.

'Is it Emily?'

I shook my head. 'We're just friends.'

'Ah, so someone new. Who is she?'

'That's the thing, Kelvin. I don't love her. I don't even really know her.'

'But?'

I frowned. 'I keep bumping into her.'

'That sounds less like love and more like stalking.'

'Ha, ha,' I responded without humour. 'The thing is, it's never on purpose. It just happens, and I don't know why.'

He studied me shrewdly. I squirmed slightly under his scrutiny. He seemed to be looking for something. I remembered why I stopped coming to church – that uncomfortable feeling as he gazed down upon the congregation, the knowing little smile, like he knew all your secrets, all your sins.

'And you want to know whether this is part of God's plan?' he asked casually.

A flash of a sheepdog circling my soul, nipping at its heels to bring it back into the flock, crossed my mind. I shook the image off. Kelvin had never given me the hard sell on religion.

'Honestly' I said, struggling to find the right way to say it, 'there is so much in my life that's random and out of control. I…'

'You want to know if this girl is part of the random, or something more.'

'I guess so,' I agreed.

He gave me a smug look. 'Well, as a priest my answer is that there is no random – everything is part of God's plan.'

It was exactly the sort of unsatisfactory thing I expected to hear.

He saw my face and laughed, holding up his hand in a 'wait a second' gesture. 'But as a man, let me ask you this. Do you like this girl?'

I looked away, not sure how to answer.

'Okay, obviously I'm starting too big. How about this, then. Do you think you *could* like this girl?'

I hesitated, thinking about the times I'd run into her – in this life, in Possibilities – and then I looked into the darkest part of my heart, the bit locked away, where feelings I didn't want to acknowledge, that I wanted to pretend didn't exist, were kept. I cracked open the door and peered inside. There was something, a tiny glimmer of light singing in the black.

I looked at Kelvin. 'Yes.'

'Was that so hard?'

Harder than he could possibly imagine.

'Then what does it matter if it's random? Does the why matter as much as the who?'

But it did matter. I couldn't explain why – not to him, not even to myself. Not always knowing what's real and what isn't, feeling like a leaf in a southerly swept along against my will, I needed to know there was something out there that was deliberate. Something that meant something. That the universe wasn't just fucking with me. And what if I just wanted to use her to fix myself?

'Troy?'

I realised tears were in my eyes, and faked a coughing fit to wipe them clear.

'It's that important?'

I didn't reply, which was answer enough.

He sighed and looked up at the wooden cross dominating the head of the church. 'Do you know what the hardest thing is about being a priest? It's living in this world. Seeing the daily horrors, the injustice of children dying, sickness, war – all the things people do to themselves, and to God's world. It's seeing all those things and still believing God has a plan. That God is great, and he will be our saviour.'

'You're talking about religion.'

'I'm talking about faith.' I must have given a look. 'We all have faith, Troy, to some degree or another.'

'I'm not sure I agree.'

'Will the sun come up tomorrow?'

'Of course.'

'You don't know that for sure, though. You're taking it on faith it will.'

'I know it will because if it doesn't we're all fucked.'

'Well, profanity aside, whether you like it or not you're referring to faith. The only type of certainty that can come from something completely out of your control.'

My hands clenched in frustration. What he was saying sounded like a fancy way of saying nothing at all. That maybe me running into Cat over and over was dumb luck, nothing more than coincidence. So what was the point? If it all was a series of random encounters, then why bother making an effort? The universe was sitting back having a laugh at the Jackson Pollack nature of my life.

'Faith, Troy, faith is a chance at redemption. A chance for hope, something to tuck away in your heart so things don't seem quite so dark. Faith is…' He paused, either for dramatic effect or because he'd run out of arguments. 'Faith is an umbrella held above us, protecting us from the world.'

I stared at him in astonishment, my mouth suddenly dry. 'What if the umbrella is broken?'

He smiled wryly. 'That's why it's called faith, Troy. You have to believe the umbrella will do its job, broken or not.'

I'd come here wanting a sign – confirmation that there was something more. And he was reciting essentially the same story Cat had told me in the doorway. As signs go it was pretty clear, and suddenly I felt uncomfortable.

'Have you been to see Sunshine?' He looked to the back of the church, where the cemetery rested.

'Don't call her that,' I replied automatically, standing up, wanting to leave before he said anything else.

'When are you going to call your mother?' Too late. 'You know, you come here wanting answers to life's mysteries. Your strained relationship is your mother's greatest mystery.'

'Thanks for the talk, Kelvin,' I said and quickly left the quiet seclusion of the church. He would tell her I had come – not the details, but that I came to talk. Mum would take it personally, and casually drop it into conversation next time I saw her, wondering if everything was okay, leaving the unspoken question out there, hanging like a balloon that was waiting to drift away or pop. I sighed and counselled myself that guys in their twenties don't normally talk to their mothers about relationships anyway. I'm just a normal guy, an average bloke with women problems. A guy sitting at the bar drinking beer and telling his mates about this girl he likes.

Only I don't have any guy friends and I hate beer. And I can't talk to Emily about these things. Sure, we've shared conversations about guys and girls, but general stuff – guys are pigs, girls are heartbreakers, that sort of thing. I offered a shoulder and a gin every time her heart broke, and she returned the favour with vodka and a *Die Hard* movie marathon for me, but this was different. For one thing, it was her friend, which is enough of a minefield for a normal guy. And I was not a normal guy.

The lack of friends is by choice. My lifestyle isn't exactly set up for close friends. Over the years, through all the Possibilities, I'd let friendships wither and die, leaving a trail of confused people and broken promises. It was easier that way. Emily was the exception. We are flatmates, which made her a constant, but it was more than that. Emily provided stability where the rest of my life hovered on quicksand. And she was there at the start.

After leaving the church I wandered the city for a while. There was something about this place, something in my DNA; this was my territory, where I felt safe, whole, complete. I'd lived in other cities, even other countries during Possibilities, but Wellington was home. I can't explain why; it's just a collection of buildings, people and personalities carved into the hills and bays. It's not the brutal southerly sweeping off the strait, or the way everyone succumbs to six degrees of separation, but something kept me here. Forces had bent in my direction over the years in an effort to carry me away – education, job prospects, women – but none of them took. Not for long anyway. Every now and then I like to amble down Cuba Street, stopping for coffee in one of the multitude of cafés, watching street performers, or bizarrely dressed couples yelling at each other for obscure reasons. It felt right.

I wasn't convinced by what Kelvin had said, despite the bit about the umbrella. Or maybe I was convinced and that scared me. Barely living, existing without hopes, desires, love, colour – it's addictive. Not like drugs, or cigarettes, or Facebook posts about cats. But it's always there, in the corner of your eye, the back of your mind, a heavy coat draped over your shoulders, providing a constant oppressive presence. And discarding the coat, after wearing it so long it seemed like a second skin, taking that coat off and putting it away, wasn't going to be easy.

I ignored the universe for a week. Saturday morning Emily went off to volunteer at the SPCA, and lacking anything to do I walked into the city and wandered around for a while before deciding to get a drink; everything seems better with a hot chocolate and a muffin. I was still choosing where to go when I found myself outside the little café Cat had taken me to on our first non-date. I don't even remember turning down the alley. The universe was pushing hard.

Before I could enter my phone rang. I didn't recognise the number so sent it straight to voicemail. A couple of seconds later the same number rang again, and this time, with barely supressed annoyance, I answered it.

Emily had left her cellphone at home and she needed it desperately. Could I bring it to the SPCA urgently – life or death, freedom of the Western world depended on it.

It took an hour, by the time I swung home first, before I arrived at the old hospital building taken over by the SPCA a few years back. The parking lot was full, prospective families excitedly choosing their newest member. Inside competing smells of antiseptic and animal food jostled for dominance.

The lady behind the reception told me Emily was showing a family some kittens, but she waved me through the employees-only door. I'd been here often enough to be mistaken for Emily's brother, or boyfriend, so they didn't seem to mind where I went. Emily spotted me over the bent backs of parents, their children red-faced with excitement, arguing over the black-and-white one versus the tabby one. Emily winked and gave me a wait signal. Bored, I wandered down the corridor, passing several rooms filled with forgotten lives. I admired Emily for working here. The emotional landscape of breath-taking mountain views as families are brought together is offset by the dark caves of those cases where adoption isn't possible. It's only for the strong-hearted, the eternal optimists.

At the end of the corridor was a closed door, with a single window set in the wood at head height. Something covered the window from the inside, blocking the room from the world. A white sign with black writing hung on a nail. Do not Disturb, Session in Progress, it claimed. I had started to turn back down the hallway when I spotted a sliver of uncovered window, big enough to fit an enquiring eye. Just a quick look, I thought.

Leaning my head against the cool glass, I peered through the gap. It took a moment to adjust to the dim light in the room, and a moment longer to understand what I was seeing. The room was bare of furniture, the barren walls a soft colour difficult to make out in the light. A small bundle of dark blankets lay casually discarded against one wall. Someone sat against the opposite wall. She wore blue tracksuit pants, a pale-blue T-shirt, scuffed and worn running shoes, and her hair was braided and draped over one shoulder. With a jolt I realised it was Cat.

She was completely focussed on the pile of blankets, staring at it with an intensity that lacked sense in the surroundings. She seemed frozen in time, a statue immortalised. Yet she wasn't completely frozen; now that I looked closer her hands were moving – slowly, precisely, hypnotically, limber fingers twisting and turning, performing an intricate dance in the air.

Fascinated, I watched as a story was woven from threads of air. That's when I realised she was signing. The random movements not random at all, but letters and words. But why? I knew she wasn't deaf, so what was going on? I was watching something intensely personal, the cover over the window intended to prevent eavesdroppers, yet I couldn't look away. I consoled myself with the fact I don't know sign language so couldn't understand what she was saying. Even so I stole a guilty glance back down the hallway to check my indiscretion wasn't being observed.

On turning back a hint of movement from the other side of the room caught my eye. The pile of blankets twitched again. Slowly a trembling nose emerged from the folds of material, followed by pointed ears, then the dark eyes of a small dog, completely focussed on Cat's hands. Her fingers paused upon seeing the emergence, but now they restarted, if at all possible more deliberate in their movement. They seemed to be beckoning the dog, imploring him to emerge from the safety of the blankets. I became lost in the beauty of their actions, wanting to move closer.

The dog agreed with me. He inched out from the blanket, then backed away, startled by his own bravery. His eyes darted from side to side, looking for danger, refusing to believe it wasn't there, then locking back on her hands.

Suddenly something grabbed me and hauled backwards. I stumbled away from the door, bouncing off the side wall and fell onto one knee. Startled, I looked up into Emily's furious eyes. Wordlessly she pointed to the sign on the door. I opened my mouth to explain but she angrily gestured for me to keep quiet, and half-dragged me down the hall. We reached an empty office and she shoved me through the door, slamming it behind us. I turned in astonishment, and looked into a face I'd never seen before – an Emily consumed with rage. I opened my mouth again to ask what the issue was but she cut me off.

'You will not talk. You will listen, and then you will leave. There's a reason the door is closed, a reason the window is covered, a reason there's a fucking sign on the door. And it's not so you can stick your nose in where it doesn't belong. What goes on in that room is none of your business. Nod if you understand.'

I didn't understand, but nodded anyway.

'No one gets to know what happens in there unless Cat tells them, and she never tells, so go home and pretend you were never here.'

I obediently went to the door and opened it.

'Wait!'

I turned back and she had her hand out.

'Phone.'

I meekly handed over her phone and left, still reeling at Emily's reaction. It seemed out of proportion to the crime. It also made me wonder if there was something more happening in that room than I'd thought.

When I next saw Emily the heat had gone out of her, replaced by an icy cold to rival the strongest southerly wind. I waited until the evening before raising the subject. For some reason it was important for me to know.

First I made sure she was settled on the couch, full of takeaway pizza and sipping on her second glass of red wine. Then I put on the latest reality show addiction, something about famous people beating each other up – I never paid much attention.

An ad break came on. 'Ems…'

She sighed. 'I'm sorry, okay? I may have overreacted.'

'May?' I raised my eyebrows.

'Okay, so I went full wolverine, but you deserved it.'

'All I did was peek into a room. You acted like I was some pervert looking in her bedroom window. It doesn't make sense.'

She sighed again and sipped her wine. The show came back on and she grabbed the remote and paused the image. 'I told you on the hill that day, I told you Cat needed you. After the attack she didn't have you to help her work through what happened. To teach her how to fight. That saved me, Troy – you gave me back some control. You helped me not be afraid any more, but Cat didn't have that. So she's coping a different way. We get some bad cases in.'

She wasn't talking about people now. I know some of the rescued animals are in bad shape – beaten, neglected, treated like trash. She never talks about it but I know when it's been a bad day; she comes home, puts on a trashy movie and drinks herself to sleep.

'We only rehome them if they can be rehabilitated. That means teaching them to trust again, that not all humans are scum. Sometimes we do it, and it's amazing, watching them come out of their shell, being welcomed into a new family. Knowing they're going to be loved again, or maybe for the first time in their lives. It's exhilarating. It keeps me going.'

'It's why you keep volunteering,' I said.

She picked invisible threads from her pants. 'Yes. I know I sometimes come home a mess, but if I can keep at it, if I can help just one animal find love, then it's all worthwhile.' She took a sip of wine, lost in her thoughts.

'And Cat?'

Emily cupped her wine glass in both hands, staring into the dark depths. 'She takes on the lost causes, the ones everyone else has given up on, and tries to show them a way back from the darkness.'

I swallowed and looked away, overwhelmed by guilt. I should have helped Cat when Emily asked me to. I couldn't see further than my own problems, my own constricted view of what mattered. I'd abandoned her – I don't even know her, but she needed me for something and I wasn't there. I felt like shit.

'She doesn't talk about it much, but she's struggling. I don't know what she does in that room, and I don't care. It seems to be helping both her and the animals, and she wants to keep it secret. If it's helping her, then good, and nothing is going to screw that up.' Her voice flashed with fire, then she gave me a crooked smile, and sculled the rest of her drink, before restarting the TV. Conversation over.

The next time I saw Cat was the following week at the trial. With the typical efficiency of the New Zealand court system it had taken some months before the two men appeared in court, charged with assault, attempted rape, and sexual assault. The prosecutor wanted both girls to testify, and I was supposed to be the nail in the defendants' coffins. The hero who swooped in and saved the day. Most people would revel in the attention, making the most of their fifteen minutes of fame, but there were two reasons for me rejecting that. The first was I still blamed myself for being late. If I hadn't been lying on that beach, wallowing in my own self-pity party, I might have stopped the attack as soon as it started. I'd never told Emily that's how I felt, but guilt is a hard emotion to shake.

The second reason was that I've had fame – and, in some Possibilities, fortune as well. It can be fun, especially the money part, but like anything, after a while it gets stale. In one Possibility I won three million dollars in Lotto, and over the course of ten years and several bad investments blew it all. In another Possibility I landed a part in a movie, a cameo – five minutes on screen, three lines – but for one of the lines I adlibbed 'Check that, Jack' and it exploded on social media. I became known as the Check-that-Jack guy, invited to parties, had sex with a lot of women who wanted to say they had fucked the Check-that-Jack guy. I won't lie, it was an awesome time, but after six months the world moved on, and the invitations stopped coming and I struggled to get work as an actor, and for the rest of that Possibility – another twenty years – I was a where-are-they-now segment on entertainment shows. Fame is fun, but only for a while. I don't need it.

Mostly, of course, it was the guilt thing.

When I saw Cat standing there, bookended by her parents, I flashbacked to that night. Her father took two steps forward and shook my hand so hard I lost the feeling in my fingers. When he finally let go her mother enveloped me in a bone-crushing hug. They both said something but I wasn't paying attention; I nodded and smiled.

Cat wore a defiant expression on her face, ready to stare down the world. If I hadn't seen her in the room at the SPCA, seen the vulnerability on her face, the exhaustion in her posture, I might have believed in it.

'Hey,' she said.

'Hey,' I replied.

'I haven't had a chance to say thank you,' she said awkwardly.

That wasn't right; I didn't want things to be awkward. 'My fault,' I grinned. 'I'm regretting all those lost opportunities for you to buy me drinks.'

She laughed, a genuine and beautiful sound that by her parents' reactions was a rare event. At that point Emily went to find the bathroom, and Steven arrived with a girl I recognised as Jessica. He was holding her hand, and noticing my glance he grinned at me. I rolled my eyes and his grin broadened.

The parents turned their attention to the new arrivals, and Cat took the opportunity to edge closer to me.

'I'm scared,' she whispered, her eyes never leaving her family.

I remembered the strong woman I'd first met, the wild and carefree one who stole my phone and was ready to sleep with me, all on the same day. Those two words made me angry that someone could take away her spirit so easily in the space of a few minutes.

'This is where you say something inspirational to make me feel better,' she added.

I looked into her eyes, trying to think of something to give her strength, dredging through multiple memories to find the perfect thing to say. But there was no perfect thing. Then I remembered something a doctor told me when I was fifty and going in for triple bypass surgery. 'You're allowed to be,' I told Cat.

'It's not who I am.' She shook her head in frustration.

'And it's not who you have to be – tomorrow, or next week, or next year. But right now you're about to face the man who attacked you, and it's okay to be scared.'

She shook a little. 'What if I can't do it? What if he gets off?' She looked like she was about to throw up.

'Do you remember what we did to him on the beach?'

Her eyes widened and a smile played across her lips.

'If you get scared in court, if he looks at you funny, think of me kicking his ass. Because I'd happily do it again for you.'

She looked at me thoughtfully. 'Who are you Troy?'

I looked at her.

'Why did you slam the door on my face that morning?'

I was spared answering by the trial starting. I waited in an adjoining room and was eventually escorted into the courtroom, where I sat in the witness chair. After I gave my oath the prosecutor began with some simple questions. I answered as clearly as possible, all the time sneaking glances at the defence table. The two men kept their heads down the whole time, but there was one moment when the guy whose nose I broke looked up and scowled at me with pure hate. I stumbled over my words, before looking away, taking a sip of water, and continuing.

I didn't look in their direction again, not even when their lawyers attempted to twist my testimony, suggesting I was the aggressor, that I had interrupted a consensual act between two couples and attacked their poor clients. But it was a shot in the dark, a vain attempt to distract the jury with wild theories. This wasn't my first time in the courtroom. In one Possibility I'd become a lawyer, and spent fifteen years prosecuting guys like these. There was nothing their defence could throw at me I hadn't seen before. And with Emily and Cat's testimony it was a slam-dunk case.

I didn't see Cat after the trial – her family whisked her off as soon as she testified – but the prosecutor told me Cat and Emily both did well. 'Even shedding a couple of tears,' she said gleefully. 'That's jury gold.'

It was one of the quickest jury decisions in months: twenty minutes to convict, sentencing to follow at a later date. Case closed, time to move on with our lives.

When I left the courtroom Emily was standing a few metres from the front door talking to a man. His back was to me, but I'd recognise my father anywhere. As I approached, Emily gave him a hug, then told me she would meet me in the car.

Dad had a grim expression on his face, but it softened when he looked at me. 'Rough day, son?'

'I've had worse,' I replied.

We stood in awkward silence. I wanted to take Emily home and be done with the day. I shifted restlessly and he picked up on the signal, but obviously had something to say.

'Why didn't you tell us this happened?'

'I didn't want to worry you and Mum.'

He snorted. 'That ship's long sailed, Troy. Besides, don't you think it would have been nice for us to find out from you rather than the newspapers? After all, she's practically family.'

I looked at him blankly.

'Emily, son. We've known her for ten years, she's like a daughter to us, and we have to find out from some reporter that she'd been attacked, almost...' He broke off and looked away.

My face flushed. Once again, while trying to do the right thing I'd done exactly the opposite. 'I'm sorry, Dad, I didn't think.'

He waved a hand. 'You don't want to talk to us about what's going on with you, then fine. I'm not happy about it and it upsets your mother, but it's your life so fine. But don't shut us out completely. That's unacceptable. Understand?'

I nodded mutely.

His expression softened and he looked at my hand. 'Emily told me what you did. Are you all right?'

'I'm fine. Hardly hurts any more.'

He nodded. 'I'm proud of you, Troy.' He looked embarrassed by this outpouring of affection, and before I could respond he turned and marched off.

The one after the trial

Moving on from the trial started with alcohol.

I'd suggested dinner out but Emily said the only people she wanted around her were me, Cat, and gin and tonic. I didn't think Cat would come – her family had been so protective of her at the trial – but just after 7pm there was a knock on the door. Emily was busy pouring drinks so I padded down the hallway and opened the door. Cat stood on the top step, dressed in old jeans and a zipped-up tracksuit top. Her hair hung loose and she clutched a big brown shoulder bag which clunked a little when it moved. Over her shoulder I saw her dad in the car; he waved at me and I lifted a hand in response.

'At least you have clothes on today,' she said mockingly.

'I made an effort,' I responded, pointing at the paint-stained tracksuit pants and grey, faded T-shirt with unidentifiable stains.

'Me too.' She indicated her own ensemble.

I opened the door wider, she took a step in, half turned and waved to her dad, who waved back and drove away.

After I shut the door behind Cat I locked it and put the security chain on, then turned around to see Cat looking at me. 'Emily prefers it now.'

Her shoulders relaxed a little, releasing tension I wasn't even sure she knew was there. I led her down the hallway and into the lounge where she went straight over to the single La-Z-Boy chair and sat down, curling her feet under her, all in a single fluid movement of familiarity.

Before I could comment Emily came in carrying two tall glasses filled to the brim with liquid and ice, topped with a slice of lemon. She handed one to Cat and sat down on the couch with the other.

'It's on the bench,' she said in response to my expression.

In the kitchen I approached the filled glass on the counter with caution. Emily could be a generous pourer at the best of times, and this was not the best of times. My hesitation was warranted; the first sip was pure vodka with a hint of lemon. The alcohol burnt my throat, eliciting a small coughing fit. From the other room I could hear Emily laugh. It was such a good sound to hear I forgave her for trying to poison me. I emptied half the glass and topped it up with lemonade from the fridge. The second sip was much more palatable. I carried my drink into the lounge and sat at the other end of the couch, putting my feet up onto the coffee table because I knew it annoyed Emily. She shot me a look and I put on my best blank expression.

Disgusted, she turned her attention to Cat. 'How you feeling, El?'

I kept forgetting her actual name is Elissa.

Cat shrugged and took a big drink before answering. 'Like shit, really.'

Emily looked at her friend with concern, then down at her own drink. 'Yeah, me too,' she admitted.

I kept quiet. We sat in silence for a while, sipping our drinks, lost in our own thoughts.

'Not much of a celebration, is it?' Emily said jokingly.

'I'm not sure there's anything to celebrate,' Cat replied.

'We won, Elissa. They're going to prison, hopefully for a very long time.'

She shook her head. 'I know, but…' She seemed to sink further into the chair.

'Troy, give us a minute,' Emily ordered.

'Troy, stay,' Cat countered and I paused halfway out of my seat. 'I don't want to talk about it, Ems. I want to forget it all.'

With no further instructions from Emily I sat back down.

'I'll get the chips then,' Emily stated and we both watched her leave the room. I looked at Cat and she looked back at me.

'You're quiet,' she said.

'It didn't happen to me,' I said.

'But you were involved.'

I glanced down at my hand; it ached sometimes. 'It's not the same. I was the aggressor, not the victim.'

She pulled her feet out from under her and leaned forward. 'But you were affected,' she insisted. Reluctantly I nodded and she appeared satisfied, then asked, 'So how did you get over it?'

'It's not the same, Cat. Why aren't you asking Emily?'

She leaned back in her chair and looked at me thoughtfully. 'Why do you call me Cat?'

Because the first time we met you refused to tell me your name, is what I wanted to say. Only it hadn't happened to her. Which makes conversations really awkward.

'You remind me of someone I once met and it's kind of stuck in my brain now. Does it bother you?'

She thought about it. 'Does it bother me you would rather use the name of another woman instead of my own? Yeah, kind of.'

'Fair enough. I'll call you Elissa from now on.'

'Is there going to be a from now on?' she asked.

'There's always a from now on,' I said bitterly.

'Is there?' she replied quietly. I didn't pick up on it, not until later.

Just then Emily came back in, juggling chips and dip and a bottle tucked under one arm. She placed the food on the table with a determined thump and pulled out the bottle, revealing it to be schnapps.

'If we're not going to celebrate then we're going to commiserate.' She pulled three shot glasses from her pocket and laid them out in a row on the table. She filled each one and handed them around. 'To surviving,' she toasted. Cat and I raised our glasses as well, although I noticed she was a little slow to bring hers up, and we all drained our glasses.

Emily refilled them. 'To Troy breaking his hand.'

I looked at her.

'If you hadn't…' She faltered over the words.

'To Troy breaking his hand,' Cat said.

We drank. Weirdest toast I'd ever done.

Emily filled the glasses again. 'To those motherfuckers rotting in prison.'

We drank.

'To being messed up,' Cat said.

We drank.

'To surviving being messed up,' Emily toasted.

I hesitated on that one but drank anyway. My insides were beginning to feel nice and warm, and my head felt lighter on my shoulders.

They were both looking at me expectantly and I realised they were waiting for me to toast.

'To fluffy slippers,' I said.

They looked at me in amazement.

'Never underestimate the importance of fluffy slippers,' I added.

'To fluffy slippers,' they both said.

We drank.

'I need to stop,' Cat said in a slightly slurred voice.

'I need to throw up,' Emily informed us.

She left in an unsteady hurry and I heard the bathroom door slam shut.

'Will she be all right?' Cat asked.

'Sure. She'll make some space, drink some water and be back ready for the next round.'

'It's funny, I've known Emily for two years and this is the first time I've seen her drunk.'

I'd seen her drunk plenty of times. Emily prefers to get drunk at home, rather than lose control in public and rely on others to send her to the right home with the right person.

'Can I ask you something?' Cat started. She was hesitant, unsure now. 'Can I…can I hug you?'

I wasn't expecting that and she read the surprise on my face. 'It's just … since the attack I haven't been able to relax near a guy. My dad goes to hug me and all I can think of is that man on top of me, tearing at my bikini, and I freeze up. I know it hurts Dad because he doesn't understand, and I'm tired of feeling bad, and guilty, and I was hoping you would let me hug you because I really want to feel normal again, and this is safe, you're safe, and I really want to hug you.' She trailed off. There were tears on her cheeks and her hands shook.

I stood up and walked slowly over to her chair. Her eyes followed me apprehensively. I reached out a hand and cautiously she took it. I didn't pull her up, letting her rise at her own pace. We stood still, my hand in hers, a few inches between us. She took a tiny step forward and stopped. Then another. We were virtually touching but I didn't move. Hesitantly she leaned forward and rested her head on my chest. Carefully I put my free hand around her and rested it lightly on her back. She froze, time froze. The only sound was my breathing, slow and steady, her breathing, short and ragged, and the tick of the clock above the TV.

Suddenly the spell was broken. She grabbed me with both arms and clung tight, as if wanting to melt into me. After a moment I rubbed her back, a small gesture of comfort. She went rigid, then tore herself lose. She looked at me wildly and I put up my hands in a placating manner. Another wrong move. She stumbled backwards, caught her knee on the corner of the chair and tumbled to the ground. Tears filled her eyes as she hyperventilated.

'What the fuck is going on?' came Emily's voice from behind me.

'Nothing,' I assured her. 'She fell over.'

Emily stepped around the table and helped Cat to her feet. 'I can see that, idiot. Why did she fall over?'

'It was my fault,' Cat told her, wiping the tears off her face. 'I got up too fast and went a bit dizzy. So actually, Emily, it's your fault for giving me all that alcohol to drink.'

'Well, if it makes you feel any better I've already been punished. Whose idea was it to mix gin and schnapps?'

'Yours,' I reminded her.

'In that case it was a wonderful idea but poorly executed.'

Cat plonked back down into her chair and Emily and I resumed our positions on the couch. The rest of the evening was spent mostly in silence, watching a terrible movie on television and alternating large sips of water with small sips of alcohol.

I offered to take Cat home, but she said her dad would come, and he showed up suspiciously quickly once she called. We said our goodbyes at the front door, Emily and Cat with a quick hug and a peck on the cheek, Cat and I with an awkward half-wave and a mumbling see ya later. We watched her climb into the car and let it pull away from the kerb before closing and locking the door.

'What happened between you two?' Emily asked casually.

Cat obviously didn't want Emily to know, otherwise she would have told her, so it wasn't my place to say anything, but I also didn't want to lie outright to my friend. I settled for something in the middle.

'She wanted to hug me, to say thanks for saving her. But like she said, when she got up all the blood rushed away from her head and she fell over. No big thing, Ems.'

She looked at me shrewdly, or maybe drunkenly; it was difficult to tell. Then she staggered off to bed.

Lying on my bed later, I struggled to find sleep. I wasn't sure how to help Cat. I could teach her to fight, like Emily, and that thought triggered a wave of guilt. I had helped Emily, but ignored Cat. By trying to protect myself from getting too close I hadn't done what I should have for someone else. Been a friend.

Frustrated, I pulled the pillows out of the way, exposing a hole in the protective shell of cotton and wool, opened the bedroom door, padded down the darkened hallway and clicked on the light in the bathroom. Standing in front of the mirror, I studied my face. Every angle, every line, hair, the dark pupils – it all screamed normal, average, nothing to see here. Only that's not what I saw. I saw pieces, tiny fragments making up a collage of every Possibility I'd been through. A sand sculpture at the mercy of the tide.

I thought about when I was young, before this thing started, when I was normal. I struggled to remember what I was like. All these Possibilities I've lived, collectively they've moulded me into someone different, each one chipping away at my personality, replacing it with something else, something fractured. It sounds clichéd but I don't even know who I am any more. There've been so many versions the core of me is warped, and unrecognisable.

I searched the mess of memories, filtering out ones I knew to be from other lives. A picture began to emerge of a teenage me – kind, helpful, generous. Someone who wanted to be accepted by his friends, who wanted to grow up to play basketball for New Zealand, marry a supermodel and live in a ridiculously big house. Someone who would have helped Cat from the beginning. It would have been nice if that person still existed.

The next morning Emily was gone by the time I got up. I made a mental note to text her later and ask for Cat's contact details. I showered, dressed and headed for work. As I walked to the bus stop the old couple were at their letterbox again. It occurred to me this was the only place I ever saw them. They were arguing over something, and as I went past the woman grabbed my arm.

'You there, which one is better? This monstrosity – ' she held up a picture of a black wrought-iron gate, more decorative than functional ' – or this one.' The second picture was a plain wooden gate.

I pointed to the wooden one and she gave her husband a triumphant look and released me.

I felt buoyant all the way to work, and not even a sudden urgent deadline was enough to bring me down. Around mid-morning I remembered to text Emily. Then I buried myself in the project, not realising I'd skipped lunch until my stomach protested.

I grabbed my jacket and was about to head out the door when my cell rang. It was Emily. 'Hey, what's up?' I asked. She was crying. 'Ems, what's wrong?'

I ducked into an empty meeting room and closed the door. I didn't understand her at first, but enough came through the garble to ignite a chill inside me. I told her to take a couple of deep breaths. Then she started again, but I knew what she was going to say before the words came out.

Because instantly I recalled the night before – words said, looks made, things I'd recorded in my memory but hadn't noticed at the time. I knew, and I felt sick, felt like being sick. I bolted to the bathroom, smashed open the door, and diverted at the last second to the sink, the toilet a step too far.

They buried her three days later. It was held at the same church my parents go to, the service taken by Kelvin, another link between Cat and me, except now it was too late to explore the reason why. The place was packed. Cat was obviously loved, by the tears and disbelief displayed.

Emily sat next to me quietly throughout. She hadn't said much since the phone call. I'd catch her staring into space a lot, doing things on automatic – eat, dress, breathe, sleep – her body and mind having shut down all but essential life-support functions.

I didn't speak to Cat's family at the service, or afterwards. There were opportunities to, but I didn't know what to say. I should have picked up on the signs; I could have stopped this from happening.

I'd said that to Emily three days earlier and it was the only time she'd showed any energy, when she called me a dickhead and told me to stop being stupid. I told her what I'd seen but she argued back that I'd been drinking, and even if I hadn't there was no way I could have predicted the outcome. In the end I told her she was probably right, but I didn't believe it, and I'm pretty sure she didn't believe it either.

I snuck back to the cemetery later, after everyone had gone, and sat next to her grave. I thought about the Cat I'd first met, even though it was in a Possibility rather than real life – the strong, independent, slightly mad version of her. It seemed unimaginable she could go from that to this. I lifted some dirt off her grave and let it fall through my fingers. Watched it settle and become still again.

Then suddenly I wasn't looking at the dirt, I was studying my fingers. I'd never looked at my hands this closely, other than checking for indicators of age. Now they seemed different – not just instruments to grip or turn, but something infinitely more. I remembered Cat sitting in the room at the SPCA, talking to the dog, creating words with her hands.

A thought flitted in on the breeze, catching the corner of my mind, nudging it insistently. It was a what-if thought. I tried to ignore it, to focus on wallowing in my self-pity, but it kept butting at me, like a puppy insisting on attention. Finally I brought the idea to the centre of my mind, studying it, turning it over, exploring its purpose. I scraped away at its edges, smoothing and refining it, until the picture was clear. And it made me realise how stupid I've been – not just now, but for years of Possibilities.

When I told Emily what I was going to do she looked at me for the longest while, then smiled for the first time since Cat died.

The next day I enrolled in two sign language classes, because I didn't know how much time I had, in case this was a Possibility and it ended too soon. I've never been good with my hands, which my third-form woodwork teacher had gleefully stated in my school report. But I picked up sign language quickly. There was something natural about it, something that felt comfortable, and within two weeks I could hold a basic conversation. I was driven, consumed by an insatiable hunger, practising every waking moment. After a month I could hold my own against experts – although not without the occasional mistake, like asking someone if they would like goat's milk on their hamburger.

It was time for the second part of my plan. Emily had already cleared it, so the next Saturday morning I sat waiting in the room. It looked different from the inside, colder, and more barren. The wall felt hard against my back as I sank to the floor. The floor felt hard too, come to think of it.

The door opened and Emily carried in a small brown dog. It quivered, pressing against her, eyes wide and darting. She stopped in front of me. 'This is Tigger,' she said quietly. She took him over to the opposite wall and tucked the dog into the bundle of blankets that were already there, carefully arranging them so he could see out, but could also hide within their safety.

Then Emily straightened up and walked to the door. In a soothing voice she warned me, 'Don't fuck this up,' then left the room, closing the door with a quiet click.

I sat for a few minutes. Now the moment had arrived I felt a bit stupid, unsure. What if this was a waste of time? What if this is my real life, and not another Possibility. What if Cat really was dead? Then I realised that instead of thinking it I should have been signing it. The bundle of blankets barely moved, but deep in the recesses I could make out an eye watching me. Carefully I raised my hands, flexed the fingers and blinked…

And stood on my front doorstep. Emily was beside me, and we were watching Cat get into her dad's car.

'Hey!' I called out to her.

She paused, half in the car, and looked up at me.

I struggled to fit thoughts together, shuffling through memories.

Don't do anything stupid, I signed to her. Her eyes widened. *Please*, I added.

She stood motionless for a moment, then gave a slight nod, disappeared into the car and her dad drove off.

'What the hell was that?' Emily asked as we went back inside.

'Nothing, I just told her to hang in there,' I replied.

'Since when do you know sign language?'

I shrugged. 'I picked a bit up here and there.'

'No, Troy, you pick up a bit of Maori here and there, or Spanish. You don't pick up sign language like that,' she insisted.

'I learnt it a few years ago, okay? It's no big deal. I thought it would be fun. When I saw Cat at the SPCA the other day it brought some of it back to me.'

She looked at me suspiciously, then decided to let it go. We said our goodnights and went into our respective bedrooms. I fell asleep straight away and didn't wake until the alarm went off.

The one that got away

The next morning when the old lady stopped me I picked the wrought iron gate option, much to her disgust. I figured the old man deserved to have a win every now and then.

I didn't hear from Cat the next day, but I also didn't hear from Emily, at least until she texted in the afternoon asking me to buy milk. The tricky thing about Possibilities is even if I change my decisions other people might have different ideas. Taking her own life might have been a fleeting thought that Cat acted on, or a fifty-fifty call that fell on the side of death. If the latter was the case, then I hoped my message was enough to push her in the other direction. If suicide was something she'd been thinking about for a while, festering inside her like a dark virus, then she might still be on that path. So part of me was afraid to ask for her number in case doing so set off a chain of events that ended the same way as before. I spent the day waiting, jumping every time the phone rang. When the working day was over I went to the gym and distracted myself with a spin class for an hour, stopped at the supermarket, and got off the bus two stops early, before eventually arriving home. Emily was in the kitchen, her work clothes protected by an apron, shoes carelessly discarded by the door.

'Hey,' she said as I entered.

'Hey, yourself. Good day at work?'

It hadn't been, by the following ten-minute rant about dealing with imbeciles. I sympathised but also took it as a good sign. If anything had happened to Cat she wouldn't be telling me about idiots who couldn't format a spreadsheet to save their lives.

When Emily ran out of steam I casually asked if she'd heard from Cat.

'No, I haven't,' she replied. 'Have you?'

'I don't have her number.'

'Why don't you text her now?' She indicated her phone on the corner of the bench. I picked it up, waited for Emily to unlock it, and pulled up her messages. There was a conversation thread with Cat I desperately wanted to read, but out of respect for both of them, and lack of time, I opened a new message, typed a few words – just general stuff: hey, how's it going? – and pressed send.

Emily and I chatted over dinner, a typical night in our flat, only I kept stealing glances at her phone. Not very well as it turned out.

'If you're that worried why don't you call her?' Emily finally said.

'Why don't you call her?' I shot back.

She rolled her eyes and dialled the number. At first it seemed like Cat wasn't going to pick up, the phone rang and rang. Then I heard a click, then some background noise.

'Where are you?' Emily asked.

I couldn't hear everything being said, but heard enough to know by the time Emily hung up something had happened, or was happening. 'Everything ok?' I asked.

She looked thoughtfully at her phone. 'Yeah, everything's fine,' she finally said. 'Elissa is going to Australia for a while, to stay with friends.'

For some reason I was devastated by the news. 'When is she leaving?'

Emily looked at me. Was there sympathy in that look? 'Now. She's just landed in Sydney.'

'Wow. That was quick.'

Emily frowned and got up from the table. She carried her plate over to the bench, scraped it under the sink tap, and loaded it into the dishwasher. It was only then I noticed she was crying.

I got up from the table and went over. 'What's wrong, Ems?'

'Nothing,' she replied.

I waited. This is how it goes with her. You wait until she wants to talk. The more you push, the more she resists.

'She's running away,' Emily said angrily.

I understood my reaction, but couldn't figure out why Emily was mad. 'She's obviously doing what she thinks is right.'

Emily rounded on me. 'She's not going to get better by running.'

'Who said she was running? Maybe she needs to get away from the reminders for a while.'

That upset her more. 'You mean me,' she said bitterly.

'And me,' I reminded her. 'And the city, and her family…'

'We could have helped her. I got better here, so could she.' She stopped, too frustrated to speak.

'Are you?' I asked hesitantly.

She looked at me in confusion.

'Better,' I clarified.

She didn't answer for the longest time, instead focused on wiping the bench clean, scrubbing at invisible spots.

'Ems…?'

'I don't know,' she said, working at the surface fastidiously. 'I thought I was getting to a point where it wasn't consuming my every waking thought. Where in the future a man could touch me again without me bursting into tears. Then the trial brought it all back. Seeing those … Fuck.' She dropped the cloth and began wiping her hands on her apron. 'Seeing them again, all I could think of was that night. His hands on me, the way he smelt, the way he hurt me. So maybe I'm not as all right as I thought. And the only one I can talk to about it, really talk to, is Elissa. And she's gone. And I don't know what to do.' She was crying again.

So was I. Her pain was open and raw and I didn't know what to do. I desperately wanted to hug her, but wasn't sure how she would react and didn't want to make things worse. Then she solved the dilemma by coming around the bench and opening her arms for a hug. I guess in this situation I don't count as a man. I held her while she cried, we stood for a long time, then she pulled away, grabbing a tissue from the box on the edge of the bench, and blew her nose.

'Well, this is a fun dinner,' she said in an attempt at humour.

'You know you can talk to me, Ems, about anything.'

'I know,' she said with a wan smile.

'Except makeup,' I added.

This time she laughed.

'Or that stupid reality show you watch.'

'It is not stupid. It's high-quality rubbish. And it's on in ten minutes so you can do the dishes.' She was halfway out the door when I called after her.

'You should talk to a professional Ems. Someone to help you through this.'

'That's what you're for,' she shot back.

I shook my head. 'Anyway, she'll be back, Ems. She'll visit friends, get away from it all for a while, and then she'll come back.'

Only she didn't. A couple of weeks went past without us hearing anything. Emily sent her a text but didn't get one back.

Then by chance I ran into Steven's Jessica at the supermarket. At first I couldn't place her when she smiled at me – I thought she was just being friendly – but then she said hi and it came back to me. I said hi back and, social graces satisfied, we were about to go our separate ways – her to the next aisle, me to choose from the multitude of cheeses on offer – when she turned back.

'Shame about Elissa, eh?'

My heart froze. 'What about her?' I replied in a forced calm voice.

'You know – that she's staying in Oz.'

I released my breath. 'Oh? I hadn't heard.'

'Yeah, I guess she doesn't want to come back to Welly. Too many bad memories and stuff. It's a shame – I liked her.'

'Yeah, me too. Say hi to Steven for me,' I replied, but she was already gone, gossip successfully disseminated.

I had wondered if this was going to happen, so wasn't as devastated as I might have been. Anyway, this might not be real – it might be a Possibility so no sense getting upset about it. Telling Emily would be a difficult conversation, though. As I wandered the rest of the supermarket I briefly considered flying to Sydney to see Cat, but that was borderline stalker. I needed to trust this wasn't real, that I would blink it away soon.

Only I didn't. Not for ten long years. By that time I was living alone. Five years after the attack Emily fell in love and got married. He was a good guy – a little suspicious of the single man she'd flatted with, but we got on okay. She moved to Auckland and had two kids, Chris and Rose; I suggested the girl's name. I was godfather for both of them, which meant flying to Auckland and putting on nice clothes to stand in a church and make promises.

Emily and I talked a couple of times a week, and each time she asked me when I was going to get a grown-up relationship. I didn't tell her I was biding my time, waiting to blink and leave this Possibility. I also didn't tell her that the more time went past the less sure I was this was a Possibility. That I was just wasting my real life.

I still lived in our old flat. I never got a new flatmate – I earned enough at the bank to make it unnecessary, and I liked living alone. At least that's what I told Emily. The truth was we had flatted together for so long I couldn't be bothered breaking in a new flatmate.

I did briefly talk to Cat. Well, the 21st century version of talking. A few weeks after I found out she was staying in Australia a message popped up on Facebook. An apology, and an explanation. The apology was for leaving. The explanation was a little more complicated.

It turns out when we hugged she felt for a moment like everything was going to be okay. Then I rubbed her back and all the fears flooded back, and in that instant she decided she was going to kill herself. It was something she had considered several times since the attack, but that moment was enough to send her over the edge. Basically she lost hope things would ever be okay again. Then I signed to her, told her not to do anything stupid, and it helped her climb back over the edge, or at the very least cling on by her fingertips. But she couldn't stay; she needed to get away from the constant reminders – her family who meant well but tiptoed around her, and her friends who'd decided pretending nothing happened was the way to go.

So she left, and once she was over there she felt better, less afraid. And I got that, I really did. I was bitterly disappointed, having pinned something – hope maybe – on having Cat in my life, but not if it meant she was a shadow of herself. That wasn't the person who first sparked my interest.

I responded to her message, told her I understood, and said if she ever wanted to talk then she knew where I was. I never heard back from her.

Then in 2027 some maniac walked into a branch of KiwiBank and blew it up. Apparently the bank had forced the sale of his house after he lost his job and couldn't make the mortgage payments. Instead of bitching and moaning about it, then moving on, he wired himself with homemade explosives and killed thirty-five people.

The prime minister called it the greatest act of domestic terrorism in New Zealand history. The cynical wondered why it had taken so long – every other country had experienced similar attacks so why should we be any different? The political opposition blamed it on the government, the government blamed it on the banks, and the banks blamed it on one sick individual who, according to them, they had tried to help in every way possible. None of which was particularly comforting for the families of the dead. And none of which brought back the man standing right behind the bomber – Cat's dad.

Emily was the one who told me. I hadn't clicked on the name – afterwards I wasn't even sure I'd known his name. I hadn't thought about Cat for a while, and hearing the news brought it all back. Okay, that's a lie, I still thought about Cat all the time.

I went to the funeral – not to pay my respects to her father, but to see her. I'm not sure if that makes me a bad person or not.

The service was at my parents' church, attended by a considerable number, including politicians and police. It was a little hard to distinguish those who genuinely knew the man from those who were there for public show.

I'd picked Emily up from the airport that morning and we sat together near the back. To her credit she didn't spend the ride to the church berating me about my lack of social life. She looked great; motherhood had changed her for the better.

The service itself was fine, a typical sort of funeral: he was a great man, loved by all, gone too soon, the standard sort of stuff. I know that sounds callous, but I'd been to so many funerals over the Possibilities it was hard not to become desensitised to it all.

We caught our first glimpse of Cat when she and Steven got up to say the eulogy. She wore dark glasses, and her hair was cut short, and Emily remarked she was wearing a lot of makeup. When she first spoke a little spark of electricity ran through me, the familiarity of her voice igniting memories. Steven must have been in his late twenties now, and he was a big boy – like gym-built big. He wasn't wearing sunglasses so I could see him sneaking glances at someone in the front row, but it was impossible to see who. They both spoke well, given the situation, painting a picture of a loving, generous, and supportive father. It made me wish I'd known him.

Kelvin looked frail, although his voice still filled the church, inspiring people with its strength and conviction. He was in his early eighties now, long past the age at which most people consider retirement. He often joked he wasn't going to retire, he would keep working right up until he died – in fact his casket was out the back, and he had pre-recorded his own funeral service, not prepared to risk someone else failing to meet his standards.

We'd last spoken about six months ago, catching up for coffee one morning, and I was shocked at how much he'd aged since then. At one point during the service he spotted me and a ghost of a smile crossed his face. He would be considering my coming to church a personal victory for him, regardless of the reason.

Afterwards the attendees were invited to join the family in the church hall, a building so similar to every other church hall in the country you'd think they were mass produced. Refreshments were provided by the church social group, including my mother. She stood behind the table, directing volunteers – more jam and cream scones there, more milk for the tea here. She was in her element, and for a while I just stood and watched her. Our relationship was better than it had been ten years ago. Not as good as she would have liked, but I made more of an effort. She spotted me and for a moment looked surprised, then went back to supervising. I started across the room but Emily beat me to it. She and Mum hugged and immediately started gossiping. I think Mum was secretly disappointed when Emily got married, destroying her visions of Ems and me tying the knot and producing lots of grandkids. She never got our relationship, being from a generation where if you lived with a woman it was because you were in love with her.

Mum became distracted by a question from one of the volunteers and Emily looked over my way. She gave me a mocking look, then winked, before turning back to Mum, no doubt to talk about my lack of ambition, motivation, etc.

'Hey, Troy.' Steven was standing beside me.

'Hey, Steven. I'm sorry about your dad.'

'Thanks,' he replied automatically. I imagine he'd heard that a lot over the last week.

He looked around the crowded room, searching for something, his eyes coming to rest and his face lit up. I followed his gaze. A woman stood talking to Cat and Steven's mother. She looked about the same age as Steven, and in her arms she held a baby. I suddenly realised it was Jessica, and glanced down at the plain gold band on his ring finger.

'Congratulations,' I said.

He turned his smile my way. 'Cheers,' he said. 'You know I owe it all to you.'

'Hey, man, I never touched her,' I said.

He laughed, and for a moment we were just two guys chatting, and not at someone's funeral.

Then he sobered. 'No man, me and Jess. That night at your place, it gave me the courage to stand up for myself, and to fight for what I wanted. Jess and I got married two years ago, and she means everything to me. Teresa is four months old, and I've never been happier. I've never been more tired, but it's awesome. So thanks.'

'You're welcome,' I replied. I hoped for his sake this was real life and not a Possibility.

'At least Dad got to meet Teresa. Have you spoken to Elissa?' he asked.

I shook my head, scanning the room but not seeing her. 'How is she?'

He frowned slightly. 'I'm not sure. Not good, I think.'

'It's understandable – you've just lost your dad.'

He shook his head. 'There's something else going on. I'm not sure what though. You should go talk to her.'

'Where is she?'

He pointed towards the back door. 'Probably out the back smoking.'

'I'll wait till she comes back in. Anyway, she probably has a ton of people that want to talk to her.'

He grinned at me.

'What?'

'Go talk to her, numbnuts.' He laughed.

I punched him on the arm; it was like hitting concrete. He laughed again and walked off in the direction of his family.

I picked my way through the crowd and slipped out the back door. She was leaning against a tree, a trail of smoke spiralling up from her hand. Behind her, stone testaments to the long gone stood waiting to welcome their newest addition.

She saw me coming and guiltily stubbed the cigarette out on the ground. Close up I could see Steven was right – she wore a lot of makeup, but it wasn't enough to completely cover the dark mark bleeding out from the edge of her sunglasses.

'Hi, Troy.' She leaned in for a fleeting hug, but not so quick I couldn't feel the bones beneath the dark jacket and blouse.

'Hi, Elissa. I'm sorry about your dad.'

She nodded sadly. 'How've you been?'

'Can't complain. You?'

She looked away.

'Sorry. Of course you're not okay,' I apologised.

She turned back and offered me a dialled down version of the smile I remembered. 'I'm doing okay. Sydney is great. I have a great job and a wonderful boyfriend. We're in love.' Her voice had a robotic tinge to it.

'Is your boyfriend here?'

'He's inside. He's been so supportive during this.' But the way she looked over my shoulder didn't gel with the words.

'And you're an aunt.'

This time her smile was genuine. 'She's beautiful, isn't she? Steven is a big sap around her. It's so cute.'

'No kids for you?' I asked.

She shook her head. 'No. Geoff wants to wait until we're married.'

'So you're getting married? Congratulations.'

'We're not engaged yet. We will though – when he's ready.' Again there was something not quite right about her tone. 'How about you? Girlfriend? Wife?'

My turn to shake my head.

'That's sad,' she said.

'I'll find the right someone eventually.' I looked at her a little too long; she shifted uncomfortably under my gaze and I diverted my attention to the graves stretched out beyond the tree. To me each marble stone represented a Possibility, a life been, gone, never was. I didn't like cemeteries.

'I should get back inside,' she said, briefly touching my arm.

A warm feeling flooded my body. 'I offered to help you once. Do you remember?' I said softly.

She nodded, 'Of course I do. I appreciated it.'

'The offer still stands,' I told her. She looked confused. 'You're smoking, you're thin as a rake, and if I'm not mistaken you have a black eye. Are you telling me you're okay?'

'You don't know me,' she said.

'I know who you could be,' I fired back.

Again she looked confused, then angry. 'I know what you're thinking and it's not true. I have a wonderful relationship. He would never treat me the way I wouldn't deserve.'

It was a curious way to put it. 'You deserve to be treated like a queen. Is that how he treats you?'

'You don't know me,' she repeated.

'Maybe not, but I want to help you.'

She shook her head. 'Why? Because you did once before? That doesn't mean you have to spend the rest of your life looking out for me.'

'What if I want to?' Wait. Where the hell did that come from?

'You don't know me,' she said for a third time.

'You keep saying that,' I pointed out.

'Because you don't seem to be listening,' she responded with a hint of the Cat I knew. 'Look, I'm about to put my dad into the ground, so this isn't the time or the place for conversations about something imaginary you think is happening.'

'I'm sorry, Elissa.'

She lightly touched my arm again, and my skin tingled under her fingers. 'It was good to see you, Troy.'

My eyes followed her all the way back to the hall door, but my feet stayed where they were. Well done, Troy, you royally fucked that up.

She stopped halfway to the door and turned back. 'Are you still building sand sculptures?' she asked.

'Sometimes,' I admitted.

She looked into the distance. 'Sometimes I feel like the moon,' she said softly.

Stunned that she remembered the story, I took a step towards her, and she took an involuntary step back. I stopped and she flashed me an apologetic look.

'You should feel like the sun,' I told her.

'I'm here for another week. Maybe I'll see you at the moon.'

I didn't understand the reference straight away. 'You take care, Elissa.'

She made to turn, then paused. 'Troy?'

I looked at her expectantly.

'I like it when you call me Cat.' She walked inside, leaving me to ponder what the hell had just happened. I stayed outside for a while, turning the encounter over in my mind. It could be I was reading too much into it; maybe she simply liked me calling her Cat. Or maybe she was calling for help.

Hesitantly I picked my way through the older stones, faded names and memories, and came to a stop before a newer stone. Read the words, read them again, and felt the familiar swell in my throat. My eyes kept returning to the bottom two lines. 'Died in 2006' and 'Our sunshine'.

When I went back into the hall Cat stood next to a tall, solidly built man, his arm possessively on hers. I didn't try and talk to her again.

Emily and I spent the evening catching up, mainly involving drinking, and gossiping about things. Perhaps because of the reason she was down from Auckland, or maybe she picked up on my pensive mood, or maybe she thought she would cut me a break – whatever the reason, she didn't bring up my lack of love life. A huge concession for her.

She peeked into my room at one point, saw the empty corner, and asked me if I'd finally finished the painting. I lied and said I'd thrown it out a few years ago. It was wrapped in an old sheet in the back of the wardrobe.

Sometime around midnight I crawled into bed, arranged the pillows around me, and lay staring at the ceiling. As I drifted off to sleep an idea began percolating in the back of my mind.

The next day I went to the beach. It was a work day, but my boss understood the need for a personal day, especially when I played up my relationship with Cat's father. Emily offered to go with me but I said I needed some time alone. As excuses go it was pathetic, given I live alone, but she gave me a knowing look.

Traffic was light and it took only thirty minutes. The sky was bright and clear, but the day cool. The beach was mostly empty, just the occasional retired couple walking their dog. The sand felt damp beneath me as I sat and watched the water sparkle with sunlight. I waited until the sun touched the horizon. No one came.

I went back the next day. Same spot, same outcome.

The third day I dropped Emily at the airport. At the gate she hugged me long and hard.

'I hope she shows up,' she said. Nothing gets past her. She walked through security while I tried to think of a smart come-back. I needed to start stockpiling quips so I had one ready when needed.

It was cloudy and cold at the beach. Not even the dogs wanted to walk. I sat in the carpark and wondered if I was being stupid. For all I knew she'd flown back to Australia. I was about to climb out when my phone rang. For a moment my finger hovered over the reject call button, but in the end I answered it.

'Hey, Mum.'

'We didn't get a chance to talk the other day at church.' Her voice calm but tinged with accusation.

'Sorry. You looked busy,' I pointed out.

A misty rain began to fall and the outside world slowly blurred and faded.

'Fair enough, but this weekend your father and I want you to come over for lunch on Sunday. We have something to discuss.' It wasn't a request.

'What?' I asked, supressing a sigh.

'Sunday, eleven-thirty. Bring cheese.'

'What sort of…?' But she was already gone.

Irritated at the interruption, I emerged into the rain, zipping up my coat and pulling the hood over my head. I trudged over the dunes, half sliding down to the sand. The water churned and struggled its way to shore, and a lone seagull above me issued a forlorn cry across the wind. The rain lightly kissed my jacket before sliding to the sand beneath my feet.

'This is stupid,' I called out to the universe.

'Just a bit.' Cat stepped up next to me. She wore a blue rain jacket, the hood casting her face into shadow, plus faded blue jeans, and running shoes. Her hands were shoved deep into the jacket pockets. We stood in silence for a while.

'No playing in the sand today,' she noted.

'A bit wet for building sandcastles,' I said.

'I came yesterday. Saw you waiting, but I couldn't get out of the car. Silly, I know, but I couldn't do it.'

'At least you came today.'

'I felt bad for you,' she said with a hint of mocking. 'Standing alone on the beach is sad.'

'So this is a pity visit.'

'Why else would I be standing in the rain?'

'You tell me,' I said.

She didn't, not straight away. Then she slipped her arm through mine and leaned her head against my shoulder. I was too afraid to move, the last time I'd tried comforting her still fresh in my mind.

'Why do I feel so safe around you?' she asked softly.

A thousand quips formed and died on my lips.

'You don't know me,' she said in an echo of the churchyard. 'But you said you know who I could be. What did you mean?'

I thought about my response carefully. 'You're right, I don't know you – not any more – but back then I saw something in you, Cat. Some spark, some strength, some light. I don't really know how to describe it. It's like you were whole, but you were also a promise of something great.' I sighed, let down by words.

'Wow. It almost sounds like you were in love with me.'

'Wouldn't that have been a fine thing?' I said quietly.

'Wouldn't it?' she said wistfully.

I wasn't sure I'd heard her right. Maybe I was too afraid to believe the words. For a glorious moment we stood in our own world, flashes of colour in the grey, the only two people who mattered. I wanted to stay there forever. I wanted it to be our forever.

Then the spell broke. 'I have to go,' she said reluctantly. 'Geoff will start asking questions.'

'He's abusing you.'

'He gets a little over-excited sometimes.'

I felt sick. 'Are you listening to yourself?'

She extracted her arm and straightened up. 'I know how it sounds, Troy, but he loves me. He would never – '

My head exploded, darkness flooding my sight, senses shutting down … nothing. Then hearing roared back and my face felt funny. I realised I was lying on wet sand, voices jumbling and jostling in my ears. Light edged back into my eyes I took a ragged breath, inhaled sand, could taste it on my teeth, my tongue, tried to cough it out. I tried to move and failed. Nothing worked right – arms, legs, brain. I heard a scream and something fell to the ground in front of my face, a white blob with tinges of blue around the edge.

'I told you,' shouted a man. It didn't make sense, none of it made sense. My eyes refused to focus; the white blob remained tantalisingly elusive. 'I told you what would happen, you worthless bitch.'

My face was wet, the sand or the rain, or tears. I suddenly knew what was happening. 'Leave her alone,' I shouted, but it was in my head, my mouth not working. I'd failed, I didn't protect her. It can't end like this. I didn't try my hardest, I didn't save her.

Darkness nibbled at my eyes. I'd been here before, dying, and I fought it, raged against the encroaching darkness, pleaded with the universe, yet still it came.

I closed my eyes…

And opened them again. I was sitting at the kitchen table at home.

The laptop lay open in front of me. Instinctively I reached up and touched the back of my head, expecting blood and bone. My face felt damp with wet sand. The hands in front of my eyes shook badly. Nausea gripped my stomach, and I had to force bile back down my throat. I took several deep breaths and the knot in my stomach loosened. With shaky hands I grabbed the bottle of vodka from the bench and took a swig. It burned my throat but slowly warmth made its way to my limbs and I stopped shaking.

On the laptop was a message window open from Cat. This was her explanation and apology, so we were in 2016. I got up from the table and went down the hall to check on Emily. She lay buried under the duvet. I retraced my steps, sat back down at the table and stared at Cat's message. My response sat waiting to be sent. Slowly I reached out and lightly touched the back button, erasing letters, deleting sentiment, leaving a blank window, a fresh start. I sat for a long time thinking what to say.

I couldn't jump in with *Don't get into a relationship with someone called Geoff*. She probably hadn't met Geoff yet, might never meet him. It was important to keep things generic but try and get the message across. I got the vodka out of the cabinet, rinsed a dirty glass and poured some, then sat back down in front of the laptop. Nothing came. Actually lots of things came, but none of them were right. It would be easier to do this face to face, or even over the phone, but I didn't have her number. Frustrated I paced the kitchen, winding myself around the table like a spring, each revolution tightening the tension, even when I changed direction to loosen things up. Each time I passed the blank screen the cursor blinked invitingly at me, teasing me for not know what to say.

'That looks like fun.' Emily stood in the doorway. She wore her plush, purple dressing gown, and bunny slippers. Her hair was tangled from the pillow.

'Sorry, did I wake you?' I said.

'No, just had a bad dream,' she replied, coming into the room and rinsing a glass for herself. I glanced sharply at her. 'Not about that. It was about Elissa.' She poured herself a gin and sat at the dining table. 'I don't remember it, just bits and pieces. I woke up with a sense something wasn't right. What's this?' She turned the laptop around and read Elissa's message. Her face clouded, then looked thoughtful. 'Are you going to reply?'

'I'm trying to, but I can't find the right thing to say.'

'How about, please don't stay in Australia because I'm in love with you.'

I choked on my drink. She watched, amused, as I regained the ability to breathe.

'Jesus, Ems, where did that come from?'

'Ha. You think I haven't noticed how much you've been moping around since she went to Australia? You don't do that unless you have some strong feelings.'

'I wasn't moping,' I protested. She looked at me over the edge of her glass. 'Fuck.'

She laughed. 'This is a good thing, Troy, I think it's the first time I've ever seen you like this. So we should be celebrating.'

'Yeah, right,' I retorted. 'For a start I never said I was in love with her. And secondly, even if I was – and that's a massive if – what's to celebrate? She fled the country. Yay me.'

Emily looked at me with pity. 'No one said love was easy, Troy.'

'Is that why you're living with me and not the man of your dreams?' I said with half-hearted spite.

'I'm selective.'

'You're high maintenance,' I quipped.

'I'm adorable,' she shot back. Emily had brought home plenty of guys over the years. Most I met for the first time at the breakfast table the morning after. Usually they only lasted a few months. The dumping always seemed to be initiated by her. I didn't understand it, had asked her about it a couple of times, but she said she was looking for the right guy.

I threw my hands up in mock surrender and we drank, like we'd both lost some weird game.

'Do you want her back here?' Emily asked.

My lack of response was answer enough.

'Then start with that.' She kissed me on the top of the head and took her half-empty glass back to bed, leaving me alone once more with the blank page and blinking cursor.

Finally I placed my fingers on the keyboard, stroking the keys for a moment, one final hesitation, one final chance to think or rethink. Then I typed.

I think it's a mistake, I said to her, and quickly pressed send before my brain or heart changed my mind. I poured another drink, a healthy buzz now permeating my body, my mind softening at the edges.

I was about to close the messenger window down when a response popped up. Just the one word. *Why*?

Because your friends are here. We can help you.

She came back straight away. I have friends here, and it's far away.

What about your family? I typed.

They understand, she replied.

Will distance help? I asked. Really?

She didn't like that. She made me wait five minutes before responding. *Tell me about Cat,* she said.

What about her?

You said I reminded you of her. So tell me about her.

I told her all about the Possibility. From answering the door wearing a towel, to standing in the shop doorway while the rain swept the streets clean. I skipped the part about nearly sleeping together; that seemed a little too weird.

I have a confession to make, she said in response.

My mouth went dry. Experience has taught me that very little good starts with those words.

That day I came to the door. I was planning to steal some stuff from you.

Thankfully we weren't on video chat so she missed the grin on my face.

She told me all about the bet with Emily. I debated whether to act outraged or play it cool. I ended up somewhere in the middle.

The funny thing is I had some pepper spray in my bag, only I didn't know whether I was going to use it.

It was just a story, I told her.

She didn't respond for so long I thought she'd disconnected. Finally a message popped up – a Skype address, and a day and time, tomorrow night at 8pm. Then she was gone.

It seemed we were going to do this with baby steps. Fine by me; I had all the lifetimes in the world.

The one that almost wasn't

The middle of the year was performance-review time at work. I've had the same boss for three years and the review always took a similar path. You're doing a good job, let's think about career progression, where do you want to be in five years? I always have a joyless laugh at the last one.

This time when I sat down in the room with Adam something felt different. It started out familiar enough – good job, Troy, your colleagues like you, your work is good, blah, blah. Then halfway through the meeting he closed his folder and sat back to look at me. Adam was a bulky Irishman in his forties with a wild ginger beard and a liking for KFC, which he always ate at his desk on Fridays. This was evidenced by the smell in his office, and the grease stains on any paper given to you on a Friday afternoon. He was a good bloke.

'What are you doing here, Troy?' he asked.

I looked at him in surprise. 'Having my review,' I replied.

He waved his hand dismissively. 'Not in this room, you feckin' idiot. At the bank. What are you doing working here?'

Confused by the change in direction, I started the stock response of loving the environment, the work, etc.

He stopped me with a look. 'You're good at your job, but your heart's not in it. Yet you seem to have no ambition to go anywhere else. That's unusual for someone your age. Most of you pricks come here expecting to have my job in two years. With you I get the impression you'd be equally happy cleaning the office as working in it. What's that about?'

'Are you trying to get rid of me?' I retorted.

'Bank policy prevents me from saying yes.' He shuffled up straighter in his chair. 'But between us, if I thought it would get you anywhere I'd fire your arse right now.' His expression softened and he leaned forward. 'I've seen people like you, Troy. Hell, I've been you. Addicted to the pay cheque. More interested in what you take home than what you do to get it.'

'Rubbish. I care about the job.'

He laughed, his beard wobbling in waves. 'Maybe. But do you care about doing a good job no matter what, or doing this job well?' He saw my confused expression. 'There's a difference between wanting to do good work, and caring about the job. Are you excited to come to work every day? If not, what is it you want to do with your life, Troy?'

Live without these fucking Possibilities, I thought.

'You must have had something in mind when you left school,' he pressed.

My shoulders tightened. He was acting more like my dad than my boss. Then I thought of the canvas sitting in the corner of my room. Of lofty ambitions when paint first touched its surface. A face came unbidden, captured in time, then it swarmed out, to be replaced by Cat. I shook my head to jostle it away.

Adam mistook the movement. Disappointed, he looked at his hands, picking dead bits of skin from his palms. His voice turned serious. 'You need to figure it out. Do you know how hard it is waking up one day to find you're forty years old and you're trapped in a life you didn't expect?'

I had to shake my head – what else could I do?

He grunted and carried on. 'I don't expect to have this conversation again in a year's time. Meanwhile, procedure dictates I must give you a two-percent pay rise. Congratulations.' He grinned. 'Now piss off and do some work.'

If nothing else, the meeting had taken my mind off that night for a full twenty minutes. I'm not sure where the rest of the day went, other than disappearing behind a cloud of butterflies. Hell, they felt too big to be butterflies – more like bats flying around my stomach. I couldn't eat, couldn't concentrate at work.

It didn't help I'd made the mistake of telling Emily and she texted me every hour reminding me how important it was to get Cat back to Wellington. Nothing like a bit of extra pressure. It was crazy – why was I acting like a lovesick teenager?

I knew the answer, but avoided looking at it directly, not wanting to acknowledge the obvious. Because this time it was real. I don't know how I knew it, but I did. It was different because it was real, so the stakes were much higher.

And always there was the nagging thought that maybe this was just me using her to try and help myself.

I don't usually watch the news, preferring to get it on demand via the internet, but for some reason I plonked myself in front of the television that night. The lead news item was the disappearance of a girl in her early twenties. She had been hitchhiking home to Wellington and hadn't arrived. They flashed up a photo of her and for a heart freezing moment I thought it was Cat. Then I looked closer and realised she just looked like her. A memory of the man in the white car crept forward in my mind. He might have nothing to do with it, but I called the police anyway. First I blocked my number so there would be no awkward questions, then I gave them a description of him and the licence plate of his car. I found out later he was arrested and charged with the girl's murder. Part of me felt good, and part of me thought I should have called them sooner.

At 7.45pm I sat at the dining table, laptop open, Skype window ready. The next fifteen minutes ticked by like they were being held back, something standing behind them tugging on their shirts. Eventually the clock read 8.00pm.

Nothing.

Okay, that was fine – it had only just clicked over.

8.05pm. Still nothing. Sure, no problem – she was obviously running a little late.

8.10pm. Maybe she was having technology issues.

8.15pm. I checked the Messenger window for any new posts from her. Nothing.

8.20pm. Maybe the internet was out.

And so it went on, every minute accompanied by a reason, an excuse for her, all the time ignoring the most obvious – that she had simply changed her mind. I sat at the table until the clock clicked over to 9pm, then finally accepted that she wasn't calling. Complete disappointment flooded my body, like my parents had told me Santa and the Tooth Fairy didn't exist on the same day I found out Batman was only a cartoon.

Emily walked into the room, saw the look on my face, and walked straight out again. I didn't want sympathy, didn't want to be cheered up. I wanted to go to bed, forever.

Closing down the laptop, I went into the bathroom, and when I was washing my hands I suddenly lacked the courage to look at myself in the mirror. My eyes raised to the glass, instinctively closing upon seeing the broken visage reflected back at them.

Regretting my decision to look, I went into my room, carefully closed the door, and collapsed into the middle of my bed. I stared at the ceiling, and tried to pretend that maybe this wasn't real life. Maybe this was actually a Possibility and I would blink and not have to feel this pain. I barely knew her; to put so much importance on a single conversation, I was better off not having it.

I lay fighting with my thoughts for a long time. Sleep refused to come, my brain preferring to analyse, review, check things from a million different angles, over-analysing, inventing, shoving square pegs into round holes.

I'm not sure if I dozed or not, but the next time I glanced at my watch it was five past ten. Groaning, I rolled over to get more comfortable, then sat bolt upright and launched myself off the bed, stumbling over shoes before ricocheting off the door frame and spilling into the hall. Swearing, I rubbed my arm as I raced into the kitchen and threw myself at the table. Trembling fingers pushed the power button and hovered anxiously while it booted up. After an age the password box appeared, my fingers stumbling over the keys, getting it wrong, once, twice. Taking a deep breath, I forced myself to be calm, and this time the password was accepted. The Skype box was open and showed a missed call.

I swore again, repeatedly, when suddenly a notification appeared telling me there was an incoming call. A wave of nervous energy swept through me, and I laughed at the sheer craziness of it all. The sound of my own laughter steadied my nerves. I pushed the answer button, and Cat appeared on screen. She looked good, a little tired, her hair brushed but hanging loose, slight dark marks under her eyes, but still good.

'Hey.' The voice amplified and distorted by computer speakers unmistakably hers.

'Hey, Elissa.' I'd thought after I told her the story yesterday, about the Cat I knew, she might be offended, so I figured I'd better use her real name. It might have been my imagination, but she looked vaguely disappointed.

I said, 'Thanks for calling,' then groaned inwardly. What a stupid thing to say – she wasn't some telemarketer, or someone from the power company sorting out a billing issue.

'I thought you weren't going to answer,' she said.

'Yeah, sorry about that. A little issue with time difference.'

'Oh,' she replied absently. She didn't look comfortable, as if one finger was hovering over the disconnect button.

'How are you doing?' I asked.

'Okay, I guess. I'm not doing very well with this running away thing though, am I?'

'I don't know, you are in a different country,' I pointed out.

She looked around her room. She seemed to be sitting on a bed; behind her the door was closed, a dressing gown hanging on a hook. 'True, yet here we are talking. I fly thousands of Ks to get away from you, and then call you up. Not very successful.'

I was stunned. 'You were trying to get away from me? Why?'

She stopped fidgeting and looked directly into the camera. 'Because I like you. Or I think I do, or I want to. It's complicated.'

My heart started beating faster. 'Why is it complicated?' My voice cracked a little.

'Because you saved me. You were this hero who swooped in and stopped this horrible thing from happening, so I don't know if I like you because of that, or because I actually like you. And I always thought of myself as a strong person – that I would never need anyone, especially a man, to save me. Which turns out was wrong. And even if I do like you, the thought of being with you, of us being physical – fuck it, of having sex – scares the shit out of me. And I hate that, because the old me, the real me, wasn't like that. The story you told me about Cat, that would have ended with me taking you home and jumping you. Which now makes me sound like a slut, and I'm really not.'

'Elissa.'

'And then there's the fact that every time I see you it reminds me of that night.'

'Elissa!'

'And I look at your hand, your poor hand, and I feel guilty that it happened because of me, and so I hugged you, because I wanted all of it to go away, I wanted it to be okay.'

'Elissa!' I repeated urgently.

'And it was for a second, then you rubbed my back, and the real me, the ghost me, it loved the feeling, but the new me froze.'

'Cat stop!'

She paused.

'Take a deep breath.'

She did.

'You can let it out again.'

It came out ragged, with a little laugh. 'I've had a long time to think about this,' she said.

'And you've got a long time to say it, we're not on the clock here.'

She laughed again – not quite natural, but better – then turned serious again. 'How did you know, Troy?'

'What?'

'When I left your place that night I felt like the real me was slipping away for good. I didn't think I could recover, so I was going to go home and swallow a bottle of pills. But you signing to me, it got me thinking, and I changed my mind. So how did you know?'

Because I saw it as a Possibility. 'I didn't really. But you had this look on your face as you left. Like you had…'

'Given up,' she finished.

Yeah. I didn't know if I was right, but I thought … just in case.'

'That's a hell of a just in case.' Her voice was shaky and she wiped an eye.

I looked away from the computer, feeling my own tears forming, a lump materialising in my throat. I swallowed a couple of times and blinked rapidly to banish the tears, then looked back at the screen.

Cat was watching me. 'Allergies?' she mocked.

'Dust,' I quipped back.

She blew her nose on a tissue. I looked at the bottle of vodka sitting on the bench and resisted an urge to pour myself a drink. Outside the kitchen window a cat yowled in the darkness. I couldn't make it out until it leapt onto the fence and glanced back, its eyes bright beacons in the night. Then it was gone. I quickly looked back at the laptop, for a moment worried she was gone too.

Instead she was staring at me. 'Am I interrupting something?' she asked sarcastically.

'The local nightlife,' I replied. We sat in silence for a moment, neither of us totally sure which way to take the conversation. 'So how's Australia?' I finally asked.

'It's okay. I miss my friends, and my family. I'm pretty sure Steven is going to fuck up his relationship with Jessica without me there to keep him from being too much of a man.'

'If he does I can always slap him around for you.'

'Could you? That would be awesome,' she replied with a cheeky grin.

More silence. This wasn't going to plan.

'Troy, can I ask you a question? I always wondered this, but never had a chance to ask. That day on the beach – why were you building the moon out of sand? Emily told me you're not the artistic type.'

So I told her the story again. When I finished she was frowning. 'I still don't get how that translates into you spending all day on something that's going to be gone as soon as the tide comes in.'

I shrugged. 'I was killing time.'

She looked down, her hair falling across her face, shielding her from the world. She whispered something. I didn't catch it, and asked her to repeat it. She lifted her head and the look on her face was soul-destroying. 'I said I sympathise with the moon.'

No, that can't be right – she's supposed to be the sun, the brightness. I was the moon, the shattered, the disillusioned. You can't have two moons – it would rip the world apart.

'Elissa,' I began.

'Call me Cat,' she interrupted.

'Are you sure? Why?'

'Because I like the sound of the other woman. It's comforting I was like that once,' she replied wistfully.

'You could be like that again, Cat.'

She shook her head sadly. 'That old me is a ghost now. You can't bring back the dead.'

It pierced my heart, the way she said it, with finality, with acceptance. 'Maybe it's not dead,' I urged. 'Maybe you're having an out-of-body experience.'

'What, like astral projection?' she asked.

'Exactly. Right now you're looking down on yourself, separate but attached. You just need to find a way to get back into your body.'

'How?' She seemed curious, which I took as a sign of encouragement.

'I don't know,' I confessed. 'But we can figure it out.

'We? Since when has there been a we?'

'What sort of knight in shining armour would I be if I rode out of town after rescuing the damsel from the dragon?'

'Damsel?' she noted with a raised eyebrow.

'Too sexist?' I asked.

'Too old. What are you – like three hundred and fifty years old?'

'It feels like it sometimes,' I shot back.

'Then maybe you shouldn't help me. I'd hate for you to break a hip.'

'Harsh, but since you're the same age as me we can break a hip together.'

'I bet you say that to all the girls,' she said.

'Oh, sure, it's a great chat-up line. Works well in the retirement villages.' We both burst out laughing, I threw a guilty look at the door, aware of the time. 'So how about it?'

She looked down at her hands again. 'It's funny. I always considered myself to be a strong person, but with everything that's happened … maybe I was fooling myself.'

I shook my head. 'You're forgetting that you were doing pretty well defending yourself. If I hadn't interrupted you, you'd probably still be kicking the crap out of him.' I could sense her scepticism through the computer, but I pressed on. 'You're like this because you *are* strong. The stronger the substance the more pieces it shatters into.'

'The bigger they are…'

'Exactly,' I told her.

I could tell she was mulling the thought over. Eventually she looked at me. 'Why? Why are you doing this?'

'Because I like you too, and it's not because of what happened, it's just because.'

She chewed on her nail, then realised what she was doing and dropped her hand back into her lap.

'What do you say?' I asked.

She looked at me and smiled. 'Same time tomorrow night. Don't be late.' Then she disconnected the call, leaving behind a blank screen and a heart full of hope. I had the best sleep I'd had in a long time.

The one with the photo

'Hurry up,' Emily called from the car.

'I'm coming,' I replied, shutting the front door, and jiggling it to make sure it was locked. Walking down the narrow path I could see her impatiently tapping her fingers on the steering wheel. Glancing down the street, I saw a real-estate sign outside the old couple's house and made a mental note to try and find out what had happened to them.

I'd barely settled into the seat before she pulled away and merged into traffic. I understood her impatience, but that wasn't going to stop the merciless teasing for the rest of the night.

'Relax, they're not going to start without you,' I told her.

'God, why did I give up smoking?' she said, cutting off another car and earning an angrily shaken fist.

'Because it's illegal.' They said you could hear the collective hacking cough of thousands when cigarettes were taken down from shop shelves for the last time. Another swerve almost sent us into a parked car and I gripped the dashboard. 'Slow down,' I told her, 'or we're not going to make it at all.'

Her response was to push the accelerator down harder. Thankfully we were in an electric car and spared the engine's whining protest. As it was, a disembodied voice advised us we were going too fast in a residential area. She eased up slightly and our odds of surviving went from not a hope, to slim.

'If you cross the zone going too fast they'll shut down the car and we'll never get there.'

She immediately eased back to the speed limit.

'Why are you so nervous?' I asked her.

'It's a big show, Troy. This could make or break my career.'

I would have been impressed if she didn't say it every time she had a show dedicated to her work. 'You'll be fine. The critics love you, the public love you, I love you – what more can you ask?'

'Critics are fickle, the public are unreliable, and you're biased.'

I couldn't argue. We sat in silence as she navigated her way into the city and parked in her pre-booked space. The old museum was lit up with her name, and crowds milled outside the entrance waiting for the doors to open. She gripped my arm and steered me to the side entrance where her agent, Reed, waited.

He greeted us with a curt nod, preoccupied with all the minute details. 'You're late.' Reed was a tall, thin man, always impeccably dressed, with manicured nails and styled hair. I disliked him immensely and the feeling was mutual.

'Sorry,' she replied meekly.

'How's Fiona?' Reed asked as he ushered us through the door and into a narrow corridor. He was too busy to see her facial response.

'Fine,' she said coolly.

This made him look up. 'Sorry, Emily, wasn't thinking. Jack Cunnington is in attendance tonight.'

Emily paled. Even I knew who Jack Cunnington was – the most influential critic in the world. He really could make or break her career. Suddenly I felt nervous for her.

'You wait here,' Reed told us. 'I'll go tell them to open the doors.

Troy, for God's sake get her a drink.' He disappeared through the internal door, leaving destruction in his wake.

'Oh my God, oh my God, oh my God. Troy, I'm going to be sick.'

'Just breathe, Ems. You're good at what you do, and everyone knows it. Jack Cunnington knows it too, so breathe.' I pulled out my phone, brought up building services and ordered two Martinis – one vodka, one gin.

When they arrived Emily sculled hers back. 'I wish Austin was here,' she said.

Austin, her husband, had died two years ago from a brain aneurysm. Eight when he died, Fiona was now a precocious ten-year-old, but she was everything to Emily. I kissed Ems on the top of her head. She looked fabulous at forty-eight, her hair shorter now, and a few more lines on her face, but I wasn't one to judge. She wore a long blue dress that clung to her body, still in shape thanks to endless hours in the gym, and a job that resulted in shedding nervous weight every few weeks.

'There's something else, Troy. I didn't want to tell you until tonight, but you need to hear this before you go in.'

'What is it, Ems?'

'One of the –'

Reed burst through the door. 'Come on,' he said, grabbing her arm. 'It's time to start.'

Emily looked at me helplessly, and mouthed *I'm sorry* before disappearing through the door. Sorry for what? By the time I followed them, Reed and Emily had disappeared further into the gallery. I remembered when this was the Wellington museum, before the museum moved to a new purpose-built building in 2026. Since then this place had been used for a number of different things, including for a brief time as a historical-themed brothel. For the last year it had been the hottest gallery in the country. Every artist was desperate to show their work here, something guaranteed to elevate their stature in the art world, not to mention adding value to their work. A feature show was considered an unobtainable pinnacle for most of them. It was Emily's first.

No one paid much attention to me as I wandered across the ground floor, snagging a drink refill from a well-appointed waiter. The crowd emitted a nervous buzz across the ground floor. I glanced up the central stairs and caught a glimpse of Emily rushing back and forth. She didn't need to – everything had been set up hours before – but she was panicking. I knew she'd ignore any words of encouragement, so I kept quiet.

The crowd was an eclectic group, young and rich, old and well-connected, and politicians looking for a sound bite to boost relatability with voters. I recognised a few people by sight, well enough to give a head tilt, but not enough to initiate small talk. A few people recognised me and attempted conversation. I was polite but vague. I didn't know any of them; they had obviously seen my picture and read my bio.

Finally someone called for quiet and Reed appeared halfway up the stairs.

'Ladies and gentlemen, it is with great pleasure I welcome you to The Gallery tonight. We are here to see the latest work from an extremely talented photographer. Her work has been exhibited all over the world, she has twice won international photographer of the year, and she hails from right here in Wellington. What you're about to see is truly some of her best work. And I'm not saying that because I'm her agent and get a percentage of all sales.' He paused for polite laughter. 'As you can understand, Emily is extremely proud of her work, but she's also a little nervous, so instead of her saying a few words she would like to let her work speak for itself. Ladies and gentlemen, I give you Loss.' The applause was thunderous and genuine, a class-A drug to the insecure.

People began making their way up the wooden stairs to the second floor. I joined them, excited for Emily, and excited to see her work. I don't usually see what she is working on before an exhibition – I liked to be surprised. At the top of the stairs people fanned out into different directions. The stairs were in the middle of the floor, so there were lots of options. The lights were dimmed to allow the photos to have the greatest impact. Waist high, thick wooden posts dotted the floor. They were smooth and stained dark, and each displayed a photograph. I approached the first one and saw it was of an old dog, grey muzzle, coat flecked with white. It lay with head on paws, eyes clouded, the ravages of time seeping off the photo. I circled the post, noting the stiff legs, possibly arthritis, the thin torso, ribs pushing against the skin. This was a dog on its last days. The caption simply said, Companion.

A small boy, around five years old, stood open-mouthed at the image, before reaching out a hand to touch it. For a moment the picture distorted, dragged down like a finger in paint. The mother snatched his hand away and the picture re-established itself. The mother offered a red-faced apology to the rest of us and dragged the boy off.

Technology had advanced considerably in the past twenty years, particularly in optics. Photos are no longer two-dimensional snapshots – the latest cameras have holographic capability. I'm not much on how technology works; Emily tried to explain it to me once but my eyes glazed over and I pretended to snore. Basically you take a photo and when the image is prepared it creates a holographic image. So instead of seeing something flat on a page, you see it as it's supposed to be, three-dimensional, fleshed out, alive. Not really alive – the images don't move – but they look like they could. In the first year the technology was available the number of suicides rose by 25 percent. Grieving people could see a three-dimensional image of the deceased and it screwed with their minds. Some couldn't handle it. Like anything, though, once it had been around for a while people became used to it, and suddenly the old style of photos didn't cut it any more.

I moved to the next image, this one of the burnt-out shell of a house. In front of it stood a man, his head bowed, clothes singed and dishevelled. Despair seemed to radiate from him. You could virtually smell the smoke. A woman standing next to me began to cry and was immediately comforted by her companion. I felt a lump in my throat and quickly moved on. All around me people were reacting to the raw emotion in each picture. Some stood silently, reflecting on dislodged memories. Others shed their own tears. Conversation was at a low murmur, as if normal volume would offend the work. I spotted Reed across the room, leaning against the wall wearing a satisfied look. This sort of reaction was good for business. Which was good for him. As long as Emily got her entitlement I didn't care what he got, but the guy was still an arsehole.

Emily was kept busy with a steady stream of admirers, and no doubt she was too wired to enjoy it. I once asked her why she did it. Why put herself through this if it caused her such stress? She told me a story about her first holographic photograph. It had been of Fiona's doll, her very first doll, battered, dirt-stained, much loved. It was slumped down on a child-sized chair, eyes half open, one arm twisted unnaturally behind it, the other draped casually across its body. Emily said she had shown the picture to Fiona and one of her friends. Fiona burst into tears and her friend reached out for the doll, fascinated by the realism, disappointed when her hand went through it. Emily said the different reactions to the same image fascinated her, and that's what kept her going. I understood, but still had concerns about the toll these types of events took on my oldest friend.

As I drifted from one image to the next I became aware of a conversation buzz. People were talking about a picture I hadn't seen yet, in the large room off the main floor area. One woman dabbed at her eyes with a tissue, while her partner rubbed her arm in a consoling gesture. Intrigued, I wove through the crowd and slipped through the doorway. It was quieter in the room, the single image obscured by the only other people in the room. As I got closer the couple turned and stepped away, giving me my first clear view of the image.

The other person in the room noted my reaction. 'That's how I reacted too,' she said. 'Amazing, isn't it?'

I stood speechless. She patted my arm and backed away. I don't know how long I stood there, how long my brain had trouble processing what I was seeing. I didn't even hear Emily came into the room.

'I'm sorry, Troy,' she said softly from behind me. 'I should have told you.'

'Yes, you should have,' I said dully.

She moved next to me, slipping her arm into mine. 'You have to realise why I didn't. I knew this would be painful for you, even after all this time.'

And she was right. She knew me too well. Decades melted to nothing; all I could see was yesterday.

'I've asked them to close the room off until you're done.' Emotion was evident in her voice. She grieved for me. I appreciated what she said, but didn't trust my voice enough to tell her. She slipped away and I was alone with my memories. I sank to my knees in front of the image, bringing my face close, and drank in everything – the eyes I knew so well, a single tear frozen in time on a perfect cheek. It was as if Cat was staring at me, into me. Unbidden the last conversation we had replayed in my head and I imagined the words coming from the lips inches away.

I began to notice little things. She was older than when I last saw her, through the computer screen. Tiny lines crept around the corners of her eyes, and her mouth. Her hair was shorter and darker, carelessly cut. But it was the eyes I kept coming back to. I remembered them looking at me, remembered them sparkling with laughter. Now, even through the dimensional element of the image, I could tell they were sadder eyes.

I glanced down at the column. The label said sold, and I felt a pang of jealousy that someone else would have this memory in their possession. The title of the image was 'Too Much', but that's not what caught my eye. The photo was dated 2032.

A cold wave swept through me, and I stood and went in search of Emily.

I didn't get to talk to her alone until the end of the night; she purposefully dodged me. I stalked her through the crowd, but like a deer in the dense bush she remained elusive, flitting in and out of my peripheral vision.

Once the last guest left it was just Emily, Reed and me. Reed was in a buoyant mood.

'Jack Cunnington loves you, Emily. His review will send sales through the roof. You've hit the stratosphere, my girl.'

The term my girl irritated her but he was too preoccupied to notice.

'I'm tired, Reed. Troy and I are going home.'

'Of course,' he said pompously, like he was giving his permission. 'We'll talk tomorrow, Emily. You were wonderful.' He kissed her on both cheeks, then was off.

We didn't talk on the way to the car. She was nervous and I was angry and neither of us wanted to start.

She handed me the key and I punched in the security code, and slid into the driver's seat. I might be pissed off at her but she was exhausted, in no fit state to drive.

Traffic was virtually non-existent, but I took the long way around the bays. I like it better than the tunnel and hills. We were halfway around when Emily spoke.

'Pull over,' she asked.

I did and we sat in silence, me looking out the window at light reflecting off the water, her playing with the flat package she had carried from the gallery.

'I'm sorry, Troy.'

'You already said that.'

She sighed. 'You're angry with me.'

'I'm pissed off.'

'You have every right,' she said softly.

'Thank you,' I replied sarcastically.

'I've watched you pine for her for twenty years, Troy. I've watched you waste your life on a never was. I begged you to move on, but you never did – you buried it, scabbed it over. Why would I bring that up again?'

My anger cooled slightly, against my will. I wanted to be angry with her, but her words made sense. To cover my thawing mood I flicked the ambience button on the dashboard, activating the outside speakers. The sounds of the harbour, breaking water and crying birds filled the car.

'Where did you see her?' I asked.

She sighed again, pressing her head against the window. 'Five years ago Austin and I took Fiona to England – do you remember?'

I did remember. She'd been gone for three weeks, and came home exhausted and broke.

'About a week in we hired a car and drove around the countryside. Austin was over London, and we wanted to see if the old countryside still existed. You know, like the ones that used to be on the television shows when we were growing up. It sounds so clichéd but we discovered villages time forgot. Little places no bigger than a pub, a corner store and a few houses. Hell, some of them had horses riding down the main street. Austin insisted we turn off our personal devices; we were cut off and we loved it.' Her voice was bittersweet at the memory.

I switched off the outside noise and once again the whole world was inside the car.

'We saw this sign for a town, this tiny place with a village green outside the pub. It was so peaceful. We decided to stop at the pub for lunch. Elissa was working behind the bar. I didn't recognise her at first, not until she looked up and smiled.'

'She lived there,' I said, for the sake of saying something.

'Yes. She'd been there fifteen years.'

'Why?'

Emily looked at me with a mixture of sadness and pity. 'Isn't it obvious, Troy? She was hiding.'

'From what?' I asked, afraid of the answer.

'From the world. Austin took Fiona across to the green to play while we caught up. I didn't even need to ask – he was good like that.' The emotion constantly bubbling under the surface cracked in her voice. I reached over and squeezed her hand. 'She told me she drifted for a long time after leaving Australia. She hadn't known what she was looking for until she found the village by accident, and she felt safe there.'

I remembered the image at the gallery. The expression on her face. 'But not happy.'

Emily shook her head. 'No, not really. She asked about you. She sounded … regretful. But she didn't tell me what happened between you two. Neither did you.'

I remembered every word, every inflection, every gesture, even though it happened decades ago. 'I fucked up, Ems. I got frustrated and pushed too hard and she bolted. I tried to apologise, but the damage was done. She stopped returning my texts, wouldn't answer my calls. I even flew to Australia to see her, to beg for forgiveness, but she was already gone. She trusted me to be patient, to be there for her and help her heal, and I messed up badly.'

'Idiot,' Emily said.

'I know. You don't need to rub it in.'

'Not you,' she replied angrily. 'Her. She should have given you a chance. You're worth it.'

I didn't want to talk about it any more. 'I see you sold the image.'

She nodded. 'I got an offer I couldn't refuse.'

I started the car and pulled out. We didn't talk the rest of the way home, both lost in painful memories. At my place we got out of the car. I met her on the pavement and gave her a hug and a kiss on the cheek, letting her know I wasn't angry any more. She handed me the package she'd been holding.

'What's this?' I asked.

'An offer I couldn't refuse,' she said.

Speechless, I watched her get into the car and drive away. In the kitchen I carefully opened the package, fumbling over the wrapping before pulling it free. I placed it flat on the kitchen table, the image materialised and once more I looked into Cat's eyes. I felt overwhelming sorrow, and helplessness, and anger at the stupidity of wasting my life over a mistake. I went to put the image back into the box, determined to move on, but couldn't. There was something mesmerising in those eyes; I couldn't look away. Lost hope stared unblinkingly back at me, and my eyes filled with spilled emotion. I shook my head and blinked…

'Hey, are you okay?'

I opened my eyes, and found I was sitting at the kitchen table, laptop open in front of me. Tears wet my cheek and Cat was looking at me through the screen. It seemed like a lifetime since I'd seen her face, not just a photo. I reached out and touched the screen, my heart thudding through my chest.

She asked again.

'Um, sure.'

'You spaced out for a second.'

'Yeah, sorry. I was thinking.'

'Not too hard, I hope. If you're not used to it new things can hurt.'

'Don't worry,' I quipped, 'I'm not planning on making a habit of it.'

'Are you crying?'

I touched my face. 'Nah, must be the connection.'

She didn't seem convinced. 'I hope you understand. I'm almost ready to come home, I'm just not quite there yet.'

I smiled. 'You take all the time you need.'

The one with the parents

A little while later I received a summons from my parents. Originally worded as a casual text invitation to dinner, when I went back and said I was too busy, the direct response was, find time.

So the following Sunday I dutifully showed up, with Emily in reluctant support. It's not that she doesn't love my parents, and they certainly love her. But when I'd shown her the text from Mum she came to the same conclusion as me: something was up. It had taken some fast talking – and major concessions on TV viewing – before she agreed to come.

When we arrived Mum was in the kitchen, arms covered in flour, a scene that tugged at my memory and heart. Delicious smells wafted from the oven, and piles of peeled potatoes sat in a saucepan, waiting for their turn. Emily and I dutifully kissed Mum on opposite cheeks, then she sent me out to help Dad in the garage. Emily threw me a good-luck look, then turned to help Mum.

Dad was stacking boxes. We hadn't talked much since the scene outside the courthouse. I stood in the doorway for a moment, watching him work. He wore an old shirt, the colour washed away by years and detergent. The shirt's original buttons had long been replaced, and there were stitched holes in both arms and the back. Mum wouldn't let him wear it out of the house. It was his favourite shirt, and one of my constant memories from the moment I could form them. I asked him once why he didn't throw it out, and he told me it was the first shirt Mum ever bought him, so sentimental value outweighed aesthetics. I'd seen the shirt in countless Possibilities, seen him buried in it, and wear it to Mum's funeral. It was like a second skin on him. Sometimes I joked that he loved the shirt more than he loved me, and he laughed, and I laughed, and for an instant we shared the sort of father/son moment everyone should have.

He finished stacking the boxes before spotting me. 'You couldn't have helped,' he said, gesturing to the pile.

'You looked like you had it under control.'

He screwed up his face in mock anger, then waved me over. 'Well, don't think you're completely out of it. I was making space.'

'For what?' I asked apprehensively.

He grinned at me. 'For this,' he replied with a dramatic wave of the hand.

All I saw was an empty wall, with a pile of stuff to one side, including two paint roller and a drop cloth, and dammit he wanted me to paint the wall. Resigned I took off my jersey and threw it through the internal door. Dad opened the paint, a light green – Mum's choice, he replied to my raised eyebrow – and stirred it with a piece of kindling wood from the stack next to the internal door. Heat pumps were for younger people, he always said, coming from a generation that firmly believed in burning trees to keep warm.

We picked our rollers, like selecting duelling weapons, backed away from each other, then in unison touched the wall with paint-laden sweeps.

Never one for subtlety, Dad got straight to it. 'You're hurting your mother.'

I swallowed the guilt and stabbed at the wall with my roller, then realised he was waiting for an answer. 'I don't mean to,' I replied lamely.

'Maybe if we knew what was wrong we could help,' he offered.

'Who said anything was wrong?' I asked, deflecting the question.

I could see him out of the corner of my eye, looking at me thoughtfully, roller paused against the wall. He sighed. 'I figured this wasn't going to be easy,' he admitted.

'Then let's not do it,' I suggested.

'I know some things about hurting your mother,' he said softly. 'I had an affair.'

It took several moments to realise I was staring at him open-mouthed.

He offered me an apologetic look and resumed working. 'It was a long time ago, a one-off, stupid act. You were eleven at the time, I think. Anyway I'm not going into the details. Suffice to say your mum found out and it hurt her a lot. We nearly split up.' A pause while he reloaded his roller. 'We probably should have, but your mum was good enough to give me a second chance.' He said it matter-of-factly, as if Mum had offered to iron his shirts.

'I don't know what to say.'

He glanced across, then turned his attention back to the wall, his face bright red. 'My point is, I made a choice and it hurt your mother and she found a way to forgive me. So whatever the problem is, your mother can handle it.'

I still hesitated.

'She thinks she's done something wrong.'

'She hasn't,' I insisted.

'Then what is it?'

The garage suddenly seemed smaller, and warmer. Beads of sweat formed on my forehead. I fully expected to turn around and see one-way glass and an interrogation table. The internal door was a long way away, and I didn't think I would reach it alive. I resisted a sudden urge to click the main garage door up, roll under it and sprint off down the road.

'Well?' he insisted.

'I love Mum,' I finally said.

'She doesn't think so.'

My hand clenched tight on the roller handle at his stinging words. 'I guess I'm scared, Dad. Scared it will hurt too much when she dies.'

He dropped the pretence of painting and turned to face me. 'Unless you know something I don't, then you're talking about something that's years away. So what's this really about?'

I didn't answer, couldn't answer.

'Troy!'

'I've seen it,' I snapped. 'I've seen her die, more than once.' It rushed out, like the cork had popped and years of pressure erupted. 'I've been to her funeral, I've carried her fucking coffin, I've watched you struggle through the same eulogy so many times I could tell you what you're going to say. I've lost my mother over and over again, and then I come around here and there she is, in the fucking kitchen baking cookies, and it tears me apart every single time. So I'm sorry that I'm hurting Mum, but it's nothing compared to what I feel.'

'Don't swear,' Dad responded.

I laughed bitterly. 'Is that it?'

He jerked his arms in frustration. 'What do you want me to say, Troy? You're not saying anything, just spouting meaningless crazy words.'

My stomach twisted. This was the reaction I'd expected, and suddenly I wanted to rewind, hoping this was a Possibility and it would be erased from his memory.

'What does it even mean? You've seen your mother die?' His face a mask of confusion.

More silence while I figured out how much to say, how far down the rabbit hole to actually go.

'Wait, this isn't that thing when you were fifteen, is it?' His face cleared, leaving disappointment behind. 'Troy, I thought you were over that. We sent you to those doctors, you had all the medication…'

'I'm not crazy,' but my reply lacked conviction.

'Of course not, son.' I could hear the pity in his voice. 'But you are confused. Remember how you thought you were married to that girl – what was her name? Heather? And you thought you had a daughter.'

'It's real,' I insisted.

'But it's not, is it? Are you married? Do you have any children? I thought we were past all this.'

Stung by his words, I instinctively lashed back. 'The first time you met Mum she was at a bake sale at the church standing behind a plate of her chocolate chip cookies, and you've never been sure whether it was the way her hair fell over her face, or the smell of her cookies that attracted you first. Do you know how I know that? Because you tell the same story every time you give her eulogy.'

'You could have heard that story any time,' he scoffed.

'But I didn't, I heard it from you – at Mum's funeral.'

'Stop it!' he cried. 'Stop this nonsense, Troy. It's one thing to spout this crap when you're a teenager, but you're a grown man. We raised you better than that.'

It's one of the few times I've ever heard him swear.

He drew a deep breath, and continued in a calmer voice. 'If you truly believe what you're saying then you need to seek medical help.

But I think it's an excuse, just like it was when you were fifteen. You're hiding from the world, behind these fantasies of yours. You need to take responsibility for your actions Troy.'

'I am…I do. I'm trying to tell you what's happening with me.'

He slammed his roller onto the wall, sending drops of green flying across the room. One hit my cheek and began its long, slow slide down.

'This is why I've never told you,' I said bitterly. 'You'd rather think I'm crazy than actually listen to me.'

He dropped his roller and faced me, arms tight across his chest. 'Fine, I'm listening. Tell me all about it.' His voice was flat, face expressionless.

'Have you ever wished you could go back and do it over again? Not have the affair?'

He watched me through narrowed eyes, then gave a single jerk of his head. 'Of course.'

'Only if you go back it might never have happened anyway, because everything else could have changed.'

'What are you talking about?' he demanded impatiently.

I struggled for the right words. 'You made a decision to have an affair, but the other woman made the decision too, so even if you went back and changed your mind she might have already changed her mind so there was never going to be the opportunity in the first place.'

He stared blankly and I knew I was losing him. 'Look, was this your first and only colour choice?' I waved a hand at the wall.

He seemed startled at the sudden change in direction. For a moment I wondered if he was going to dismiss the conversation entirely. Then he answered, 'No, it was between this one and blue.'

'And you chose this one. And if you went back to that moment, to when you made the decision, you might choose the blue one instead.'

'What the hell are you talking about?'

'I get to go back and make different choices, but because everyone else has made different choices as well, nothing is ever the same.'

'What does that have to do with paint?'

'It was just an example, Dad.'

He threw his hands up in disgust. 'You know what? If you're not prepared to talk sensibly then I'd rather we not talk at all.'

'Fine,' I snapped. 'I'll get Emily and we'll go.'

He grabbed my shoulder. 'No, you won't. Your mother is expecting you to stay for dinner and that's what you're going to do.' I tried to pull away, but he held on tight.

Emily popped her head through the internal doorway. 'Your mum says to wash your hands and come eat.'

Dad looked at me for a long time, anger evident in his eyes. Then he released me and turned his full smile to Emily. 'Of course, we'll be right there.'

Dad and I didn't talk for a while. It should have upset me more, but I was too distracted, because a few weeks later Cat flew home. She and I had talked every night, but at her request I didn't meet her at the airport – she wanted it to be family only. Even though I was itching to see her in the flesh I respected her decision. We arranged to meet up for brunch the following day and Emily spent most of her morning, before leaving for work, laughing at my nervousness.

A southerly wind whipped off the harbour, rattling windows and bones. Rookies and amateurs struggled to keep umbrellas from being snatched into the air, like Mary Poppins on drugs. Wellington natives turned up the collars of their coats and slipped from shelter to shelter. Cat and I were due to meet at an underground food court; I guess she thought it would be better to meet for the first time on neutral ground. My disappointment in her choice was quickly suffocated by the excitement of seeing her again in person. Skype conversations were great, but no substitute for the real thing.

It was the cusp of the lunchtime rush, so there were plenty of empty tables as I descended the escalator, stepped past the sushi place, and looked around for Cat. We hadn't been specific about where we were going to meet, which suddenly seemed a mistake, given that food outlets stretched around three sides of the building, separated by shops and an elevator bank in the middle. I must have looked like a madman or a really bad spy, eyes darting in every direction, identifying and dismissing potential targets.

One full circuit later there was still no sign of her. She was only five minutes late according to the wall clock – nothing to worry about – yet with everything that had happened to get to this point my heart was beating faster than normal. I forced myself to take a deep breath, then started another circuit, this time going slower, just a normal guy trying to decide what to eat, and trying to find a girl.

The second circuit wasn't any more successful. By now she was ten minutes late and nerves were bubbling to the surface. Tables were slowly filling with smartly dressed workers, and the low buzzing of conversation began to ramp up.

I started on circuit three, walking slowly down to the first corner, the wait sapping my energy and enthusiasm.

'You know, this is fun,' came a voice from behind me. I turned to see Cat standing about a metre back. She wore a long, dark winter coat, supplemented with a black scarf, and purple woollen hat on her head.

'How long have you been there?' I asked.

She shrugged. 'Since about halfway through the first circuit.'

'So you've been behind me for the last five minutes?' I said incredulously.

She grinned at me impishly. 'I wanted to see how long I could follow you before you noticed. But I got hungry.'

'You can go back to Australia,' I told her.

'Hey, don't blame me – all you had to do was look behind you. You'd be terrible in a spy movie.'

'So would you. How many times have you seen James Bond give himself away to the baddies because he craved sushi?'

'Actually I was thinking pizza.' She stepped closer, and I could see nervous tension on her face. Neither of us were sure how to greet the other, both of us remembering the last disastrous attempt at a hug. Finally I stuck my hand out. Laughing, she shook it, holding on long enough to convey more than the formality that such a gesture suggested.

We chose and paid for our lunches. She went with the pizza option – a single slice with pepperoni – plus bottled water while I went with a sandwich and a Coke. I wanted Chinese food, but the thought of spilt rice and ending up with bits of vegetables stuck between my teeth diverted me from that choice.

We found an empty table against a wall, quiet while we arranged coats and trays, opened bottles and sampled food.

'Okay,' Cat said, 'here's the thing. I don't know what this is.'

'It's lunch,' I replied, slightly confused.

'I know what this is' – she gestured to her food – 'but I don't know what *this* is.' She waved a hand between the two of us.

'Oh,' I replied. The truth is I'd been focused so much on her coming home I hadn't given *this* much thought either. 'It's two people eating food and catching up.'

'Which sounds a little like a date,' she said, avoiding my gaze.

'Would that be a problem?' I asked hesitantly.

'Maybe. I don't know. All I know is I'm shaking like something that shakes a lot.'

I looked at her.

'Okay, not my best work, but it should give you an idea of how nervous I am.'

That made two of us. 'So this isn't a date then, it's a pre-date.'

'Pre-date?'

'Yeah, it's what you have before an actual date, to see if an actual date could occur.'

She thought about it, rolling it around in her mind to see all the angles. Slowly she nodded. 'What are the conventions of a pre-date?'

'No hand-holding, kissing, or any other physical contact,' I offered.

'Agreed. Also no talking about likes and dislikes.'

'Definitely,' I agreed. 'No sly looks checking the other person out.'

'Absolutely. Although sometimes eyes might accidentally rest on the wrong area of the other person, so perhaps we should define what that means,' she responded, clearly warming to the conversation.

'I'd say nothing in the chest area on you,' I offered.

'And nothing in the butt area for you.'

'Or you,' I added.

'Oh no. I've been working hard at the gym on my butt – I want you to check it out, but in a general admiration kind of way, not a sexual way.'

'What's the difference?'

'Length and intent.'

'That's not fair. How will I know where the line between admiration and lust is?'

'When I slap you, it's lust.'

Her eyes were brighter than I remembered, undiluted by pixels, taking in artificial light and turning it into something beautiful.

'And none of that,' she said, breaking contact and waving her hand in my face.

'Definitely none of that.' I swallowed.

With the general ground rules in place we spent the next two hours talking. A couple of times people lurked pointedly, waiting for us to move so they could swoop on the table, but we ignored them. When one particularly forthright woman told us to move Cat and I smoothly switched to sign language and pretended not to understand her. Despite the fact she had just heard us speaking she turned bright red and backed away, apologising. After she disappeared we switched back to talking.

I can't remember all the things we discussed. By some unspoken agreement we steered clear of the attack and its aftermath, so it was all general stuff – how she found living in Australia, and the news that Steven had broken up with Jessica. I felt a twinge of disappointment to hear that. He and Jessica had seemed like a good match and I felt some responsibility for getting them together. Cat didn't know all the details, but from what her parents had said it was his idea and Jessica was pretty cut up.

We talked a little about Emily. Cat expressed her regret that she hadn't stayed in touch as much as she should have. I told her Emily was doing well, mostly true, and understood about Cat leaving, mostly untrue.

At one point in the conversation I glanced around and spotted a woman sitting at a table a few feet from mine. About my age, with short brown hair and in a business suit, she looked vaguely familiar. A few seconds later I realised it was Heather, but it couldn't be. I didn't believe in ghosts. My heart stuttered and I blinked a couple of times, then realised it only looked like her.

'Who's that?' Cat asked, following my gaze.

I turned my attention back to lunch, picking at crumbs and draining air from an empty bottle. 'No one. She just looks like someone I went to school with.'

Cat studied my face. 'Crush?'

I nodded sheepishly.

'And she didn't feel the same. Ah well, probably for the better. If she'd felt the same way you might have gotten married and had a daughter, and I'd be sitting at a table talking to myself.'

She grinned, but my gaze went back to the woman, memories of Heather and I together, getting married, lying in bed, having sex, all flashing through my mind before I blinked them away.

'Sorry,' Cat said. 'I didn't realise she was the one who got away.'

I turned back to the woman sitting opposite me, more determined than ever not to let this one get away. 'She was the one who went away. Like you said, her loss. I'd hate for people to think you were crazy. Crazier, anyway,' I added.

'Touché,' Cat said with a laugh.

The lunch seemed to stretch on forever, but eventually Cat glanced at her watch and said she was meeting her mother for manicures together. She made a face at my raised eyebrows, and protested it was normal for mothers and their daughters to do that sort of stuff.

We threaded our way through the crowded tables and stopped at the bottom of the stairs leading to outside. She put on her coat and hat again – rugged up against the cold or armoured against the world, I wasn't sure which. We stood there awkwardly.

'So, what are the rules for ending a pre-date?' she asked.

I shook my head. 'I don't know. A handshake seems too formal.'

'And a kiss is too date-like.'

'What about a hug?'

'That could work, but it would depend on length and placement of hands.'

'So where does that leave us?' I asked.

'I guess it depends if the pre-date was a success. If it wasn't, then a general hand wave and a generic see you later would be acceptable.'

'And if it was?'

Someone bumped past us and I realised we were in the way of pedestrian traffic. I grabbed her hand and pulled her to one side. When I went to let go she didn't. I looked down at our hands together, feeling her warmth, then up into her eyes.

'Maybe we're overthinking this. A brief handhold seems acceptable,' she said softly.

I swallowed. 'Practically scandalous in Victorian times.'

She held on for a few more seconds, then gave my hand a squeeze and reluctantly – at least from my perspective – let go.

'Will you tell Emily I'll call her in a couple of days?'

'And me?' I asked in a light tone that didn't match the speed of my heart.

'You I'll call tomorrow. We need to start negotiations.'

'Negotiations?'

She paused halfway up the steps and looked over her shoulder. 'For the actual date,' she grinned.

'I'll have my people call your people,' I said to her back as she disappeared. I turned to see the disgruntled woman from earlier standing right behind me, the one we'd turned away from the table.

'So you can talk,' she said sarcastically.

I grabbed her arms and kissed her on the forehead. 'Take the damn table,' I said before releasing her and bounding up the steps.

The one with the acting career

Tension flowed out of the screen, infecting us with nervousness. We couldn't keep still though none of us wanted to leave the room; however my bladder was achingly full. The TV host said they were going to a break. I bolted from the room, sliding on the wooden floor before regaining traction and rushing into the toilet, yanking on my zip as I went, barely getting there before the flow started. I urged the urine to hurry, cutting it off before I should, hoping no one would notice the drops that didn't quite make it, and made it back to the lounge just as the ad-break finished.

I accepted the glass of water Emily shoved in my hand, some of it slopping over the edge onto my pants, helping conceal the damp patch. On the other end of the couch Steven and Jessica sat, recently back together for the second time. Across in the armchairs were my parents, and Cat's dad was perched on a dining chair wedged in between them. Her mother was in Melbourne with Cat. We'd caught one glimpse of them in the audience, clapping enthusiastically at the winner of an earlier category.

On the coffee table sat an unopened and chilled bottle of Deutz – the middle-class equivalent of champagne – and seven glasses, six of which matched. We'd been impatiently waiting for the last hour, sitting through endless people thanking other people that no one had ever heard of. I couldn't tell you the names of any of the winners.

Suddenly it was time. The host announced the presenter, and the presenter announced the nominees for best actress. It was the fourth name that interested me.

'Elissa Sanders, for *Lessons in Song*.'

The crowd went wild – at least the one in our room did. In the theatre thousands of miles away there was polite applause for the New Zealand nominee. While critics lauded her starring role in the drama series, newspapers and websites wrote off her chances compared to the darling of Australian television, Claudia Marshall. When I'd spoken with Cat a few hours ago she'd pretty much agreed with them, saying she was just going for the atmosphere and the autographs.

I'd reminded her only a few people get nominated each year for best actress and it was a big deal, so suck it up and take the compliment. She told me she loved me for being optimistic, and then laughed at me for being stupidly naïve and hopelessly biased. We'd ended the call gently arguing.

She looked stunning. Given the hours in makeup and hair, and getting dressed, I wasn't surprised. But then, as she had said, I was hopelessly biased, and considered her stunning in an old T-shirt and track pants.

Our pre-date seemed a lifetime ago. She'd exited the food court onto the street, only to run into her old acting agent, who convinced her to go to an audition. The audition turned into a part in a commercial, which turned into an appearance on a local TV show, which turned into a starring role in *Lessons in Song*, an Australian drama series. Our relationship was mostly via phone or Skype at the moment. It wasn't easy – something we were both aware of but mostly ignored.

'And the winner is…' Pause for dramatic effect.

I wanted to reach into the television and shake his fake tan off.

'Elissa Sanders for *Lessons in Song*.'

We went mental. Popcorn was thrown, couches were jumped on and somehow a pot plant met its untimely death. At one point I was being hugged by three different people, before Emily shushed us all. Cat made her way up onto the stage and stood in front of the microphone, grinning like a mad woman.

'This is…such an honour. The last year has been this crazy journey – it's been nonstop since we started filming the series. I've hardly had time to breathe, which is good because I can't breathe in this dress anyway. I want to thank our director Carl Silvers, who gave me a shot and believed in me, and the immensely talented Gareth McClure, who made every day on set bearable. To all the wonderful cast and crew, thank you, this is for you, for giving me the opportunity to look good. I'd like to thank my agent, and all my friends back in New Zealand – hi, guys. Especially my parents for all the love and support they've shown me over the years, particularly for letting me crash at their house when I couldn't afford to pay rent.' Music began playing in the background and she looked around wildly. 'Oh, there're so many more people I need to thank. The moon and the sun, I love you all, thank you so much.' She was ushered off the stage.

Everyone in the lounge buzzed, talking excitedly about the win and being able to brag about knowing a Logie winner. Everyone except Emily, who was staring at me.

I gave her a wink, attempting levity to offset how I felt inside. What did I expect – a romantic declaration broadcast to millions?

Actually that would have been nice, but I would have settled for a casual mention.

'I'll get the dip,' I said lightly. 'Open the bottle Ems.' But she didn't, instead following me into the kitchen. I tried to ignore her, but when I straightened up from retrieving the dip from the fridge she took the bowl out of my hand and set it on the bench.

'Stop it,' she said.

'Stop what?'

'Thinking.'

'Um, excuse me?' I said in an attempt to be vague.

She sighed. 'I know you, Troy. Right now you're overanalysing why Elissa didn't mention you in her acceptance speech. *What does it mean? Not even a casual mention.*'

I started at how accurate she was.

'And until you talk to her it's all pointless.'

'But – '

She held up her hand.

'Ems...'

She shoved her hand in my face.

I swotted it away. 'Seriously, that's fucking annoying. How can it not mean anything?'

'Troy, the history of the awards shows is littered with people who forgot to thank the people they care about the most. You and I have no idea what it's like on that stage. The pressure must be enormous – the lights, the cameras...'

'The action,' I quipped.

She gave me a disgusted look. 'My point is, don't overanalyse it. You know Elissa loves you.'

'Does she?'

'Surely you guys have said it?'

'Not in so many words,' I replied slowly.

'There are only three words involved – which one did you leave out? I, love, or you? It's obvious you're crazy about her, and she must be crazy because she's into you.'

'Gee, thanks, Ems.' I picked the dip up off the bench but she took it out of my hand and put it back down.

'Troy, why haven't you told her?'

I shifted uncomfortably on the spot. 'I haven't found the right time.'

'Jesus, Troy, you're not proposing to her. There is no right time – just say it.'

'Says the expert,' I retorted.

'I've said it plenty of times,' she shot back.

'Family doesn't count,' I said to be cruel, but she didn't take the bait.

'The difference between you and me, Troy, is I don't have anyone in my life at the moment that I want to say it to; you do.' There was a hint of regret in the way she said it. Emily was a strong, independent woman, or so she kept telling me, but she also loved being in a relationship. She hadn't been in one since the attack – apart from all those Possibilities that never happened and therefore don't count.

'You will, Ems,' I said, putting my hand over hers.

'Of course I will,' she said with a suggestion of a tear in her eye. 'I'm fabulous. But we're not talking about me, are we? We're talking about you being a typical bloke – too scared to say how you feel.'

'You're a pain in the arse. Oh, look, I can say how I feel.'

'Sarcasm is the lowest form of wit, but then I guess it's better than no wit at all,' she responded with a raised eyebrow.

I felt a little bad. 'The thing is, Cat… I mean Elissa and I, we haven't slept together.' At first I'd been determined not to push things, to let her take things slow, and then she'd had to go to Australia for filming. I'm not sure how she felt about the lack of sex, but it was becoming a real issue for me. I'm not some sex maniac, which I realise is exactly what a sex maniac would say, but most sex maniacs wouldn't have spent one Possibility living in a monastery for thirty years after taking a vow of celibacy. What I am, though, is a normal, healthy twenty-eight-year-old male who isn't having sex, and the longer it goes on the more I think about it. We've had phone sex a couple of times, but that's a fancy way of saying masturbation. 'And I don't want to say it before we do, because I don't want her to think I'm only saying it to get her into bed.'

She shook her head. 'Man, what is it like in your head?'

Before I could answer Jessica walked in.

'They sent me to find out what was happening with the snacks. But it looks like I'm interrupting so I'll tell them you'll be in when you're in.' She turned to leave but Emily grabbed her arm.

'Nope, you can help with this argument.'

'Discussion,' I said.

'Disagreement,' Emily said pointedly.

'Listen, I really don't want to get involved in your domestics,' Jessica said, trying to back away.

'All you have to do is answer a question,' Emily assured her.

'Okay,' she replied suspiciously.

'Has Steven told you he loves you?'

Jessica looked relieved. 'Oh, sure.'

'Was it before or after you slept together?'

'After – about thirty seconds after.' Jessica and Emily laughed, increasing my sense of discomfort.

'If he'd said it thirty seconds before, would you have thought it was to get you into bed?'

Jessica thought about it, then shook her head. 'Nah, by that stage I'd already made up my mind to have sex with him, and I think he knew it, so it was the icing on the cake.'

'See?' Emily rounded on me. 'Overthinking.'

'That's one opinion, Emily. Hardly conclusive scientific proof.'

'Fine. There's another woman in the lounge – let's ask her as well.'

I stopped her. 'Ems, that's my mother. You are not going to ask her anything that will make me imagine her and my father in bed.'

'Then stop being a dick.'

'What's the problem?' Jessica asked in confusion.

'Troy's all cut up because Elissa didn't say his name on television.'

Jessica looked at me thoughtfully. 'I didn't notice – I was just happy about her winning.' She picked up the dip and went in search of chips.

Ouch! It felt like she'd hit me over the head with the dip bowl. I'd been so caught up in what wasn't said, I'd completely overlooked that she'd won. All her hard work had been recognised at the highest level.

'How's that ego now?' Emily asked.

'Flatter than a pancake,' I replied miserably.

She patted me on the arm. 'Perspective, my friend. It's all about perspective.'

The logical part of my brain understood and agreed with her, but the logical part of my brain wasn't currently in charge. The emotional part was running rampage through the streets of doubt, burning cars.

The doubts remained, until my cell phone rang thirty minutes later. I could barely understand her through the background noise. I asked her to repeat it twice, before suddenly the noise subsided.

'I said, I won,' Cat said.

'I know,' I replied. 'Congratulations.'

'Thanks. I can't talk for long – I've shut myself in a cupboard, but they're looking for me. I've got more press to do. I can't believe I won.'

'I can. Didn't I tell you?'

'Yeah, but you had to say that – you love me.'

I glanced around at all the ears listening. 'Maybe.'

'Whatever. Did you get my reference?'

'What reference?' I asked.

'To the moon and the sun. To you and me. I wanted to say something special only we could understand. Tell me you got it? I've already had journalists asking me what I meant by it. You did get it, didn't you?' She sounded anxious and I felt stupid.

'Of course I got it.'

'Good,' she said, relieved. 'I gotta go, but tell everyone I'll call tomorrow, okay? Oh and I just heard they've given the go-ahead for a second season. Isn't that fantastic?'

'Yeah,' I said, trying to mean it.

'Talk to you tomorrow, babe. Bye.'

She was gone before I could respond. Suddenly aware of every eye on me, I forced a smile. 'She told me to tell you all hi, and says she'll catch up with everyone tomorrow.'

While conversations resumed, I mentally beat myself up. It was my story yet I'd been so focused on listening for my name I'd completely missed the reference.

I vaguely heard Steven talking about milking being the brother of an award-winning actress. The dads were talking about cars, in a way where neither of them really knew what they were talking about but didn't want to appear ignorant. It amazed me they had already moved on from the win, even though it only just happened. Emily and Jessica were discussing Cat's dress, wondering how expensive it was.

I sat and let the conversation wash over me. I glanced over to see my mother staring at me shrewdly. It was an insightful look, as if she could see my thoughts. I hated it when she did that. Mumbling some excuse, I got up from the couch and went back into the bathroom, closing the door quietly but firmly, the click as the lock slid home acting like a starter pistol for the emotions chaffing inside. They burst forth, brawling, tumbling over each other. I half expected to see tiny fists punching at the skin, but the face in the mirror was smooth, whole, and calm.

I felt stupid and scared at the same time. Stupid for thinking she'd forgotten about me, and for not getting the reference, our secret reference. And scared because it felt like she was so far away from me – not just geographically, but metaphorically. It was great she had won, and fantastic that more work was coming, but all of those things seemed to be pulling her in a direction that wasn't towards me. Which was selfish, but I felt like it was all slipping away.

There was a knock on the door. 'Everything all right, dear?' came my mother's voice.

I took another long look in the mirror before opening the door. 'Geez, Mum, can't a guy go to the toilet in peace?'

'I didn't hear a flush,' she said shrewdly.

'False alarm,' I replied.

'Mmm. You need to eat more fibre.'

'Mum, I'm twenty-eight years old. I hardly need nutritional advice.'

'Tough. I'm going to keep giving you advice on what to eat right up until you give me a grandchild, and then I'll give you advice on what they should eat. It's my prerogative as a mother.'

'Okay, more fibre it is. We should get back to the celebrations.'

Instead she leaned against the wall, suddenly looking tired.

'Are you okay, Mum?'

She waved it off. 'Nothing a few years off the body wouldn't fix.'

I leaned against the opposite wall and folded my arms, which brought a smile.

'You used to do that when you were a little boy.'

I straightened my arms, then realised I looked silly, fidgeted a bit before refolding them.

Mum laughed. 'You hated it when I questioned you, so you'd find the closest wall and lean against it, trying desperately to be cool. Sometimes you'd press your little body against the wallpaper so hard I expected to see an outline when you stepped away. And you'd fold your arms across your body like that. Like you were hugging yourself for comfort.'

'It was a little like the Spanish inquisition at times,' I quipped. But she wasn't far off. Leaning against the wall, I used to pretend I was a super hero who could push through the solid material like jelly, smooshing away from my mother's withering stare, through the wallpaper, through the gib board, insulation, and out the other side.

'You really like this girl.'

My brain froze at the sudden change of topic.

'You don't need to say – I can tell.'

'How?' I said.

She laughed softly. 'Call it mother's intuition, or call it the fact that this is the first one you've brought home to meet us.'

Actually I've introduced plenty of girls to my parents, just never in the real world.

'You're worried,' she added.

'I'm happy. She's in another country, and I'm a little sad I can't be with her to celebrate. That's all.'

'Are you sure?'

'Don't overthink it,' I said with a touch of irony.

She studied my face a little longer, then pushed away from the wall. As she neared the lounge door I had a sudden flash of memories – all the times she'd died crowded my thoughts like a morbid montage, sans music.

'Hey, Mum,' I called after her. She paused and looked back. 'I…' For some reason I couldn't say it. It seemed fatalistic, as if telling her would bring bad luck. We'd never been good at saying the words. I suddenly understood why I hadn't said it to Cat.

'What is it, Troy?'

I couldn't. Don't ask me why, but it seemed silly telling her. 'I do like her. She's special.'

Mum nodded. 'Yes, she is.' She disappeared through the door.

I wanted to go back into the bathroom, look into the mirror again and see if there was anything different – enlightenment perhaps, whatever that looks like. But I knew all I would see was the same face staring back at me, the same craters and imperfections. Whatever else happened, I needed my sun; I needed Cat.

Maybe I should fly over to surprise her. The idea materialised from nowhere, but the more I stood leaning against the wall the more it made sense. It was perfect, in fact – a romantic gesture, showing up at her hotel room with flowers. Mmmm, maybe not flowers; she probably had a million of them already. Something from home then, or maybe just me. There was time to work that out once I booked the flights. Shit, I'd better book the flights.

I went into the kitchen, grabbed the phone, and pressed the call button. A ring tone buzzed in my ear and I started to push buttons, then realised I didn't know what buttons to push. Dropping the phone onto the counter, I crossed to the table and fired up the laptop. My fingers tapped impatiently as it seemed to take an age. I didn't realise Emily had come in until she put a hand on my shoulder.

'What's going on?'

'I'm going to Melbourne.'

'Don't –' she started and I rounded on her.

'What do you mean, don't? I'm doing something stupidly romantic. It's the basis of every love story.'

She squeezed my shoulder. 'I meant don't waste time. I'll book the flights – you go pack.'

'Oh.' I felt foolish again.

Eight hours later I was on a flight to Australia. My luggage, stuffed in the overhead locker, consisted of all the clean clothes I could find – one T-shirt, one pair of underwear, black dress shoes, and two jerseys.

I slept most of the way, waking in confusion when the wheels thumped onto the tarmac. The taxi ride to her hotel took forever, especially because the taxi driver tried to talk to me about sports, which I didn't care about, and didn't believe me when I said one of the winners from last night's Logie Awards was my girlfriend.

It was mid-morning when we pulled up in front of the hotel. I paid the driver and climbed out in front of a pretty flash but not top-of-the-range building. The lobby was all clean lines and glass, and the staff well-appointed in dark-brown suits with white shirts and painted-on smiles. Approaching the check-in desk, I realised I didn't know Cat's room number. It was unlikely they would be any more believing of my status as an award winner's plus one than the taxi driver had been.

Pulling out my phone, I debated whether to text or call. Hard to casually drop it into a text, but then if she asked I could say I wanted to send her celebratory flowers. So I texted *Hey, wat yr rm no*? then retreated from the suspicious eyes of the reception staff and sat down on one of the couches dotted around the room.

My phone beeped. was gng to ask u same q

???? I responded in confusion.

Whr r u?

I wondered if I should be cagey. *Dwnstrs*, went my reply.

Nt likely.

Y????

Yr house dsnt have dwnstrs.

My heart dropped suddenly. *Wht???*

Wnt hme. 2 b with y.

But I cme hr 2 b with u.

So Ems sd.

Fuck.

Yep.

Sty thre, Im cmn hme, I said to avoid confusion.

K.

C U ASAP. I stood up and walked out of the hotel. My taxi still sat there, and the driver looked at me like I was mad when I told him I needed to get back to the airport.

My phone beeped again. *Troy…*

Yeah?

I love you.

It was spelt out in full, no text-talk for something so important. Tears threatened and I swallowed my emotions back down.

I looked out at the passing traffic. My first thought was to ignore it – both the message and the growing emotion inside me. Then reason kicked in. She'd said it to me; if I didn't reply at all she would think I didn't feel the same way. A flight home would take at least four hours, assuming I could get on one today. That's a long time to wait for a reply.

I let out a soft laugh, realising I was overthinking it again and I looked down to type a message – and blinked…

The one step forward two steps back

'Troy?'

Cat sat opposite me at an outside café table. Between us were half-drunk coffees and the mangled remnants of a scone (me) and muffin (her). The sun shone without heat, and we were the only ones sitting outside, both wrapped up in scarves and hats. Inside it was packed full of sensible people escaping the winter for a short time. 'Huh?' I said.

'You spaced out on me for a second. I said imagine if this lead somewhere? How amazing would it be to be a full-time actor?'

Memories snapped back into place. It was 2017. Cat had met her agent on the way out of our pre-date a week ago, and this morning she'd auditioned for a part in a TV show. Everything that happened in the Possibility was waiting to happen, or not happen. But if there was a chance that her success would take her away…

'Don't get your hopes up too much, Cat – it's a small part.'

She looked disappointed, perhaps expecting me to offer unfailing enthusiasm at her prospects for stardom. Then she shook her head a little, discarding the thought. 'There are no small parts, only small actors.'

'Is that a sizeist thing?' I said, hating myself for not being supportive.

'That comment was beneath you,' she said primly.

'Is that a sizeist thing?' I repeated.

'Shut up and give me your scone,' she demanded.

This was our second pre-date. Cat had gone home from our first one in high spirits, but then doubts had crept back in, so she'd asked for a postponement of the actual date, though she was eager to pursue further negotiations as part of a follow-up pre-date.

We'd arranged to meet for coffee. I didn't want any, and I didn't particularly want to meet in the middle of the day in such a public spot, but it was this or nothing. It might have been wishful thinking – or my imagination – but she seemed more relaxed today. It probably helped that we'd either texted or talked every day since the first pre-date.

What wasn't in my imagination was the glimpses of the real Cat appearing, the one who stole my phone allegedly to help me. She came out from behind the clouds every now and then with a laugh, a sly smile, a brash statement, so I knew she was still there. I just wasn't sure if Cat knew it yet.

We finished up our food and I suggested a walk along the waterfront. As we walked she slipped her arm through mine, a suggestion of intimacy suitable for a pre-date. We talked of inconsequential things – the latest movies we might see together, books, and it turned out we shared similar tastes in both. Despite the cold the waterfront was busy, bundled up families bustling from place to place, dogs reluctantly being walked by equally reluctant owners, lovers strolling hand in hand and laughing at things that probably weren't all that funny. We could have been one of them; I wished we were. Overhead seagulls sat on the wind, waiting for dropped morsels to scrap over. It was a good moment.

As we walked Cat's phone beeped. She slipped her arm free and dug it out of her jacket pocket. She flicked a couple of buttons and frowned.

'What's up?' I asked.

She read a bit more before replying. 'It's about this guy I met in Oz, Geoff. We went out a couple of times.'

My mouth went dry. 'He's no good,' I blurted out. She looked up at me in confusion, and I strove to find the right words to explain the outburst. 'You know, never trust a guy called Geoff,' I said lamely.

She switched her attention back to the screen, tapped out a brief reply and pressed send. 'That was my friend Angela, telling me Geoff has been arrested for domestic abuse. Apparently he hit his new girlfriend during a fight.' She looked me in the eye. 'So you were right, he was no good.'

The strength seemed to leak out of her, so I guided her over to a seat.

She admitted, 'I always thought there was something a little strange about him, but I thought it was me.'

'Did he…?' I hesitated, not sure how to phrase it.

'No.' She shook her head. 'He never hit me, but if I hadn't come back – that could have been me.' She shivered with the thought and pressed into me. I put my arm around her, it felt natural. 'How did you know?'

'I didn't – how could I? It was a guy thing, you know? You mentioned another guy so I immediately went into offence mode.' Even I didn't buy that bullshit, so it wasn't surprising when she pressed further.

'But it was so instant. It's like you recognised the name, like you knew something about him. Do you? Do you know Geoff?'

'No, I don't.'

She sat up and looked at me.

'I really don't.'

'Did I mention him to you? I don't remember doing it, but maybe I said he'd asked me out.' She sounded unsure, suspicious.

I imagined scenarios running through her mind, possibilities of why I might know Geoff. I could hardly tell her that her abusive Possible boyfriend murdered me on a beach. 'You're overthinking it, Cat. It was a throw away comment. You could have said any other guy's name and I would have said the same thing. How on earth could I know this guy Geoff was a violent ex?'

She mulled that over for a while, then relaxed her body. 'I guess you're right. Sorry. It's just … I can't help thinking it was a narrow escape.' She gave a rueful laugh. 'I guess you saved me again.'

'Must be my destiny.' I grinned at her.

'God, I hope not,' she retorted.

My face fell at the bluntness of her words.

She looked up in time to see the tail end of my expression. 'Sorry, Troy, that came out wrong. What I meant was I don't want to be the sort of person who constantly needs saving. That's not who I was, and it's not who I want to be.'

'Who do you want to be?' I asked.

'I want to be Cat. I want to be that girl – she sounds awesome. She sounds like the sort of person who isn't afraid all the time. I want to be her.'

'Good,' I said firmly. 'Frankly, I'm more interested in her anyway.'

She punched me on the arm. 'Then go spend time with her,' she said.

'Can't.'

'Why not?'

'She doesn't exist anymore,' I said calmly.

Cat sat up and looked at me. She brushed wind-blown hair from her face. We were agonisingly close to each other, our lips separated only by self-control and fear. My heart told me to bridge the gap, to press my lips against hers, but my head screamed at the disaster that could follow for not showing restraint.

She trembled slightly, possibly suffering the same dilemma. 'You sound sad,' she whispered.

'Reflective,' I said.

'Would you rather be with her?'

'She's a ghost,' I replied. 'There's nowhere else I want to be.'

She searched my eyes, looking for something – reassurance, sincerity, hope? Only she knew. Slowly she leaned in and for a heart-stopping moment I thought we were going to kiss, then she moved her head to the side and pressed her cheek against mine. It was cold, but soft, and she smelled slightly of vanilla.

'Thank you,' she whispered.

'For what?'

'Being patient.'

We stayed that way for a moment longer, then she pulled away, and a stab of loss shot through me. Cat leaned back in the seat, and taking her cue I leaned back as well, and together we watched the world move forward.

'Do you think we're the only people here on a pre-date?' she asked in a light tone. I recognised she wanted to isolate the intimacy, and return to easier things.

'Most likely. The concept hasn't really caught on yet. Although those two maybe?' I pointed to a man and woman passing by. As we watched the man casually stretched out to take hold of the woman's hand and she, equally as casually, moved her hand away.

'Oh, dear, he doesn't know the rules of pre-dates,' Cat commented.

Undeterred, the man tried to put his arm around her shoulder, but she slipped out from under it, then slid her arm through his and held on, a compromise he seemed content with.

'He'd better give up or there won't be an actual date,' I noted.

'Some people don't get it,' Cat replied sadly. 'What about that couple?'

An older couple, both probably in their sixties, strolled towards us.

'Married,' I said dismissively.

'No wedding rings,' Cat pointed out.

'Maybe they aren't married to each other.'

'Ah, a secret rendezvous, a romantic tryst.'

'Not so secret.' I indicated our surroundings.

'Maybe they're just bad at it,' she suggested.

'You'd think once you get to that age you'd be good at keeping secrets.'

'It's like riding a bike – you have to keep it up or you get rusty,' Cat replied.

'I see.'

'Tell me a story?' she asked.

'When I was twelve…'

'No, not a real life story. I'm not trying to bond over childhood experiences. Make one up.'

This girl was killing me with her demands on my creativity. I made up a story about retired spies walking along the waterfront one day who get drawn into an afternoon of intrigue and danger. It was terrible, but Cat withheld all criticisms.

She didn't talk at all for a long time, finally looking me in the eye. 'So, Troy Messer, what secrets are you hiding?' She said it lightly but there was an importance to the question.

For a fleeting moment I thought about telling her everything, laying it all on the line. But I'd tried that before, with different people, in different Possibilities, and it never ended well. Besides, it's not the sort of thing you bring up on a pre-date. It's more a second or third date – or never – sort of thing.

'I have never learned to ride a bike,' I said flippantly.

'Not even a tricycle?'

'I'll never keep a secret from you, Cat,' I lied.

She looked for truth in my face and seemed satisfied.

'Unless it's a surprise birthday party. Then I'll have to.'

'Fair enough,' she replied.

I felt bad for lying to her, but I'd feel worse if she ran away screaming. We sat in comfortable silence a little longer, occasionally breaking it to make observations on passers-by. When I reluctantly conceded it was time to go I walked her back to her car, parked in a little side street off Customhouse Quay. Cars circled the block like waiting sharks, looking for empty spots, but there wasn't much foot traffic and for a moment we had the footpath to ourselves.

'What's the appropriate resolution to a second pre-date?' I asked with a mixture of hope and nerves.

Her expression mirrored my feelings. 'I'm not sure,' she admitted.

'A hug?' I suggested.

She shook her head. 'Too generic.'

'A kiss?'

Again her head shook. 'Too intimate.'

'On the cheek?' I offered as an alternative.

She considered this for a moment, then nodded. I leaned forward, and after a micro-hesitation so did she. Gently I placed my lips on her soft cheek, felt her lips on my skin. Then they were gone, leaving a warm impression, a source of heat that slowly spread across my face and down my neck. She winked at me and we both laughed, maybe from relief, maybe from something else.

After she got in her car and started the engine I waited for her to put it into reverse and pull out of the park, but she sat there. Through the glass I could see her studying me. Finally she wound the window down.

Puzzled I walked around the side of the car and she looked up at me thoughtfully.

'Tomorrow night, 6.30, dinner, you and me.'

'Okay,' I replied calmly, as if my insides weren't jumping around.

'I'd rather do it tonight but I've got this family thing, and I think we should do it sooner rather than later, before I change my mind again – don't you think?'

'Sure,' I agreed.

'Right, tomorrow, 6.30, dinner, you and me. It's a date.'

'An actual date?' I wanted to be clear.

'A real-life date,' she replied. 'Watch your feet.' She put the car in reverse and I stepped back on the footpath and watched her disappear around the corner. Suddenly tomorrow seemed like more than a lifetime away.

I wanted to skip down the road in giddy joy, but settled for grinning like an idiot. As I turned the corner into our road I could see the old couple once more at their gate. The old woman made to grab my arm but I'd already stopped.

'You there, wipe that stupid smile off your face and tell me which one you prefer.' She held up two photos of puppies. One was a Dalmatian, the other a Terrier.

My smile widened. 'Neither. My friend volunteers at the SPCA and she can find the perfect dog for both of you.'

'I don't want a mongrel,' the woman said primly.

'We're all mongrels,' I replied with a wink at her husband.

The smile didn't leave my face until I walked up the path to my front door.

My phone rang; it was Kelvin. 'Could you swing by, if you're not too busy?'

'I just got home.'

'Great, then I'll see you in half an hour,' he replied, hanging up before I could answer.

With a sigh I turned around and made my way back into the city. Kelvin was sitting in the front pew when I entered the church doors. He didn't react to my arrival, and for a moment I wondered if he was asleep, or worse.

I sat down next to him. His eyes were closed but his beard trembled as air went in and out of his mouth.

'Do you believe in God, Troy?'

It was an uncomfortable question. How do you tell a priest you don't believe in something that is at the core of who they are?

'There is no right or wrong answer,' he added, sensing my hesitation.

'Really? So it's okay to say I don't believe God exists?'

He opened his eyes, turning them towards me. 'God knows you exist,' he said with a wink.

'Did you ask me here for a theological discussion?'

He shook his head. 'Your father rang me. He's concerned about you.' He saw the flash of anger cross my face and held up his hand. 'He rang me as a friend, and because he loves you.'

'So did he tell you he thinks I'm crazy,' I replied bitterly.

'He has concerns,' Kelvin admitted.

I stood up, fists clenched in frustration. Kelvin placed his hand on my arm. 'Sit down, Troy. I'm too old to come after you if you storm out dramatically.'

I slumped back onto the seat, and he patted my arm encouragingly. 'Your father doesn't think you're crazy. But he's worried about you and asked if I would talk to you.'

'What did he tell you?' Bitterness twisted my words.

Kelvin paused, weighing his words carefully. 'He told me that you seem confused sometimes about what's real.' He held his hand up again as I opened my mouth to retort. 'These are his words. He's worried you're running away from something. Are you, Troy?'

I shook my head. 'I'm not confused.'

'But you are running,' he replied.

I shook my head again. 'I'm not running from anything; it's running from me.'

'What is?'

'The world.'

'I'm not sure I follow,' he admitted.

'Tell me something, Kelvin. Is everything we talk about confidential?' When he nodded I checked. 'Even from my parents?'

'No one will know what we speak of except me and God.'

So I told him everything. At the end I waited expectantly for the look of sympathy, or fear that a completely bat-shit crazy man was sitting next to him.

Instead he appeared thoughtful. 'I'm sorry, Troy,' he said. 'That sounds like a very lonely existence.'

'That's it? You believe me?' I asked, stunned.

'I believe that you believe it.' It was more than I'd hoped for. 'So what's it like, living with these … what did you call them? Possibilities?

I looked around the empty church, picturing it full of people, waiting to celebrate their faith, to rejoice in their belief that there was a higher power, that something was waiting for them when they moved on from this world. I felt more disconnected from them than ever. Kelvin was waiting for an answer and I said to him the most honest thing I could think of. 'It's like the whole world has amnesia.'

'How does that make you feel?'

'Tired,' I replied.

He studied my face, and I turned away from his gaze. 'You say some of the things that you live in these Possibilities actually happen. Have you considered the possibility you're psychic?'

I had, but the research I'd done didn't back it up. Psychics are generally vague about things, sensing someone is near water, that sort of thing. I'd scoured the internet, searching for anything that would point to others who suffered the same thing as me, and always came up blank. I shook my head.

'I'm sure God has a reason for this, but I'm not privy to his innermost thoughts so I can't determine what it is. What I will say is this. If these things are happening to you, there are two ways you can go. You can let them isolate you – strip you of friends and family and everything that matters so you can protect yourself. Or you can embrace it, treat it as a gift to be used to make this world a better place.'

'It's more like a curse,' I said angrily.

'Sometimes things are both. It can appear a curse to you, because you've been given this burden. But if you can use it to help just one person, then it's something wonderful as well.'

Further conversation was halted when a group of parishioners came into the church, looking to steal Kelvin away for tea and absolution.

'What are you going to tell my parents?'

'What I always tell them. That their son loves them very much, and to be patient.'

I breathed a sigh of relief as he was swept away in a sea of cardigans and perms. The silence that fell was disconcerting, the words Kelvin said troubling. I stared at the altar and tried to will away the frustration building inside me.

'Is this you?' I said quietly, my voice lost amongst the wooden pews. 'Is this you?' I repeated louder. 'Did you do this to me?'

I stood up, fists clenched. 'Why? Why would you do this? What could I possibly have done to deserve this thing?'

The only sound was my own voice echoing back at me.

'WHY?' I screamed.

It may have been God's house, but it seemed he wasn't taking questions.

'Fuck you,' I said bitterly and left, vowing never to return.

The one where I ran

The waitress delivered our drinks. His was in a takeaway cup and I revised my assumptions about the purpose of the meeting. The musty smell of wet clothes mingled with roasted beans, while conversations mingled into an unintelligible heavy cloud of noise above us, waiting to burst and deluge words onto damp heads.

'I never had a chance to properly thank you,' Cat's dad said. He'd summoned me here via phone call the night before.

'There's no need.'

'I disagree. My children are extremely important to me. One of them was in trouble and you helped. It was rude of me and I apologise.'

My body relaxed and the breath I'd been holding eased out into the world. 'You're welcome,' seemed a lame response, and his smile acknowledged the awkwardness of the situation.

'Elissa is doing well. She's very strong.' His voice was tinged with pride. 'But she's not back to her true self, not yet. It would be a shame to have progress halted.'

My mouth went dry. 'Why would it do that?'

He shrugged. 'Any number of things, I expect. Ill-timed words, opportunists, misplaced intentions.'

'This is about our date,' I realised, wondering why it hadn't clicked sooner.

'This is about the timing of your date,' he replied.

I looked around the café, searching for the right words.

'Good,' he nodded. 'You're not protesting. People who protest too quickly and too loudly lack sincerity, don't you think? I work in parliament, and I'm around insincerity every day. It's very *troubling*.' He emphasised the final word.

'No doubt,' I responded. 'But I'm not a politician, and I genuinely like your daughter.'

He searched my face, poking at my words for suggestions of duplicity, and seemed satisfied with the results. 'I believe you though I can't speak for whether those feelings are reciprocated. But liking someone doesn't negate the possibility of something going wrong. In fact, it's likely to increase the odds in my experience.' He sipped his drink.

'Saying the wrong thing can happen any time, regardless of the situation.'

'Perhaps, but I have a little more experience in these matters.'

'Age and experience don't always go hand in hand,' I shot back.

'No,' he agreed. 'But age usually brings clarity about your actions.'

'My head is clear,' I told him.

'Are you saying you won't hurt my daughter?'

'I'm saying I like your daughter, and have no desire to hurt her in any way, ever.'

'Then I should return to work.' He stood, shrugged his coat on, and picked up his umbrella. 'I hope you know what you're doing Troy. And I hope you know why you're doing it. And I hope this doesn't end badly for her – and worse for you.' Without waiting for a response, he wove through the tables and out into the winter's day.

After he left certainty slipped away with him, and as my coffee cooled my brain heated up. I had become singularly focused on the assumption I was the one to fix Cat, or at least make her Cat again. But maybe I wasn't. Maybe all I would do was make it worse for her. Be a constant reminder of what she went through. What if she never became Cat again because of me? Worse, what if her feelings were a result of me saving her from the attack, and not genuine?

After finishing my drink I returned to work, and spent the rest of the day distracted by disturbing thoughts. Several times my colleagues asked if I was all right, and I pleaded ill health. Around lunchtime Cat texted and suggested a restaurant – Italian – or as an alternative, a Malaysian joint off Courtney Place. I said sure to the Italian, and offered to pick her up. Several messages went back and forth with the details, and all the time my mind was looking at the issue from different angles. Was it even a problem? I hadn't decided by the time I left work.

I got home about 5.30pm. Emily was at the gym and I was glad for the silence, although she did text a few minutes later to say good luck, and not to screw it up. Sometimes the feeling of love is overwhelming.

I wanted a shower, but decided against it – our antiquated system would have taken too long. So I settled for splashing water on my face, reapplying deodorant, and for good measure a couple of squirts of cologne. That done, I checked my face in the mirror – first looking directly forward, then slowly moving my head from one side to the other, changing from full to half, to crescent. It left me unsatisfied, and with more doubts. All excitement about the date was gone, all the energy from the day before submerged in molasses-like uncertainties.

Disturbed, I turned away from the reflection and went into my room, wondered what I'd gone in there for, then walked out again.

Meandered into the kitchen, once around the dining table, then out into the hallway again. I realised I was procrastinating, delaying my departure even though time moved forward, creeping towards the moment between being on time and being late. I checked my phone, even though it hadn't signalled a message. I was hoping she would cancel, that she would resolve the turmoil for me. Abruptly I grabbed the car keys off the table next to the front door, went outside and shut the door behind me. The click of the lock seemed to calm the doubts. I strode more confidently to Emily's car, gunned the engine and screeched away from the curb in a fuck-you to the uncertainties.

My newfound buoyancy dripped away the closer the car got to her house. Each turn, each traffic light sapped my confidence.

I pulled up and put the car in park, but left the engine idling. Behind her front door she would be waiting patiently, maybe excitedly, maybe nervously. I turned my attention to the rear-vision mirror, twisting it around to see my face. The eyes of the moon stared back at me, dark and shadowed. Did I want those eyes, that face, and the problems resting behind it, to infect Cat with their shadows?

Disgusted, I put the car into drive, pulled away again, and drove straight to the closest pub, turned my phone off, and drank myself into oblivion.

The next morning I woke up in my own bed, fully dressed and still drunk. Squinting through blurry eyes at my watch revealed it was midmorning. I'd slept through my alarm, and Emily leaving for work, neither of which was usually quiet. My phone lay on the table next to the bed, but the screen remained stubbornly blank when I pushed buttons. A vague memory of turning it off filtered through the haze.

When it powered up there were eight messages and four missed calls. All from Emily and Cat. I deleted them without looking, guilt overpowering the alcohol. As if she somehow knew I was back in touch with the world, Emily called. I let it go to voicemail, then drifted back to sleep.

The next thing I knew something hit me in the face. Jolted awake, I felt as if the world swam in and out of focus for a moment before something rushed at my head and my face received another battering. I raised two hands as a shield, then realised Emily was standing next to the bed, pillow in hand. Her expression was disgust mixed with disappointment. She'd never looked at me that way before, and it hurt worse than a pillow to a hungover head.

'Kitchen, now,' she ordered.

Getting vertical took longer than expected. The first attempt induced a wave of nausea so strong it took all my willpower not to spill my guts on the bedroom floor. When it passed I took a hesitant step to the door, immediately followed by a stumble, then another step. After what seemed an age I managed to get to the kitchen and collapse onto a dining chair. The room stopped spinning after a minute. In time to see Emily put a glass of water down in front of me.

'Thanks,' I croaked.

'It's not out of sympathy. I want you awake enough to hear what I have to say.'

I took a couple of sips, the water sluicing away the taste of bile and alcohol and possibly cigarettes. 'I know what you're going to say. I fucked up.' My voice still cracked but was at least recognisable.

'You left fucked up way behind on this one.'

'Is she mad?'

'That's between you and her.'

'Then why are we talking now?' I asked sullenly, wishing the world wasn't so loud.

'Because I'm mad.'

Something in her voice made me look up. Her face rippled with barely controlled anger, her cold eyes penetrating my skin and tearing at my soul. I wilted under the look and slunk back to staring at the glass of water.

'What were you thinking? Scratch that, you weren't thinking. Of all the selfish...' She stopped, rage evident in her expression. She paced the room behind me, then walked around the other side of the table and sat down. 'Look at me, Troy.'

I raised my bloodshot eyes and met her gaze. Her hands were placed flat on the table, knuckles white as she pushed them down, possibly to stop herself from reaching across and slapping me.

'We've known each other for a long time, and I've gone through every emotion during that friendship – happy, sad, worried. I've been proud of some of the things you've done, and concerned about things you haven't done. But today...' She looked away, struggling to continue, then turned back. 'Today is the first time I've been disappointed in you.' Those ten words tore me to shreds, and the tone they were said in burnt the pieces and scattered the ashes to the wind.

'Ems, please...'

She shook her head. 'Elissa was relying on you to be a nice guy. I told her you were a nice guy. I told her you would never hurt her, and she believed me. Hell, *I* believed me, so you have one shot to redeem yourself. Tell me what happened.'

The light from the windows behind cast her face in shadows and stung my eyes. I dropped my eyes back to the drink in front of me. 'I'll be bad for her,' I said weakly.

She slammed her hands on the table, causing me to jump. 'Bullshit,' she hissed. 'Fucking bullshit.'

'It's true.'

'Fucking bullshit,' she repeated. 'Why are you always putting yourself down? It's getting old, Troy.'

Tears appeared without warning, running silently down my face. 'It's true, Ems. I'll be bad for her. I'm bad for you. I –'

'What?' she said, anger sharpening her voice.

'I have too many ghosts.'

'What the hell does that even mean?'

Words stumbled and caught on my teeth, none willing to escape into the world. I shook my head.

A chair scraped as she stood up. 'Fix this, Troy. Fix it now or…'

I looked up at her. There was something ominous in the words she left unspoken.

'Just fix it. I'm going back to work.'

She left me nursing the glass of water and a shattered soul.

A little while later I managed to stand up, without much protest from head or stomach, and staggered into the bathroom. The mirror drew me forward, the refrain from *Snow White* slipping through my brain: Mirror, mirror on the wall, who's the biggest dickhead of them all? The answer was in the red eyes and the face that wore all those Possibilities. The cracks and flaws were sharper, harsher in the artificial light. Today, more than any other day I could remember in this life or any of the Possibilities – today I was the moon.

Something bubbled inside me, and the longer I stared into the mirror the stronger the feeling got. The mirror was the beach, and what does the moon do to the beach?

Raising my hands up, I slammed both fists into the glass. Nothing happened, other than a jolt through my knuckles and through my wrists. I slammed them again, and again, felt a crack and joyfully thought it was glass, but it was only a bone. Again, again, hammer, slam. There, a tiny crack in the glass. Redoubling my efforts, blood smearing the glass, more cracks appearing. Sweat appeared on my forehead, slipping into my eyes, stinging them.

I blinked it away.

The one where she runs

And I was sitting in my car staring into the rear-vision mirror, the engine running. Through the window I could see Cat's front door closed against the world.

A quick glance at my watch confirmed it was 6.30pm, date time. My fists ached with phantom pain from the Possibility. I expected them to be covered in blood but the skin was unmarked. I wiped away sweat that wasn't there, then put the car in park and turned off the engine.

The most disturbing part of the Possibility was Emily's reaction. It might have been deserved, but still seemed excessive, and I made a mental note to ask her if she was all right. Shame and a desire not to have Emily ever look at me like that again was enough to dampen the doubts. Taking a deep breath, I opened the car door, at precisely the same time as my phone beeped.

It was from Cat and it wasn't a where-are-you message.

Sorry, can't do it. Talk to you tomorrow. Don't hate me.

I didn't know what to think. Considering the Possibility I'd just lived, and how close I'd come to bailing, it was hard to get upset with Cat, but I still felt disappointed.

K, went my reply. It was childish not to send more, a part of me knew that – the response should have said, No problem, talk to you soon. Let her know it wasn't an issue. But the pissed-off part of me was in control of my fingers and that's all they would let me type. *Let her stew on that*, I thought vindictively.

Turning on the engine, I took one more glance at the house, and saw a curtain twitch, knew she was behind it – possibly wondering what the one letter actually meant, and maybe feeling terrible. *Fuck*, I thought, picked up my phone, and sent a follow-up message. *No problem, talk soon.*

Feeling better for her and worse for me, I left, the drive back home seeming to take forever.

Emily was sitting in the lounge when I walked into the house. 'What did you do?' she asked.

'Why do you assume it was me?'

She gave me a look that said of course it was my fault.

'She cancelled when I got to her house.'

'Really? Huh.' Emily got up and left the room.

I'd expected more, so I followed her into the hallway and through to the kitchen where she picked her phone up from the counter. Manicured fingers flew over keys and seconds later a message was sent. Immediately a response came back.

She studied it for a moment then looked at me with a mixture of pity and apology. 'You need to give her more time, Troy.'

'I don't need to do anything.'

'Don't be a dick.'

'Okay, so I give her more time. We've already had two pre-dates – what's a little more time?'

'Exactly, she wants this. She's just scared,' Emily said.

I sighed. 'What do you want for dinner?'

She studied my face, and didn't seem satisfied. 'It's important you know I know you changed the subject, but I'll allow it.'

'You'll allow it? What are you, a judge now?'

'I am your superior in every way,' she replied with a toss of her hair. 'Now make me some of your pasta, and don't go heavy on the garlic – I'm not trying to repel vampires.'

She perched on the edge of the bench and watched me as I worked, putting a pot of water on the stove to heat, and chopping vegetables. It was a comfortable, normal scene in the flat.

'What if more time isn't enough for her?' I asked, crushing cloves of garlic, then dumping them into a hot frying pan.

'It will be,' she replied. There was something steely in her voice that caused me to glance up. It wasn't the same reaction to the last Possibility, but something was definitely bothering her. I got the sense that Cat and me being together was important to her.

'Ems, what's going on?' She didn't reply as I added the vegetables to the sizzling pan. 'Ems?'

'Nothing's going on, Troy. Now shut up and cook me dinner.'

I leaned over the pan to get a whiff of the fragrant smell, and steam hit me in the face, causing me to blink.

The one where we both ran

And I was sitting in my car again. What the fuck? This had never happened to me before – to experience so many Possibilities so quickly. I was used to them taking months, years, lifetimes, not hours. It's like the universe was throwing everything at me, trying to stop Cat and me from having this date.

Looking at the rear-view mirror wasn't worth the trouble – the reflection wouldn't be any different to the last two times.

Who was I to argue with the universe? I sent an apology text to Cat and drove aimlessly for an hour, exploring backstreets on autopilot. Outside the world turned, life went on, people dated, fell in love, or into bed. Cat didn't reply.

After procrastinating as long as I could, I pointed the car home, parked and went into the house. Emily was watching TV. I flopped down next to her, mentally preparing for the barrage about to come.

'I'm sorry, Troy,' she said.

'For what?'

'Cat texted me. Said she couldn't go through with it.'

I checked my phone. There was nothing from her. 'But she didn't say anything to me.'

'No, she went to a friend's house. Her dad was supposed to tell you. Didn't he?'

Confession time. She couldn't be pissed at me if both Cat and I bailed. It was almost funny. So I told her what I'd done, or not done.

She shook her head in disgust. 'You two. What the hell am I going to do with you?'

'Ask Cat. That's the second time she's bailed on me.'

She looked confused, and I remembered the last time had been a Possibility. 'Counting pre-dates,' I added.

'You both need your heads slapped,' she said bitterly, abruptly standing up and storming out of the room.

Seriously, what was her problem? It was true though, we both probably needed our heads slapped. This was getting too hard, and it shouldn't be this much work getting together with a woman. But now I was home, in the safety of familiarity, I had doubts about my doubts. Why did I leave Cat's house? Why didn't I just get out of my car and walk to the front door? All the reasons for running seemed immaterial now, inconsequential. The universe? Fuck the universe. Kelvin was right – it was time to fight for what I wanted, what I needed.

A warm feeling spread through my stomach at this revelation. I blinked.

The one with the actual date

And I was sitting outside Cat's house. Without hesitation I got out of the car and strode to the front door. It swung inwards before I could knock, and for a moment I thought it was an automatic door, not seeing anyone standing in the hallway. Then Cat appeared from behind the door and my step faltered. She was stunning. Her hair flowed over her shoulders like silk, blonde contrasting against the dark blouse and black skirt. Black heels completed the outfit.

She laughed at my expression. 'Either you're trying to catch flies or you like what you see,' she said.

'I don't like flies – too many carbs – and you look amazing. I feel like a servant standing in front of the queen.'

She smiled slyly. 'You are, boy. If you remember that we'll get along famously. Now escort me to the carriage.'

I gave a mock bow and held my arm out for her. She placed her hand regally on top of my arm and we glided to the car in royal fashion. After I opened the door for her she kept up the game by sitting down, then swinging her legs into the foot well. By the time I got into the driver's seat her belt was done up and she was looking at me expectantly.

'What?' I asked.

'Drive on, servant.'

'You know they used to overthrow the monarchy,' I said darkly.

'You wouldn't overthrow me, would you?' she asked sweetly. When I glanced over she batted her eyelids.

'Oh, my God. This is going to be a long night.'

She laughed. 'But hopefully a memorable one.'

Shaking my head in resignation, I set off for the restaurant.

Dinner was a blur of laughter, and pasta, and more laughter. No alcohol by mutual consent – me because I was driving, her because she wanted to remember every detail although I suspected a deeper meaning. Before we knew it two hours had passed and we were walking back to the car. The only spoilt moment was when hurried footsteps behind us made her shrink into me, laughter dying on her lips. A man brushed past my shoulder, hurrying somewhere, but the sound of his feet, the uncertain, unknown, was enough to trigger Cat's memories. As he disappeared around the corner without a backward glance she relaxed a little, but stayed close. Her hand found mine and gripped it tight. I squeezed it reassuringly and she smiled weakly.

'Sorry.'

'For holding my hand? I'm not,' I replied, deliberately misinterpreting her comment.

She gave a grateful look – more wattage, less fear.

'Imagine if the press saw us now,' I said. 'Royalty consorting with the peasants.'

'I'm prepared to risk the scandal.'

Just then the skies opened up without warning and we darted into a shop doorway to shelter. In seconds the ground hissed with bouncing raindrops, puddles springing from nowhere. The scene induced a feeling of familiarity, of the first time Cat and I met. The doorway was different, but everything else was similar enough to raise goose bumps. I realised Cat was looking at me.

'Do you believe in déjà vu?' she asked.

'Sometimes. Why?'

She shrugged. 'I have a sense we've been here before.'

The goose bumps erupted into mountains. 'Maybe we have,' I joked, 'in a different lifetime.'

'You think we're star-crossed lovers? Destined to find each other across multiple lifetimes?'

'Something like that,' I replied with a grin.

'I need to thank you, Troy.'

'For what – sounding crazy?'

'For being patient. For not running away.'

'I could say the same thing to you.'

She looked out into the driving rain. 'I almost did a couple of times.'

'Why didn't you?'

With the rain came a drop in temperature. She shivered slightly so I took off my coat and put it around her shoulders. Chivalrous, perhaps, but it also left me cold.

She gratefully accepted the warmth, then slipped her hand back into mine. 'I guess I don't want to spend the rest of my life running from things. That's not who I was, and it's not who I want to be.'

A warm feeling spread through my body, repelling the chill, tingling my fingertips. Cat let out a tiny yelp and snatched her hand away.

'What's wrong?'

'I got a shock off you.'

'Weird,' I replied, but honestly, everything about this was weird. What was one more?

Cat hesitantly reached out her hand again. We connected; no shock this time.

'Very weird,' she said.

'No quips about us being electric?'

'Well, I've got the power?' She laughed.

'It's electrifying.'

'Your life is far from static.'

'Okay, I'm out of puns,' I admitted.

'Then you'd better kiss me,' she said.

The mood instantly changed, and electricity was in the air, or at the very least tension. I leaned down and she tilted her head up. Slowly our faces drew together, and I gently placed my lips on hers. They were warm and soft and I wanted to stay there forever. After a few seconds though I pulled away.

'Is that it?' she whispered in a voice mixed with relief and disappointment.

I leaned forward and rested my forehead against hers. 'I don't want to trigger your flight responses.' I watched her face as she struggled with the same things – push on and maybe go too fast and wreck things, or hold back and take things at snail pace.

'How'd you get to be so sensitive?' she whispered.

'Practice,' I replied truthfully.

'I think my flight responses can handle one more kiss.'

So we did, and it was longer, and better, and sweeter, with a hint of tongue, and when we broke apart this time we were both disappointed.

'God, I'm going to hate it if you're right all the time,' she said.

'I promise to be wrong every now and then,' I replied.

'Why do I think that won't be much of a problem?' she said teasingly.

With mock resignation, I looked out at the rain falling in ceaseless sheets of cold. 'This isn't going to end any time soon. I think we need to make a break for the car.'

'Okay, I'm game,' she replied, and reached down to pull off her shoes.

'Are you going to give me my coat back?'

'Not a chance, buddy,' she replied and dashed away laughing.

I caught up with her at the corner and we splashed our way to the car, delayed in our escape from the rain while I struggled to find the car keys, before remembering they were in my coat pocket, around Cat's shoulders. By the time we finally got inside we both resembled deep-sea divers, soaking wet and panting from the effort. Wiping the water from my face with a hand only transferred moisture from one place to another. Meanwhile Cat shed my coat and was relatively dry underneath.

'I'm not ready for today to be over,' she said.

'What are you suggesting?' I cranked the car heater up to maximum.

'Let's get you out of those wet clothes.' She laughed at the expression on my face. 'Easy, tiger, you're not getting lucky tonight, but I don't want you catching pneumonia on my watch. Let's swing past your place so you can change, then figure it out from there.'

It was difficult to argue with the logic; especially since uncontrollable shivers were beginning to wreak havoc on my hands, which made the drive home an interesting one. We made it in one piece, more through luck than skill. Emily was watching some reality show, in front of her a half-empty glass of wine and a half-full bowl of popcorn. She wore her slobby clothes – tracksuit pants, an old T-shirt and slippers. She seemed surprised to see us, and shot me a dirty look as I excused myself to change. She obviously assumed I'd done something wrong.

After pulling on some dry clothes I emerged into the hallway to catch the sounds of laughter. That couldn't be good for me.

A glass of wine now sat in front of Cat.

Emily grinned up at me. 'Elissa was telling me how you were a perfect gentleman. Who knew you were capable?' They both laughed as I dropped into a chair.

'Isn't the girlie debrief supposed to wait until after the date, not during it?'

'Girlie debrief?' Cat raised her eyebrows.

'Yeah, you know – where you talk about me, and all the things I did wrong.'

'We could wait until tomorrow, but it's more fun doing it now in front of you,' Emily said.

'Oh, joy,' I said sourly.

Emily suddenly said, 'I'm glad you two are finally getting on with it.'

We both looked at her.

'You sound like the fate of the world rests on us dating, Ems,' I said.

She looked a little sheepish, yet defiant at the same time. 'Not the whole world, just mine.'

Cat and I looked at each other in confusion.

'Look, forget it.' Clearly embarrassed, Emily stood up and strode out of the room before we could say anything else.

'What was that about?' Cat asked me.

I shrugged. 'Let's go find out.' We followed Emily into the kitchen, where she was doing the dishes, a clear sign she was avoiding something.

'It's silly,' she said before we could ask. 'So can we drop it?'

'We didn't bring it up,' I pointed out.

'What's going on, Emily?' Cat asked.

Emily stopped what she was doing and sighed. 'It really is silly.'

'Then tell us so we can laugh at you,' I said.

Cat punched me on the arm. Then she went around the bench and put an arm around Emily. 'Is everything okay?'

'You guys aren't going to let this go, are you?'

'We will if you want us to,' Cat replied.

'No, we won't,' I said. 'If you don't want to talk about it, it must be juicy, so spill.'

'If she doesn't want to talk about it she doesn't have to,' Cat told me.

'She's the one who brought it up in the first place,' I replied.

'So what? Now she's changed her mind.'

'But it's still bothering her or she wouldn't be washing dishes.'

'*She* is standing right here,' Emily interrupted.

We fell silent while Emily struggled with herself for a moment, then sighed again. 'Okay, fine, but mock me on this and I will kick you in the balls.'

'Cat doesn't have balls,' I pointed out, then wilted under the combined venom from two ladies.

'I just want you guys to be happy.'

We waited, there had to be more to it than that.

'I guess…it's silly, but I thought if you two got together then something good would have come from this shitty thing that happened. Then I could have happy memories and not…the ones I have.' She looked at me defiantly, waiting for the mocking to start.

I was stunned.

'Well?' Emily said.

Cat gave her a hug, then looked over at me. I walked around the bench, but Emily put her hands up to stop me. 'If you hug me I'll cry.'

I held my own hands up. 'I was going to slap you on the back of the head.'

'I'll just cry anyway, and punch you,' Emily retorted.

I put my hands behind my back. 'Then let's settle for this.' I pushed through her hands, leaned in and kissed her on the cheek. 'You're not silly, Ems.'

Cat leaned in and kissed the other cheek. 'Not even a little.'

Emily started crying. 'You guys,' she choked out.

'But that's a lot of pressure on our relationship,' I pointed out.

'True,' Cat agreed. 'I mean, it's only our first date and suddenly the future happiness of our friend rests on there being a second one.'

'Mmm. Well, technically the first one isn't over yet. Although we did kiss, which is usually the end of the date.'

'Not necessarily. I've had dates where the kiss is just the start,' she mused.

'Really? Do I want to know about them?'

'Do you?'

Emily had been turning her head back and forth like she was watching a tennis match. Now she stopped. 'Wait a second – you guys have kissed already?'

We ignored her.

I protested to Cat, 'And here I thought I was special.'

'You don't think it was special?' she asked.

'It felt special,' I admitted.

'For me too.'

'Seriously wait – you guys have kissed already?' Emily tried again.

'Sure,' Cat told her before turning back to me. 'Then why are you getting so upset about stuff from the past?'

'I'm not upset,' I said defensively. 'I simply don't think it's appropriate to talk about previous relationships while you're on a date.'

'When did this happen?' Emily interrupted.

'In a shop doorway,' I informed her.

'You seem upset, which is strange, because I assume you've kissed other girls and I'm not getting all up in arms about it.'

'I wasn't upset until I learned the future happiness of my best friend rests on the next kiss.'

'There won't be a next kiss if you keep this up.'

'Oh, my God – stop, please. I never should have said anything.'

'But it was a great kiss,' I said.

'Magical,' she agreed.

'Electric, even.'

'Guys, please,' Emily pleaded.

'Should we let her off?' Cat asked me.

'I think she gets the point,' I agreed.

Emily looked at us in amazement. 'You mean this was for my benefit?'

'Not all of it,' I admitted.

'We actually did kiss,' Cat confirmed.

'And it was special,' I added.

'I hate you both,' Emily declared and stormed out.

'You know her better than I do. Was that too much?'

I shook my head. 'Nah, she'll be fine.'

'You don't feel any extra pressure on this?' She gestured between us.

I thought about how much pressure I was already piling onto this relationship and shook my head, 'Nah. You?'

She thought about it for a moment, and I wondered what was

going through her mind. Then she shook her head as well. 'Nah,' she grinned, 'but I think we should call it a night. Frankly, anything after this would be anticlimactic.'

I drove her home, where we kissed once more – another sweet, lingering contact of lips. Then she disappeared behind the solid wooden door of her house.

Emily was in her room, the closed door a sign she hadn't yet forgiven me. She'd be fine by the morning. In the bathroom I brushed my teeth – a difficult thing to do when you're smiling. As I finished up and rinsed my mouth a curious thing happened. On my final glance into the mirror something had changed. I studied my reflection, not sure what it was. It looked the same, but there was definitely something different, something…better. Shrugging it off as post-date euphoria, I turned off the light and went into the hallway, hesitating outside Emily's door. I felt bad for teasing her. It wasn't something we'd planned – it'd been natural, organic, and thrilling. The connection and the way we'd naturally bantered was a great sign.

I knocked on the door. 'Ems?'

There was no response. I placed my hand flat on her door, wanting to push it open, to rush in and say sorry to my best friend for being a dickhead. But I didn't. This was an Emily I had seen before, although rarely, and it was better to wait until the morning. 'I'm sorry, Ems.'

The rest of the evening was spent watching the newest reality show to hit TV. Not out of interest, but so I could talk about it with Emily later, as a peace sign.

The next morning was cold, both inside and outside. Emily finally came into the kitchen as I was cleaning up my breakfast dishes. For a second it was like a scene from a Disney movie – ice forming as she walked. I could see my breath, and actually shivered at the look on her face. It would have been easy to become a statute under that gaze; instead I held out a cup of coffee. She looked at it suspiciously, like it was a lump of poison, then begrudgingly took it.

'I really am sorry, Ems.'

'I heard you,' she replied.

'But I'm going to keep saying it until you forgive me.'

She cupped her hands around the hot drink, raised it to her lips and blew gently. 'You're a wanker sometimes,' she sighed before taking a sip. The room temperature rose considerably.

'I've never denied that. Look, we didn't mean to make fun of how you were feeling.'

'But you did.'

'And I'm sorry. But, Ems, I'm worried about you.'

She looked surprised. 'Why? Because I'm pissed off at you? It'll pass.'

'I know it will, and that's not the problem.' She looked at me and I chose my next words carefully, wanting to find out the truth but unwilling to reignite the cold war. 'I want this thing with Cat to work, and I think it's great you do too, but it seems important to you – too important – which makes me wonder what else is going on.'

She took another sip of coffee. 'Who said anything else is going on?'

'Me. As you keep pointing out, we've known each other for a long time. I know when something is wrong, Ems.'

She took one more sip, then put the cup down on the counter. 'The only thing wrong is I'm going to be late for work. Thanks for the coffee, Troy.' She grabbed her handbag off the back of a dining chair and walked out of the kitchen.

'This isn't over,' I called after her.

'Yes, it is,' she called back, the slam of the front door her final word.

I brooded over the problem all the way to work, interrupted only by a five-minute period of euphoria as Cat and I texted, both expressing our enjoyment over the unqualified success of our first date. We promised to talk that night – in her words, to initiate negotiations for a follow-up date.

Slipping the phone back into my jacket pocket, I looked out the bus window and turned my thoughts back to Emily. After the attack I'd been worried about her – whether she would bounce back, recover to become who she was, or be changed forever. She had seemed to be back to her normal self. Occasionally I would catch her looking off into the distance, an expression of pure sadness on her face, but then she would shake it off and be Emily again.

Now it seemed she wasn't as good as I'd thought, which worried me.

The one with Emily

After lunch Emily texted, just two words: 'I'm sorry.' I took it at face value, and replied, 'Me too, see you tonight.' She didn't respond but that wasn't unusual.

Work occupied my thoughts for the rest of the day. A major presentation was due at the end of the week, so it was seven o'clock by the time I got home. The lights were on, but when I called out there was no response. Checking the kitchen, I found her bag on the bench but there was no sign of Emily.

'Ems?' I called again.

Her bedroom door was closed. I knocked on it; no response. Knocked harder; still no response. Turned the knob and pushed it open.

Her room was dark. I flicked the light on, and saw it was empty. The clothes she'd worn to work that morning were laid carefully on her bed, shoes together beneath the outfit. There was nothing unusual about the scene but a chill swept through me.

Re-entering the hallway, I noticed the bathroom door was also closed. Knocked on it. No response. Tried the door. Locked.

'Ems!' I called, banging loudly on the door.

No response. My heart thumped in my chest and ears.

'Emily, open the door.'

No response.

Taking a step back, I kicked the door. In the movies this would have resulted in the door exploding inwards, in reality it did nothing but hurt my foot. I kicked again, and again, and on the fourth try the door burst open. I stumbled forward and sprawled onto the ground, scrambled to my knees, and saw Emily in the bath. She was naked, and judging by the skin on her hands she'd been in there for a while. She was leaning back in the water, face barely above the surface, her eyes unseeing.

Frantically I searched for signs of injury, then signs of life. There was no blood, no empty pill bottles. I ripped the plug out, then grabbed her shoulders and shook her with a gentleness contrary to the turmoil I felt inside.

'Ems.'

Nothing.

'Ems!'

Still nothing.

'Emily Rose Tostra, look at me.'

There was a small flicker in her eyes, then nothing.

'Emily, please,' I pleaded.

The water gurgled down the plughole. I grabbed a towel from the rack and wrapped it around her as much as I could, hands slipping on her wet skin. She felt cold.

'Emily!' I slapped her lightly on the face. Nothing. 'Come on, mate, don't do this. Come on, Ems.'

My phone rang. I ignored it, then realised I needed help, yanked it out of my pocket and pressed the answer button.

'Hey, I thought we could discuss details for date number two,' Cat said.

'Call an ambulance Cat. For our place.'

'What's wrong?'

'It's Emily. Just call.'

'Done,' she replied without further questions.

I dropped my phone, heard the clatter on the floor. Now that help was on the way, two things went through my mind – one, I needed to warm her up, and two, she would be mortified if the ambulance people found her naked. Leaving her was difficult, but lifting her wet, limp body out of the bath by myself wasn't an option. I grabbed a pair of tracksuit pants and a T-shirt from her room. Absurdly I rejected the first T-shirt I pulled out because the colour clashed with the pants. That was Emily working through me. By the time I wrestled the clothes onto her there was a banging on the front door – the ambulance had arrived.

The next few minutes were a blur of questions and calm, efficient people working on Emily. They threw jargon around, which stirred memories of my Possibility life as a paramedic, but I wasn't paying close attention because at that point Cat arrived, a look of horror on her face as she saw Emily being wheeled into the ambulance. One of the paramedics, a solidly built man in his late thirties, asked if I wanted to go to the hospital with them. I nodded and Cat said she would follow in the car, giving my arm a reassuring squeeze before I climbed into the back of the ambulance. As we pulled out into traffic the paramedics continued to work on Emily, checking her vital signs, relaying information to the driver. I absorbed as much of it as I could, at one point hearing the words catalepsy and depression. I racked my brain for knowledge but my fear for Emily made it difficult to focus. I knew they weren't good words though. I felt nauseous, silently pleading to Emily to come back, thinking I should have seen this, should have known something was wrong, should have been there for my best friend, should have…

I blinked…

The one with the flatmate

And was sitting at my desk at work. I still felt nauseous, bolted into the bathroom and vomited into the toilet. My heart pounded, and fresh images of Emily lying in the ambulance, staring at nothing, brought more vomit. Once my stomach settled and I'd rinsed my mouth, I glanced at my watch.

The 'I'm sorry' text from Emily had just arrived but she didn't answer my call. I checked with her work and they said she'd gone home sick. My boss didn't take much convincing that I wasn't feeling well, my episode in the toilet having been overheard by several co-workers.

Spurning the slowness of a bus, I grabbed the nearest taxi and offered an extra twenty dollars if he got me home as fast as he could. He made a lewd comment about the girlfriend waiting for me and I wanted to punch him in the head, but since we were going sixty kilometres an hour I gritted my teeth and said nothing. Traffic was slow and we seemed to hit every red light along the way, but eventually we pulled up outside the house. I paid the driver, less the extra tip which he grumbled about, but I told him not to be so rude next time, or words to that effect.

The house was quiet when I burst through the front door. Passing Emily's room I saw her work clothes laid neatly on the bed. The bathroom door was closed. I didn't stop to test the lock, instead launched a kick and smashed the door open. Emily stood naked in front of the mirror, a pair of scissors in her hand.

'Troy! What the fuck?'

I turned away, face flushed. 'Ems, shit, sorry.'

'Get out!' she ordered.

I retreated to the kitchen, and a few minutes later she followed, dressing gown tightly wrapped around her, and demanded, 'What the hell was that?'

'I'm sorry, Ems, I thought…that you might be in trouble.'

'So you thought you'd give me a heart attack. Jesus, Troy.'

'I'm sorry, Ems,' I repeated, feeling foolish.

'Why did you think I was in trouble?' she demanded.

I picked up an apple and began cutting it into pieces to avoid looking at her. 'I don't know. I couldn't get hold of you, and you haven't been yourself lately, so I…panicked.'

'You think?' She poured herself a glass of water, her hands shaking slightly, and I suddenly wondered if I hadn't been far off the mark after all.

'Are you okay?' I asked.

'When my heart stops racing, sure.'

We sat in uncomfortable silence.

At last she said, 'There has to be more to it than that. It's not like we're in constant contact. You wouldn't have freaked out like that if there wasn't something else.'

This was going to be tricky. 'I got a feeling,' I said lamely.

She stared at me incredulously. 'A feeling? What sort of feeling?'

'Just that something wasn't right. That you were in trouble.'

Far from looking at me like I was crazy, Emily seemed shocked, then troubled, then thoughtful. 'Why would you think that?'

'What were you doing with the scissors, Ems?'

'Why would you think I was going to hurt myself?'

'Why were you in the bathroom with a pair of scissors?'

'You're not answering my question.'

'And you're not answering mine.'

We stared at each other, neither of us willing to give in and speak first. Finally she looked away, wrapped her arms around herself and shivered.

We were on dangerous ground. Through all our years of friendship there had been disagreements, the occasional fight, but mostly about silly stuff, not counting all the Possibilities. Something hung in the air, and one wrong word or gesture could have serious consequences. The silence drew out like a bow string looking for a target.

The tension broke with the sound of the doorbell. We looked at each other, then I went and answered it.

It was Cat. I stared, then asked, 'What are you doing here?'

'I had some spare time so I thought I'd check on Emily.' She pushed past me, and I followed her down the hall and into the kitchen.

Emily was equally surprised. 'What are you doing here?'

'I was passing and thought I'd drop in and say hi.'

Emily just looked at her.

'Okay, that sounded unbelievable to me too. I was worried about you. I got a feeling something might be wrong – you seemed really pissed off last night.'

Emily looked between the two of us. 'Great, another one with feelings. Troy had some sort of psychic flash I was in trouble.'

Cat studied me with interest, but I wasn't paying attention. 'Psychic flash,' I repeated. 'Does that mean I'm right?'

Emily wouldn't meet my eyes. 'I refuse to have this conversation naked,' she declared and left the room.

'So what sort of feeling did you have?' Cat asked me. 'Was your spidey sense tingling?'

'You're a fine one to talk,' I shot back.

'Woman's intuition,' she replied smugly. 'Is Emily going to be okay?' she added.

I glanced at the door and frowned. 'I hope so.'

Emily came back in, and with a start I realised she was wearing the same track pants and T-shirt I'd dressed her in during the Possibility. Without a word she sat down at the table, Cat and I automatically taking two of the other seats.

'Okay, I want a serious answer,' Emily said. 'Why did you think I was in trouble?'

'You're my friend, Ems. I knew something wasn't right, and when I couldn't get hold of you I …thought the worse.'

'Is that it?'

'Does there have to be anything else?'

'I don't know.' She sounded unsure.

'What is it, honey?' Cat asked.

Emily took a long time to answer. 'I was sitting at my desk this morning, and I realised I'd reread the same thing twenty times. And somehow it led to the thought that it was all too hard, and the next thing I knew I was coming home and taking my clothes off and going into the bathroom. And I truly don't know what I was going to do. This little voice was saying, *Just cut all your hair off, go for a new look*, and this other voice was saying, *What's the point? Lie down in the bath and stay there forever*. And then Troy burst through the door and scared the hell out of me, and saw me naked – we'll talk about that later – and I guess I want to know that there was a reason for it, that maybe there is something in the universe, something bigger than us, that has a plan, and the plan includes me being okay.' She trailed off, looking a little embarrassed, and lost.

I looked out the window, struggling with the right words. I desperately wanted to help her, but there's only so much truth I could reveal without forever changing the way they looked at me. I was finally connecting with Cat, and it could easily fall apart at this early stage. In the end I said, 'I sometimes get these images. Like snippets from a movie. And then they happen, like déjà vu.'

'Are you saying you're psychic?' Cat asked.

I searched her face for scepticism, for a sign she had one foot out the door, but she just seemed interested. 'No, nothing like that. It's just sometimes things come to me. And today I got this clear image of you, Ems, lying in the bath. You were catatonic, like you'd laid down to die, and when I couldn't get hold of you I came home.'

Emily stared at me in astonishment.

'I don't know if it was the universe. Maybe it's because we've been friends for so long. But something brought me here.'

'I don't know what to say,' Emily said.

Cat looked at me shrewdly.

I offered, 'How about, Hey, Troy, that sounds crazy. I'm putting a lock on my bedroom door in case you decide to murder me in my sleep.'

She looked troubled and I was worried I'd said too much.

'I don't know how to handle this,' she finally said. 'I don't see the world the same any more.'

The laptop was sitting on the dining table, so I turned it on. The girls both looked at me questioningly. I clicked on a couple of buttons and a picture filled the screen. It was of a butterfly on a yellow flower, the creature's vivid red-and-black wings open to the sun.

'That's beautiful,' Cat said.

'Who took this?' I asked Emily.

'You know I did.'

'She's thinks it's beautiful. Do you?'

'Yes, of course,' she answered in a bewildered tone.

'Why do you think it's beautiful?' I demanded of Cat.

She watched me thoughtfully. 'It's a perfect moment in time. That butterfly has such a short life that it's probably dead by now, but this photo captures who it was.'

I went out of the room, returning a short time later with Emily's camera. 'If you can't see the world the same, then don't look at it the same. Use this instead.'

'Did you go into my room?'

'Focus, Ems. You have a talent with this thing, so use it.'

Cat rummaged around in her bag and pulled out a business card. 'You also need to talk to someone. This is a wake-up call, Emily. You need to get help. This is the woman I've been seeing – she's a great listener and she will help you get better. She's helped me.'

Emily took the card from her and looked at the writing on it. 'I thought I was getting better. Troy taught me how to fight and I felt stronger, less afraid. But I guess all I did was push everything down and pretend.'

Cat reached over and squeezed her hand. 'Pretending only works for so long. Call her,' she urged.

Emily looked thoughtfully at the card, then nodded and pushed it to one side.

'No,' said Cat firmly. 'Now. We'll wait.'

Emily sighed and picked up the card, carried it over to her cell phone and dialled.

Cat said quietly to me, 'Images, huh?'

'Are you rethinking date number two?'

She shook her head. 'Hell, no. You just got way more interesting.'

I couldn't figure out if that was a compliment or an insult so didn't respond.

She laughed. 'How about Friday night? Movie?'

'I'll check my social calendar.'

'You do that,' she said with a twinkle in her beautiful eyes.

'You're in luck – a slot seems to have opened up for Friday night.'

'I thought it might.'

Emily sat back down at the table. 'I have an appointment for Thursday at 10am.' Her voice betrayed a nervous excitement.

'Awesome, we can go together – my appointment is after that. Now I have to get back to work. It's a crap job but I don't want to lose it until I become a mega-rich, wildly famous actor.'

I walked her to the door and we shared a quick hug, a slower kiss, and a promise to talk later.

Emily was still sitting at the kitchen table. 'So … psychic. All this time we've known each other and not a word.'

'I'm not psychic. I just get feelings sometimes.'

'Troy, have you not watched any of the psychic murder shows on TV? That's what a psychic does. This is amazing.'

'No, Ems, it's nothing we're going to talk about again. Ever,' I said sharply.

She looked at the expression on my face. 'Hey, of course. If you don't want to talk about it, that's fine.'

It wasn't. She was dying to ask me questions. She was already looking at me differently, which is the one thing I never wanted to happen. I resolved never to talk about it again with her or Cat, no matter what the circumstances.

'I do have one question, though,' she said. 'How come you haven't made me fabulously rich? Would it have killed you to slip me some Lotto numbers?' My face said it all. 'Okay, just kidding. I'm going to lie down. Suddenly I feel tired.' She kissed me on the top of my head, then left the room.

I hoped this was a Possibility, not real life, so it would all go away. I knew this would eat at Emily and she would eventually want to talk about it, but I couldn't. I just couldn't do it because she would think I was crazy.

I'd seen that reaction before. From my parents when I told them what was happening to me. From the doctors when I tried to convince them I wasn't mad, though all the time I was wondering if I was. It had all happened during Possibilities, but it had convinced me never to try again.

The one with more dates

Emily and I spent the next few days watching each other intently while trying to pretend we weren't. I think she was waiting for me to put a finger to my head, or touch something and jolt with a psychic vision. Meanwhile I was checking to make sure she got to her appointment on Thursday, which she did. Although to be absolutely certain I got Cat to pick her up. The thing with lying to people is you're always suspicious they're lying back to you.

Emily didn't want to talk about the session, but she seemed happier, and assured me it had helped. I believed her.

The next night Cat and I had our second date. We went to a movie, which she chose, and ate popcorn, which I chose, and spent the first five minutes of the movie working out the logistics of trying to comfortably hold hands while eating popcorn. At some point the logistics failed and popcorn ended up on the floor. We were shushed by the woman behind us when we found that hysterically funny. I spent the rest of the movie creating popcorn angels with my feet.

Afterwards we grabbed a late dinner at the food court – McDonalds for her in the form of a Big Mac combo, while I settled for a chicken kebab dripping in garlic mayo. Cat looked at my choice of food and suggested chewing gum might be in order before I kissed her again. Over the next ten minutes we dissected our meals and the movie in alternate bites. Cat declared she was a much better actor than the lead, and using chips as props proceeded to recreate a pivotal scene. When she was done the table of four sitting next to us broke out in applause. She turned red, then gave a half-bow of acknowledgement.

This time the date finished at her house. During the evening she'd told me she was thinking of moving out, getting a flat somewhere, since she found living with her parents again a bit stifling. I took it as a good sign, that she was returning to the normal state of someone in their twenties. But for now the evening ended at her parents' front door, where we settled for several kisses, each touch of lips allowing us to learn something about the other – what we liked, how we tasted, how we felt. I left disappointed. It's not like things were going to go any further, but knowing the opportunity was taken away by the threat of parents hovering in the next room was the frustrating stuff of teenagers.

The next three weeks were busy ones. Cat and I went on four dates, each ending at a front door with soft kisses and growing frustration. Emily continued going to counselling and the results astounded me. I'd thought she'd been getting better before, but now I could see the real Emily back – in three dimensions, not the pale copy I'd been living with for months. I apologised a lot during those days, feeling I should have seen the signs earlier. Eventually she told me to shut up or she'd move out. A hollow threat she'd used on many occasions, but a good sign she was on the right path.

She also threw herself into photography, finishing the course I'd given her for her birthday. She then joined a photography group that went out most weekends to take pictures of flowers and birds and stuff I thought was pretty boring, but she loved it.

Emily hadn't raised the whole psychic thing again, although I sometimes saw her look at me sideways. I suspect she was wondering if I could make her rich by winning Lotto. The truth is I had made us rich before, in a Possibility, by winning Lotto and splitting it with her. She'd blown half a million dollars in a year on clothes, first-class trips around the world, and friends that materialised at the start but vanished like ninjas into the night when the money ran out. Even if I could do it again, I wouldn't.

One thing happened that didn't help dissuade Cat and Emily of my mystical ability. A week after our second date I ran into Steven during a lunchtime walk. The weather was cool, but not raining, so we stood to one side of the pavement and exchanged the usual heys, and how's it going. He made some crack about me seeing his sister, and I asked him about his relationship, and that's when the tone changed.

'It's okay,' he said reluctantly.

'It's okay?' I repeated. 'Those aren't the words of a boy in love.'

'I never said I loved her,' he shot back. There was something else though, something that should have gone on the end of the sentence.

'But she said it to you,' I guessed. By the look on his face I'd hit the bullseye. 'Do you love her?'

The goofy grin was a good sign.

'Figure it out, numbnuts. I've seen you with her, and without her. You're better with her.'

'You've barely seen me at all. How would you know?' he retorted.

I shrugged. 'I just do. Look this could go a number of ways. She said she loves you, which is a big thing. If you don't feel the same then end it – right now. If you do, then tell her – now. I can't predict the future, but if you stay together then who knows what could happen? You could get married, have a baby girl, name her Rose…'

'Hey, dude, settle down. I'm still at school, I don't know what I'm going to be doing next week, and you have me married with kids.'

'Only the one kid.'

'Whatever.'

'I don't know what you're going to be doing next week either, but I do know who you could be doing it with.'

He looked at me thoughtfully. We said our goodbyes and I watched him start to walk off, pulling his phone from his jeans pocket.

'Hey, Steven…'

He turned at the sound of my voice.

'Don't tell her over the phone, you idiot.'

He looked down at his hand, then gave me a guilty look. That's exactly what he'd been about to do.

On the way back to the flat I stopped to pat Tigger through the wrought-iron gate. He looked happy in his new home.

When Cat and I talked that night she told me Steven had come home from seeing Jess, and had told his parents he loved her and they were going to move in together. Oh, well, things don't always go according to plan. Apparently Steven hinted to his parents that I'd been the one who'd suggested this. When I explained to Cat our conversation she promised to relay the information to her mother, who was currently out for my blood.

We were on date number seven by the time we were having this conversation. I'd got no sense that anything would be different about tonight – there was no flashing neon sign above her head, no blatant words or seductive looks – but something had changed. A new tension between us. After dinner we went back to my place to watch TV and cuddle on the couch. Emily was out with friends so we were alone. I felt her body against mine, slightly tense, laughter higher than normal, with an undercurrent of nerves. Being a male I had no idea what was going on, so I asked.

She sat up and looked me in the eyes. 'I told my parents I was staying over…here…for the night.'

My mouth went dry. 'Oh…cool,' was all I could get out.

'Is that okay?' she asked nervously.

'Absolutely,' I replied quickly, in case she thought there were doubts. 'But now your parents are really going to hate me.'

She looked relieved and nervous at the same time. I took her hand in mine and gave it a light squeeze.

She explained, 'Only, this is my first time. Not my first, first time – I've had sex before, lots of times. Okay, getting off point here. I mean this is my first time since the attack. And I don't know if I can do it, and I don't want to keep leading you on, and I really, really want to have sex with you, but I'm so scared right now…' She trailed off and looked at me apologetically.

I stood up, pulling her up with me and hugged her tightly. 'If it helps, I really want to have sex with you too,' I replied, as if the evidence growing in my pants wasn't obvious. I shifted a fraction, still holding her tightly above the waist but allowing some space below. My attempt at subtlety was a complete failure as she laughed into my neck, her breath not helping the below-the-waist situation. My body vibrated with excitement while my head thumped with doubts. 'But,' I went on, 'not tonight.'

She stiffened and pulled away, and I held on to her hands. 'Here's the deal,' I told her. 'I think we should approach tonight like a pre-date scenario. Ease into the actual sex with some pre-sex activities.'

'Pre-sex? What did you have in mind?'

'So maybe tonight we just sleep together – only sleep.'

She looked down at my pants with amusement. 'Do you think that's possible?'

'I'll admit the talk of sex has me a little excited, but my brain is in control.'

She looked at me with that wide smile that had my heart warming up for an Olympic sprint.

'Mostly,' I added.

'Okay,' she said.

It was a few seconds before I realised she was saying okay to the plan and not being sarcastic. Holding hands, we walked out into the hallway, then I nipped back to turn the TV off, then nipped back again to turn the lights off. By this time Cat was cracking up and the tension evaporated, only to return when we were standing in my bedroom, door closed, on opposite sides of the bed.

'Perhaps we should set the parameters of pre-sex sleeping together,' she said in a voice vibrating with nerves.

'Sure,' I replied, my voice matching hers. 'Shoes off seems sensible.'

'Agreed.' We removed our shoes, and in an unspoken agreement socks too.

'I don't normally wear my shirt to bed,' I said. We shed the layer, my fingers fumbling over buttons I'd undone without trouble hundreds of times before. With a shrug of her shoulders she slid her blouse off, revealing smooth white skin and a black, lacy bra.

'I don't normally wear pants to bed,' she offered. We both sat on the edge of the bed and I pushed my pants down, struggling to get them over feet that had grown to the size of a giant's. Over my shoulder I heard her pull the duvet back, and when I turned she lay covered up to her armpits. I copied her and we lay next to each other, not touching, our body heat seeping into the cold sheets, and pooling in the middle.

'I'm not an expert, but it might be easier to sleep with the light off,' she observed. I looked over at the switch on the wall, next to the door. Sighing, I slid out of the bed and took two steps, flicked off the light, then leapt back into the warmth.

'So, does pre-sex sleeping together include kissing?' she asked.

Hell, yes, I thought. *I have an almost naked, hot girl in my bed. Of course it includes kissing*. 'I don't think that's a good idea,' I replied regretfully. 'Kissing could shred what little self-control I have left.'

'Maybe that's okay,' she replied.

My eyes adjusted to the dark and I looked over at her.

She looked back at me. 'I mean, now we're here the idea of sex doesn't seem quite as scary.'

'Not to you, maybe. I'm terrified,' I admitted.

'Why? Surely you're not a virgin?'

'Hell, no, I've slept with plenty of women, not plenty, a lot. I mean enough. This is going well don't you think?'

She laughed. 'Then what's the problem? I get why I'm scared, but why are you?'

I turned over onto my side, wanting to reach over and touch her, struggling with the urge, and finally dropping my hand onto the mattress between us. Even in the pale light her beauty was obvious. 'Anything I say is going to sound corny.'

'Oh, now you have to tell me.' She propped herself up on one elbow and looked at me expectantly.

'I don't want to hurt you. I never want to hurt you, and the possibility of that happening is vastly increased because of what's led us to this point. So what if I do something wrong, or don't do the right thing, or what if we have sex and you don't enjoy it? There's a lot of pressure to get this right.'

She looked at me for a long time, then leaned across and kissed me lightly on the lips. 'Who are you, Troy Messer?'

'What?'

'You're always there when I need you, and you always seem to know the right thing to say. Somehow you know what I need to hear, or feel. It's like you really are psychic.'

'I'm not.'

'Then what are you? I've met plenty of guys and you are not like any of them. Who are you, Troy?'

I looked at those lips, wanted to answer her with a kiss – with more than a kiss; my groin was uncomfortably hard, trapped inside cotton. 'I'm just a guy who really, completely, totally likes you,' I whispered.

She leaned back a little and searched my face for sincerity, seemed satisfied with what she saw, and leaned back in, the gap narrowed between us, her body dancing with electricity. 'You know, you're terrible at getting women to not have sex with you,' she whispered, her warm breath caressing my face.

'Who says I always say the right thing?' I whispered back, and we kissed, closed mouths parting, tongues exploring gently at first, then with more urgency. Her hand rested on my chest, fingers dancing across my skin. I hesitantly placed my hand on her side, waited for a reaction that didn't come, then used my own fingers to trace lines on her smooth skin. Our bodies moved instinctively, pressing against each other, and she rolled onto her back, pulling me with her, my body pressing onto her – and that's when it started to go wrong. I felt her tense, freeze, shrink into the mattress, break lips, panting slightly from a beating heart, instantly changed from passion to fear.

Quickly I rolled off her, reinstating the distance between us. Neither of us said anything, hearts slowing, thoughts clarifying, frustration and fear coursing through me in equal parts.

Her body shook and I realised she was crying. 'I'm sorry,' she sobbed.

I reached out and grabbed her hand. 'You should be – you're really bad at this pre-sex, sleeping-together thing.'

She choked a little, released my hand and punched me in the arm, before linking her fingers in mine again.

When she spoke her voice was light and natural. 'What can I say? It's my first time.'

'You'll get better at it,' I replied.

'I hope not,' she said.

What did that mean? Did she regret staying or was she rethinking the whole relationship? I wanted to ask but couldn't.

'I'm going to sleep now, and tomorrow morning we'll laugh about this.' She sounded hopefully optimistic.

I squeezed her hand in reassurance. 'I'm going to brush my teeth,' I said softly. 'Be right back.' In the bathroom I did brush my teeth, but first I masturbated. I might be an understanding and sympathetic male who was happy to wait things out, but I also had a hot girl in my bed whom I wasn't going to sleep with.

When I slipped back into bed I thought she was asleep. I closed my eyes and rolled onto my side.

'You know, I could have cleaned your teeth for you,' she said in an amused voice.

So much for subtlety. 'Now you tell me.'

She laughed, the last sound I heard before drifting off to sleep. Such a good way to leave the day.

The one with Kelvin

I woke slowly, becoming aware of sounds and smells and light pushing against my closed eyes. I wondered how old I was. Some days it was hard to tell.

Eyes still shut, I moved first one leg, then the other. No pain. Flexed my fingers; they felt strong and supple. Finally I opened my eyes and looked at my hands. They looked young, wrinkle-free, yet slightly callused, with a malformed knuckle.

I became aware of a figure next to me. She lay on her stomach, long blonde hair draped across her face like a demure mask, her eyes watching me.

'Morning,' she said.

'Morning.' I grinned at her. 'How long were you watching me sleep?'

'A while,' she said, reaching out and putting her hand on my chest.

'Stalker,' I quipped.

'Are you real?'

'What?'

'I guess I'm afraid this is all a dream. A great dream, but one I'm going to wake up from. Tell me I'm not going to wake up.' She rolled over and stretched an arm up, the sheet falling away from her firm breast.

'God, I hope not.'

She laughed. 'You idiot. I'm serious.'

'So am I! Listen, lying here next to you, this is where I want to be, every day, so if this is a dream I don't want to wake up.' It would break my heart, I thought, shatter it into a million pieces under the weight of the moon.

'Me either,' she replied. 'Thank you.'

I looked at her questioningly.

'For pointing me in the right direction, back to the real me.'

'You did all the work.'

'Take the compliment.'

'Okay, then you're welcome.'

'I need to say something. Last night you told me you really, completely, totally liked me. I just want to say…ditto.'

'Ditto? Wow, I'm overcome with emotion.'

'Ass.' She let out a breath I hadn't been aware she was holding. 'So what's with the painting?' she asked, and we both looked over to where the canvas leaned against the wall. She turned to me when I didn't reply.

Finally I said, 'It's something I painted when I was a teenager.'

'And you never finished it?'

Our eyes naturally drifted to the top left-hand corner, dull white, devoid of paint. 'I haven't got around to it.'

'Fair enough. I guess you've been really busy for the last … what, ten years?'

'You can't rush perfection,' I replied to deflect the conversation.

'You also can't achieve it if you don't actually try.'

I reached across and put my hand on her thigh.

She squirmed, then removed the hand. 'Keep your paws to yourself, you leech,' she said primly.

'Leech?'

'It's a word. Look it up.' She removed herself from my temptation by climbing out of bed and walking over to the painting, although from where I lay that only added to the distraction. She picked it up and came back, sitting on the edge of the bed and putting the frame on her legs. Her hair hung over her face as she traced the paint.

The picture was of the top of a hill surrounded by green grass and small bushes. The middle of the picture was of the sky, cloudless and a dull blue. In the top right-hand corner, peeking in from the side of the canvas, was a sliver of the moon.

'This is really good. What's supposed to go here?' she asked, pointing at the blank space.

'The sun,' I replied, surprising myself. This was the first time I'd ever told anyone.

She raised her eyes to meet mine. 'So why isn't it there?'

Her gaze looked past my façade, past the memories, all the Possibilities. It seemed natural to tell her. 'The sun went away.'

'What does that mean?'

'It means I used to see the sun and now I don't.'

'How long has it been gone?'

'Ten years,' I said.

She leaned the painting against the bedside table, climbed back into bed, and lay down in the crook of my arm. 'That's a long time to be in the dark,' she said, her finger tracing my chest like a paintbrush.

'Yes,' I replied, lacking a better response.

'Is that why you told me the story?'

I didn't answer.

'So which one are you – the moon or the sun?'

A pause.

She took my silence to mean that the deep-and-meaningful time was over. 'So, does pre-sex sleeping together come with breakfast in bed?'

It did, and lunch as it turned out, but we parted in the afternoon since she had family things to do. Emily had wandered into the kitchen as I prepared breakfast, seen the two plates, and asked if one of them was Cat's. When I said it was she'd nodded in satisfaction, like everything was going according to her plan, and disappeared back into her room.

Cat and I talked every day, but didn't see each other again until the following Friday, which followed a similar pattern – dinner out (Thai food this time), then back to my place. The same result as the previous week: in bed together but no sex. This time I was expecting it, so didn't need to brush my teeth, or get her to.

The next morning as we were lazing in bed my cell phone rang. It was my mother. I was going to let it go to voicemail but Cat insisted I answer it. Through a shaky voice Mum told me Kelvin had passed away. He'd gone into hospital for a routine procedure and never came out.

When I hung up the phone Cat asked me what was wrong and I told her. She wept tears for both of us while I fought the maelstrom of emotions inside.

So the first time Cat met my parents, again, was standing next to me in church. True to his word, Kelvin had written his own service. It was filled with laughter and nostalgia, and during the eulogy Kelvin's son Grant read out a quote – something along the lines of, even when we think the opposite, God still gives us the tools to do his work. It was Kelvin's way of getting in the last word.

Kelvin had wanted me as one of his pallbearers and I felt out of place amongst his sons and nephews. By the time we carefully placed the box down in the cemetery sweat had my hand slippery, and I felt moisture on my forehead despite the cool day.

Afterwards there were refreshments in the church hall. The last time I'd been in here was for Cat's father's funeral, a thought that sat uneasily, with her standing next to me holding my hand. Mum was firmly planted behind the refreshment table, dispensing soothing words and scones in equal measure.

'You should go talk to her,' Cat informed me.

'Yeah. Want to come?'

'Nope. I'm going to introduce myself to your father.'

'I'll come with you.'

'Nervous? You should be,' she said with a grin, before pushing me away.

I weaved through the crowd. Mum must have seen me coming because by the time I got there she was holding out a scone. A trail of strawberry jam had slipped down the side and pooled onto her finger.

'Thanks, Mum,' I said, taking the food.

She signalled for someone to take over and came around the table. 'I'm glad you came.'

I nodded. 'I liked Kelvin.'

She smoothed her jacket and fixed a non-existent stray hair. 'He was fond of you.'

'Even for a spy?'

She flushed and looked across the room to where Dad was deep in conversation with Cat.

'Mum, it's okay. And … I'm sorry.'

Her gaze snapped back to me. 'For what?'

'Being…'

'Distant?' she prompted.

'A dick.'

'Let's go with distant,' she replied primly. 'So, am I ever going to find out why?'

My turn to look away. 'Does it matter?'

'It might.'

'Nothing I say can justify hurting you, Mum.'

'So you're not going to tell me,' she replied with a hint of frustration in her voice.

I looked at her. 'Let's talk about it this weekend. How about you guys come around for dinner on Sunday?'

She searched my eyes for something, then looked back across the room. 'And will your friend be joining us?'

'I'll ask her.'

Mum patted my arm. 'It's a start,' she murmured.

After everyone had left I sat alone in the church. I couldn't remember a time when Kelvin hadn't been part of this building. His character seeped out of the walls, his muted voice whispered from the altar. I sat in the front row, waiting for something, half-expecting him to appear from the back room, sit down next to me and pierce my soul with his eyes.

A single tear found its way down my cheek. Not only had I lost a friend, but also a confidante, perhaps the only real one I'd had. He was the only person who'd accepted at face value what I told him without considering me a candidate for mental assessment or exorcism. I pressed my body down hard on the wooden pew, suddenly afraid that I would float away, that I was less substantial without Kelvin there as an anchor. Everything seemed too difficult, a future with Cat slipping away like grains of sand through my fingers. Nothing was going to be enough to stop this crazy thing that was my life.

There was a rustling sound and someone sat next to me. A hand stole into mine and gripped it tight. Cat and I sat without talking for a long time.

The one with the freak-out

The following Friday we went to a movie, then back to my place. Emily was in the lounge, so we sat and chatted with her for a while. She'd been to a few counselling sessions now and was doing well, to the point where she had started talking about this guy from work, Austin, whom she thought was cute. I bit my tongue.

When I closed the bedroom door it was like a switch went off in Cat's head. She started pacing, agitated.

'What's wrong?'

'I want to know what your end game is,' she said.

'What?'

'No one is this patient. The first time I met you, you came to the door naked. Now for two weeks you've had me in bed, and stopped when I said I wasn't ready. No man is that understanding. So what's your end game? What are you hoping to get out of this?'

'What…?'

'Shut up. You're too nice. There has to be more to it than this.'

'That's crazy,' I protested.

She stopped pacing, the bed a barrier between us. 'Why? Why is it crazy?' she said, her eyes narrowing.

'Because it is. I've never lied to you, Cat.'

'That's another thing. You don't even use my real name. Why?'

'I told you why.'

'You told me some bullshit. Why do you call me Cat?'

'Because you told me to,' I said hotly.

That stopped her. 'What? No, I didn't. When?'

'Do you want me to call you Elissa? I will, if that's the problem. Tell me what the problem is and I'll do anything to fix it.'

'Why?'

'Because I really, completely, totally like you,' I said calmly.

'Why?' she repeated.

I stepped to the end of the bed. She took a step back. I took another step forward and this time she stayed put. 'Because you're beautiful, and smart, and confident, and quirky. Do you want me to go on?'

'No...yes, keep talking.'

'Because when I first met you, you were the sun. You were so bright I was afraid I would get burnt on you.' I took another step forward, now at the edge of the bed, nothing separating us.

'And now?'

I abruptly turned and walked out of the room, and came back with Emily's handheld mirror from the bathroom. Cat hadn't moved.

I held the mirror up to her face. 'What do you see?'

She looked at me, then into the mirror. 'What am I supposed to see? It's my face.'

'Is it a good face?'

She moved closer to the glass, moving her head from side to side to study the image. 'I like it.'

'What does it say to you?'

'It's a face, Troy. It doesn't say anything, unless I open my mouth.'

I dropped the mirror onto the bed and stepped closer, raising a hand and lightly tracing a finger down her cheek. 'Do you know what it says to me? When you cry it's like the sun has gone behind a cloud, and when you smile…when you smile I can't breathe and I like breathing, but I'd stop breathing forever if it meant seeing your smile'

She looked troubled, picking up the mirror and staring into it once more. 'The sun, huh?'

I nodded.

'Even now?'

I took the mirror out of her hands again and pulled her into my arms. 'I see a face emerging from the clouds. I see the sun coming up again.'

'No one has ever called me the sun before,' she replied.

'More fool them.'

'What do you see when you look into the mirror?' she asked. I tried to pull away but she held on tight. 'Uh-uh. Answer the question, buddy.'

There was no easy answer. The thing is, I'd noticed changes over the past few weeks. The hatred of my reflection I'd felt for so long was dulled. I still thought of my face as dark and cratered, but I was coming to see something different as well. Something better. 'I see the moon.'

'Didn't you say the moon hated its reflection?'

'So you do listen to me.'

'Mostly. You talk a lot, but some of it gets through. So do you? Do you hate your face?'

'What do you see?' I challenged.

'I see a man who doesn't want to answer the question. But okay, I see a handsome face – with eyes that have seen too much. There's so much sadness in those eyes.'

'Then why are you here?' I asked in a thick voice.

She slapped me lightly on the cheek. 'Because I want to be.'

'Then what the fuck was that all about?'

She sighed and dropped down on the bed. 'I don't know. I guess I've been freaking myself out for the last few days.'

I sat down next to her. 'About what?'

'About you, and me. I started thinking that maybe you were just trying to have sex with me. And that spiralled into other thoughts, like maybe you're not as nice as you seem. I mean, you're definitely hiding something from me, and it became a snowball, and when we came in here I freaked.' She looked at me, embarrassed. 'So … my first freak-out with you. How'd I do?'

'I'd give it a seven.'

'Only a seven!' she replied indignantly.

'I could be persuaded to go higher.'

She laughed. 'I do, you know.'

'Do what?' I asked.

'Really, completely, totally like you. Despite your harsh marking. It feels like we've known each other for such a long time. Does that sound weird?'

'Completely normal,' I assured her.

And then there was no more talking. Our lips touched – gently, then with urgency, and we were lying down, hands exploring each other above and under clothing. Layers were shed, thrown carelessly across the room, my lips found the soft skin of her neck, and she sighed happily. Underwear joined the rest of the clothes and for the first time we were naked, our hands exploring new areas, bodies responding to light touches.

There was an unexpected interruption while I scrambled around the bedside drawer for a condom, then struggled to open it, my concentration shot by her firm grip on a part of my body more used to my own hand in recent times. She laughed at me fumbling like a teenager with the condom. Her laughter faded as I lay down next to her, one leg draped across her. She tensed, waiting for me to move onto her.

Instead I pulled her on top of me, giving her control, her hair falling across her face as she kissed me in appreciation. Slowly I entered her and then we were moving together. Our movements became more frantic, our breaths shorter, heat radiating from our bodies as we moved closer. Tonight was basic, primal. With a shudder I climaxed and she collapsed on top of me. We lay unmoving, her face nuzzled into my neck, my arms wrapped tightly around her. I wanted to stay there forever, but she slid from me and we climbed under the covers, and lay in each other's arms.

'You okay?' I asked.

'I am,' she replied. 'I really am.' She snuggled in closer.

'Happy?'

'No, I'm miserable. Idiot.'

'It was a legitimate question,' I protested.

'Shut up and hold me.'

So I did.

'Tell me a story,' she murmured.

'Once upon a time,' I began.

'No, not a made-up story. Tell me a story about you.'

I told her about how I fell out of a tree when I was twelve and broke my arm, and halfway through her breathing changed. I couldn't see her face, to check if she'd fallen asleep. 'Cat?' No response. 'You asked what I was hiding. I'm scared you'll think I'm crazy, but I want to be honest.'

So I told her everything, right from the start. It took a while, and I left nothing out. It was probably cheating not telling her when she was awake, but it was a start. After I'd finished I held my breath, waiting for her to say, 'Hey, I'm awake after all, and you're a nut job, so thanks for the sex but see ya never.' All she did was sigh, and wriggle a little bit against me.

I let the breath out, and with it all my anxieties – all the tension I'd been living with for the last eleven years, all the countless Possibilities. As I drifted off a single thought flitted through my consciousness: I hadn't lived a Possibility since Cat and I spent that first night together.

Unless this is a Possibility, came the evil afterthought.

I'm not sure any more

I woke slowly, becoming aware of sounds and smells and light against my closed eyes. Like every other morning, I wondered what my age was. Eyes still shut, I moved first one leg, then the other. No pain. Flexed fingers; they felt strong and supple. Finally I opened my eyes and looked at my hands. They told me nothing.

Memories flooded back, catching like leaves on the rocks in my mind. The other side of the bed was empty. It shouldn't have been, but if today was the day after yesterday then I knew why. My silent prayer went unanswered as I checked my phone for the date and saw the numbers 2022. I stared at the ceiling, devoid of energy or desire to leave this safe haven. Out there was heartbreak. In here, I was a normal guy enjoying a sleep in.

Except for the teddy bear. It sat on top of the chest of drawers – a small brown bear with a pink bow around its head, and wearing a pink dress. Its dark eyes bridged the gap across the room and bore into mine. I rolled away from its relentless stare and touched the pillow next to me, a single blonde hair serving as a reminder of the head that should be resting there.

'Cat,' I whispered. 'Come back to me.' Tears threatened and I slammed them back down inside. There had been plenty of tears over the last week and I was tired of crying, tired of everything. I wanted to blink and get out of this Possibility and was terrified this wasn't one – that this was my life. I closed my eyes, praying for sleep to take me away, but my brain refused to allow the escape.

Reluctantly I got up, put on some clothes, and went into the kitchen. The bench was clear, the kettle cold, the chilly air undisturbed from the night before. Morning sun pushed at the windows, casting elongated shadows over the chairs and across the floor. I felt the same way, stretched out of shape. I switched on the kettle, pulled mugs and coffee from the cupboard and milk from the fridge like a pre-programmed robot. The milk had expired yesterday, and I stood dumbly holding it until the sound of the kettle boiling pulled me from the trance. I made two cups of coffee, then dumped the rest of the milk in the sink.

Steam rose off the drinks and I cupped both hands above them, soaking in the heat, waiting for it to permeate through the rest of me, before giving up. Too much to expect from simple drinks.

I sighed and carried them down the hallway to the closed door. The few centimetres of wood might as well have been a mountain of rock. My stomach clenched and coffee spilt over the cup edges onto my trembling hands. I barely noticed my skin blistering. This was true fear, the sort that clings to your soul and clouds every waking thought. I didn't need a mirror to know the moon was back – that what I would see would be cracks, and craters, and darkness, and despair. I knew what was on the other side of the door. It wouldn't change, whether I opened the door or not. But opening it, pushing against the solid smooth surface, watching the truth reveal itself in sharp silence… I put one cup on the floor and backed away, a coward.

An hour later I still sat at the kitchen table, cold coffee in front of me. The shadows were gone; the sun had done its work, leaving a warmth that filled the air and flowed around me without penetrating the numbness of my skin. I vaguely heard the front door open, and someone come in.

'Making an effort this morning, I see,' she said. She came around the table and sat down opposite me, studying my face for something, and appearing dissatisfied with the result. 'When did you last eat?'

I couldn't remember, but the faint taste of chicken came to me. 'There was that chicken you brought around,' I croaked.

'Fuck, Troy, that was two days ago! Are you telling me you haven't eaten since then?'

I might have done but memories refused to present themselves.

'Where is she?'

I looked at the door and she followed my gaze, then said, 'I'm going to make you some breakfast.'

'I'm not hungry.'

'I don't care,' she replied.

Swept away by her determination, I sat there while noises happened around me, smells materialised, and a plate of toast was put on the table. It smelt good, even though the thought of eating made me nauseous.

Emily disappeared out of the room, came back shortly after, and sat down, glaring disapprovingly at my untouched food. 'Eat,' she demanded.

'Ems…'

'No talking. Eat.'

I did. It was easier than arguing. Emily didn't attempt conversation until the plate was empty. Then she made more toast and made me eat that as well. When she got up a third time I held my hand up and she sank back into her seat. She seemed more satisfied with what she saw.

'Have you been into the room yet?' she asked.

I shook my head.

'Your parents rang me.'

That surprised me, although I guess it shouldn't have.

'They're worried because you won't return their calls. I know you're hurting, but so is everyone else. So am I.'

Tears threatened again and this time I couldn't banish them. She came around the table, put an arm around my shoulder and held on tight while I cried into my hands.

'Shit,' I said, wiping my face. 'Every time I think I've got a handle on this thing I start crying again.'

'Got a handle on it? It's only been a week since the funeral, Troy. Cut yourself some slack. And you were never the stoic type anyway. The only macho thing I've ever seen you do is kick the shit out of two guys who deserved it, and that was five years ago. We're worried – Austin, Elissa's family, me, we're all worried.'

I suddenly realised what this was – Emily the spokesperson, the elected ambassador, delegated to check on the state of Troy. Annoyance swept through me, then left on the same tide that brought it in. I couldn't fault people for caring, but I didn't need to be treated like a broken toy, fragile and worthless. I wasn't broken, I was hurting.

'When was the last time you showered?'

I shrugged.

'Go have a shower, and brush your teeth for God's sake.'

I did what she told me to do – it was easier than thinking for myself. The world disappeared behind steamed glass and the constant hiss of water. Dirt and dead skin cells were sluiced from my body and disappeared down the drain. Memories receded into the mist of the bathroom; nothing existed any more, no thoughts or pain, just the rhythmic in and out of my breath. I stood like a rock until the water ran cold, and the illusion of normality evaporated with the steam.

When I emerged from the bathroom, newly cleaned but still bone tired, Emily was nowhere to be seen. I glanced down the hallway at the closed door, then headed in the opposite direction.

Emily found me a little later, sitting in the lounge staring at the blank television.

'Most people find it more entertaining to turn it on,' she commented as she sat next to me.

I didn't answer.

She sighed and cradled my hand in hers. 'Troy, look at me.'

I reluctantly turned my head, not wanting to see what was in her eyes.

'Tell me.'

'Tell you what?' I asked dully.

'Tell me how to help you. I want to help you, Troy. I want to be there for you, like you're always there for me, but I don't know how. You're hurting, and so I'm hurting.' I turned away again, tried to take my hand back but she clung onto it. 'No. You need to grieve and I'll let you have time for that, but I won't let you shut yourself off from me. That's not going to happen.'

'It wasn't supposed to be like this. This life with Cat was supposed to be my happy ever after.' Tears flowed again, and this time I did nothing to prevent their fall. 'I went through the shitty stuff, I went through a million unhappy days, had my hopes raised and shattered more times than I should have. Don't I deserve a happy ending?'

'Of course you do, Troy. We all do. I don't know why these things happen, but sometimes life has other ideas, sometimes shit happens. It stinks, it's not fair, and there's nothing we can do but ride it out. But,

Troy, you're not alone. This horrible, shitty thing didn't just happen to you – we're all hurting too.'

'I don't have the strength for anyone else.'

'You don't have to be strong, but you have to be there.'

I knew she was right, and added guilt to the emotional sandstorm raging inside me.

'You need to go into the room, Troy.'

I nodded.

'Do you want me to go with you?'

I shook my head.

'Okay. Call me later.' She kissed me on the cheek, and crossed the room to the door.

Later I stood at the end of the hallway, staring at the same few centimetres. Behind its plain exterior was the end of something, possibly the end of everything unless I could find the strength to fight. The door handle was cool beneath my skin, smooth and clean, unyielding against my grip. I didn't want to go in. I wanted to turn and run, and keep running, and find a hill to climb and pray the other side held better things. Instead I turned the handle and pushed the door open. For the first time in a week I crossed the threshold into the room.

The first thing that struck me was the brightness. I guess I expected the curtains to be closed, but sunlight invaded every corner. A tall set of dark wood drawers sat to one side, its top bare of clutter. On the ceiling a mobile of toy moons and suns gently twisted. Directly ahead stood a wooden change table, disposable nappies neatly lined up underneath it, a cloth nappy draped over one end. On the opposite wall sat a cot, blankets lying flat, the side door unlatched and slid down. I stared at it for a moment, an unwanted picture forcing itself to the front of my mind. The walls whispered with memories.

Tearing my eyes away, I finally looked at Cat. She sat in the wooden rocking chair, her hands folding a cloth nappy. She looked at me, I looked at her, neither of us able to say anything. I took another step into the room and stopped. Everything screamed at me, a headache materialised from nothing into a ceaseless hammering. My stomach clenched and rolled, and I felt the toast preparing to surge upwards. I swallowed a couple of times and it settled, but I wanted to bolt from the room and find that hill.

'You need to eat,' I said.

'Emily fixed me something while you were in the shower,' she replied.

'You need to come out of here.'

'Why?'

I didn't know why, but being in here wasn't the right thing. 'Emily said your family are worried about you. You should call them.'

'Later,' she said absently, already withdrawing from the conversation. She finished with the nappy and placed it on the shelf under the change table. Looking at her empty hands, she reached out and swept the tidy pile onto the floor, picked one up and began folding it.

I looked at my wife and saw myself; like the walls of this room we were both memories. She wore the same clothes as yesterday, blue tracksuit pants, and a maroon T-shirt. She must have spent the night here. 'Have a shower, then come back.'

'Soon,' she said in the same voice, and it was possible she hadn't even heard me.

I crossed the room and knelt down before her. 'Look at me, Cat,' I said, echoing Emily's earlier words to me.

She gazed at me with unfocused eyes.

'We'll get through this.' I cursed the lack of conviction in my voice.

'It wasn't supposed to be like this, was it, Troy?' I wondered if she had overheard my conversation with Emily. Then I realised it was simpler than that. Cat and I were the same, we wanted the same thing – we needed this to work.

'We'll get through this, babe,' I repeated.

She finally focused on my face. 'Will we?' she asked in a heart breaking voice.

'Go have a shower, Cat. This will all be here when you're done.'

She looked around the room, then down at her clothes. Without speaking she got up and left the room quickly, as if every second gone was another chance it would vanish without her here to anchor it to us. I heard the shower start up, and in the stillness of the room around me, a room that should have been full of new life, my tears fell. Then I thought of my wife, and more tears came, because the distance between us was greater than the few feet of physical ground. I desperately wanted to believe we would get through this, but experience, and Possibilities, suggested otherwise, and it was a painful, piercing thought.

When she came back my reserves of strength were depleted. She now wore her dressing gown, and when she picked up the breast pump from beside the chair I fled the room, closing the door behind me, shutting out Cat.

We drifted for a few more days. Emily came back every evening to check on us. On the fourth day she persuaded Cat to come into the kitchen for something to eat, the first time she'd eaten outside the room in over a week. We sat around the dining table in awkward silence, picking at our fried rice and noodles.

After Emily left Cat went to go back into the bedroom, but I blocked her way.

'Get out of my way, Troy.'

'No. You've spent enough time in there, Cat.'

'I'm doing what I need to do to survive,' she replied.

'That's not living.'

'Well, neither is she!' she shouted.

'I know,' I shouted back.

We faced off against each other, anger contorting faces beyond recognition. Then the emotion drained from her face and she was the woman I loved – only not, because her eyes spoke of the deepest despair. This time when she pushed past me I didn't stop her. The sound of the door clicking shut echoed through the hallway, an ominous sound that somehow meant more than it should have.

The next morning when I went into the hallway, the bedroom door at the end stood open.

'Cat?' I called out.

The room was empty. So were the bathroom, lounge and kitchen. She was gone. A shiver that had nothing to do with the cold wracked my body. The house seemed dead.

That's when I noticed the note, carefully placed on the edge of the kitchen bench. Her handwriting cast in blue ink simply said, 'We'll talk later.' That's all it said. Not, 'I'll be home later' or 'I love you.' There was no comfort in those three words.

Going back into our bedroom, I looked for anything missing – clothes, shoes, a bag – but it all seemed there. That was a small measure of comfort. I went into the bedroom at the end of the hall. The rocking chair seemed less substantial without Cat.

I lowered myself onto it, felt the hard wood beneath me, caught her faint scent. I thought of all the nights she'd sat here. Sometimes I would sit on the floor, leaning against the drawers, watching them. We would talk excitedly of the future, but none of the plans had ended like this. I'd lost children before, in Possibilities, but this was different. This was with Cat; this wasn't supposed to happen in a happy ever after.

I glanced up at the mobile, the moon and sun slowly shifting against each other. An idea began to form.

Emily insisted on coming, and since Cat had taken the car I needed transport. It seemed like every two minutes she asked me if I was sure about this, and my reply was always the same. Sure? No. Hopeful? Yes.

After what seemed like forever, we arrived at the car park. Suddenly this seemed like a stupid idea, but I clung to it desperately because it was better than the alternative. I paused at the bottom of the path, glancing back at Emily in the car, suddenly not sure, then walked down to the beach.

It was a cold, dull day and the water churned and rolled, sending white froth onto sand washed clean from the day before. Overhead a seagull sat on the wind and cried mournfully, constantly searching for food. The only visible sign of life apart from the bird was scrabbling around on the sand, moving it from spot to spot. As I drew closer I realised Cat's movements weren't random; she was making something. She didn't acknowledge me when I dropped onto the sand next to her.

'What are you doing?' I eventually asked.

She paused with hands full of sand, and looked at me. Her face was calm, but there was a glint in her eye – a hint of life that had been absent for the last few days. 'Do you remember what you were doing the day Emily and I got attacked? It didn't work because you were trying to prove to the moon it was wrong. That was a mistake – it's not going to change its mind. What you should have been doing was showing the sun how right it is. How bright it is, how important it is to us.'

'It won't bring her back,' I replied.

'I know.' Her voice was full of regret and despair. 'But she was my sun.' She stared up into the sky, searching for the real thing, but it remained stubbornly hidden behind layers of grey. 'Will you help me?' There was desperation in her question.

In answer I picked up handfuls of sand and slapped them down, shaping them as directed by Cat. We worked in silence for a long time. At one point I saw Emily watching us from the top of the beach, but when I looked over again she was gone.

'You know Emily is pregnant,' Cat said.

I stopped, hands dripping sand, and looked at her. 'What? When did she tell you that?'

Cat shook her head. 'I could tell, the way she holds her stomach, the excitement she's trying to hide from her face.'

'It could be a stomach bug,' I objected.

Cat gave me a scornful look, and for a second the real her emerged. Then she disappeared back into the shadows.

'Why didn't she tell me?' I asked.

Cat didn't deign that stupidity with a response.

I looked over to the sand dunes and thought of Emily. I wanted to be happy for her, but happy was a lone grain of light in the emotional darkness.

'This must be agony for her,' Cat said, using her hands to scrape at the sand.

She was right. It should have been the happiest time for Emily; instead she had to keep the news from her friends, and watch us go through the sort of hell parents dread. Part of me wanted to go and find her, to give her a hug and say it was all right, that her baby would be fine, but I didn't want to lie to her. And a tiny part of me, a part I instantly loathed, was angry and jealous that she was going to have something that had been so cruelly snatched away from us.

My mouth filled with bile, and a nauseous frenzied wave of emotions threatened to crash onto the sand. I worked with increased vigour, smashing the sand down, burying my pain with each dull thud. Cat glanced over but I ignored her. Despite the cold I warmed up quickly, sweat forming and cooling on my forehead.

Even with the two of us it took another hour to finish. The finished product was huge, about two metres wide and half a metre high, as close to a circle as we could do, with long lines coming out of it, representing the sun's rays. It was a child's version of the sun, a crayon drawing on a crumbling canvas. We sat next to it, exhausted. Her hand crept into mine and I clung onto it as if afraid the tide would sweep her away.

In a quirk of timing the sun broke through the clouds and bathed our sculpture in light. I held my breath, waiting to see if the sun would accept our offering. For a moment hope smouldered in the ruins of our fairy tale, then cruelly the clouds reasserted their control of the sky and the light slipped away, Cat's hand going with it.

'Where do we go from here?' she whispered.

'On,' I replied. 'We go on.'

'How?' she said in tears. 'Tell me a story where this ends well.'

I took a deep breath, not knowing how to answer. Then it came to me. 'I never told you everything about that day. What happened after I finished the sculpture.'

When I looked over at her she gave no sign she was listening but I kept going anyway. 'I tried to stop the tide taking it. I fought against the water until exhaustion and nature beat me. So I lay down and waited for the tide to take me instead. I figured if the tide was the work of the moon and I felt like the moon, then I should embrace the tide and go with it. Then I heard Emily.'

She was looking at me now. 'Why did you never tell me?'

I shrugged. 'It's not the sort of thing you bring up, is it? By the way, I almost committed suicide on the night I saved you from being raped.'

She thought about that for a while. 'If you'd finished five minutes earlier, or we'd been attacked five minutes later, then…'

'We wouldn't be here now,' I finished.

'Would that be a bad thing?' she said.

I know she was talking about the reason why we were there rather than being here with me, but it still shredded my insides. 'We can get through this, Cat.'

'I don't want to get through this. That means I have to accept it, and I don't.'

'She was my daughter too. You're acting like you're the only one hurting.'

'How am I supposed to act? Tell me? I've never lost a child before, Troy, so please tell me how this is supposed to go.' She scrambled to her feet and I followed her.

'I don't know, but I don't want to lose you too.'

'I don't want to lose you either,' she snapped.

'Then why does it feel like you're already gone?'

She reeled back as if I'd slapped her. 'I can't…' She turned and ran off down the beach.

I stood unmoving and blinked…

And was on the beach watching Cat retreating along the sand. I blinked again…

And stood on the beach. 'Fuck!' I screamed. The clouds picked that moment to pull back their grey curtain and let the sun shine onto our pathetic offering. I blinked…

And stood on the beach. No, this can't be real life – this has to be a Possibility. This can't be what happens with Cat. I blinked again…

And again…

And again, each time staying exactly when and where I was.

The sun disappeared behind clouds again and anger narrowed my vision to pinpricks. All I saw was the pile of sand in front of me. The one we'd spent so long lovingly crafting into a beautiful offering to the universe. Only to have it rejected, like mine had been all those years ago. I kicked out, sending sand flying, and again, and again – destroying, ripping, shattering, until it was a sodden pile of nothing. Chest heaving, I dropped to my knees amongst the devastation and stared out into the ocean in despair. I'd thought I was all cried out, but they came anyway.

I blinked them away…

And was on the beach. This was real life. It was horrible and shitty, and I hated this moment more than any other moment I'd ever experienced. And I hated that I'd thought there could be a happy ending. There was no happy ending for the moon; it was fated to keep tearing at the beach for eternity. I should have known better.

I looked down the beach to where Cat had disappeared. I should go after her, fight for her, but I was done. It had all been an illusion, thinking Cat and I were meant to be together, and I couldn't do this any more. It was too hard.

In the carpark our car had gone, but Emily's was still there. It was empty, though as I approached it she appeared from the café across the road, holding a takeaway cup of coffee. We looked at each other and she read something in my face that caused her pain.

'Brush the sand off before you get in,' she said. I did, then slid into the passenger seat. We didn't say anything for the first five minutes.

'Are you supposed to be drinking coffee in your condition?' I asked.

Her hands trembled and the car swerved a little before she corrected the steering. 'How did you know?'

'Cat.'

'I didn't want to tell you, not yet.'

'I know. That's why I love you.'

'Do you want to talk about it?'

I shook my head. 'No, Ems, I really don't.'

So we didn't, instead sitting in silence the whole way home. When we pulled up outside my house there was no goodbye, she just reached over and squeezed my hand. I squeezed back, then climbed out of the car.

The house looked different, colder – not a home any more. The key echoed in the front door, and the air inside the house was still and lifeless. The empty driveway had told me what to expect; even the new note on the kitchen bench failed to spark anything inside me. The promise that she still loved me did nothing to stop the shaking.

I picked up the teddy bear from the top of the drawers in our room, took it down the hall, and lowered myself into the rocking chair. For a moment life hung suspended in a single second, then I began to rock. A soft voice broke the silence. I stopped rocking and the sound ceased. For a brief craze-filled moment I thought it was Cat – or better yet, our daughter. I don't believe in ghosts, but that doesn't mean they didn't believe in me.

I started rocking again, waiting without breathing for the voice to start again. Nothing happened. My breath stuttered out with disappointment.

Then the voice came again, only this time I recognised the voice as my own. 'You with the sad eyes...'

The teddy bear sat on my lap, staring with unseeing eyes at the room that should have been its home. I blinked...

And was lying in my bed, alone. As I picked up my phone to check the date, the bedroom door opened and Cat slipped through. She wore my T-shirt, and by the looks of it that was all.

'Sorry,' she whispered. 'I didn't mean to wake you.'

'That's okay. I don't think I was sleeping.'

She grabbed my dressing gown off the back of the door and shrugged it on. 'Emily's home, so I'm going to have a quick chat.' She came over and kissed me. 'Don't worry, I won't talk about your performance.' She laughed and disappeared out the door.

I closed my eyes, waiting for my heart to slow, waiting for the fresh memories to subside, and for the feeling of utter devastation to disappear. I opened my eyes again. It wasn't working. I looked over at the closed door and a flash of the bedroom door from the Possibility crossed my eyes. I wanted to blink it away but was afraid the act of blinking would sweep me away again. I checked the date, it was the same night Cat and I had first had sex.

I got out of bed and paced to the door, then stopped, suddenly conscious I was naked. My pants were somewhere on the floor; turning on the light made it marginally easier to find them discarded in the corner of the room. Once they were on I looked for my T-shirt and it took me a while to remember Cat was wearing it. I pulled a new one from the drawer and gently cracked open the door.

Low voices came from the kitchen. I stepped into the hallway, aware of how much the floorboards creaked in this old house. The voices continued unabated, so I slid my feet along the floor and into the bathroom, easing the door closed behind me. I used the toilet, then washed my hands, afraid to raise my eyes to the mirror, then as if compelled by an outside force, raising them anyway. The face looking back at me was dull and shadowed, cracked and full of flaws. It was the same face that used to stare back at me before I met Cat. The ground seemed to shift beneath my feet and I looked down, expecting to see a gaping hole of despair, but it was the same crappy lino.

When I slipped out of the bathroom the voices still murmured from the kitchen. I stopped halfway along the hall, where their words were clear. Eavesdropping wasn't something I normally did, but after the Possibility I made an exception.

'...thought you guys were never going to get together,' came Emily's voice.

'Me too,' Cat replied. 'Luckily he was willing to be patient.'

'Willing is probably too strong a word.' Emily laughed.

Cat laughed too. 'Okay, so he was getting a little impatient, but you've obviously had a good influence on him, Ems. He showed a huge amount of restraint. Poor guy slept next to this for weeks and kept his hands to himself.'

'He's a saint,' Emily quipped.

'Not too much of one, I hope – I have plans.'

'So things are good?'

'I think he loves me,' Cat said.

'Of course he does.'

'You don't sound surprised.'

'I live with the guy – it's been obvious to me for a long time,' Emily told her.

'You couldn't have said anything?'

'Hell, no. Not my place.'

The voices trailed off and for a second I thought one of them was about to walk into the hallway, but then the conversation continued.

'So do you love him?' Emily asked.

I held my breath. She took so long to answer I almost ran through the door and shouted *Answer the damn question.* I pushed myself back against the wall to prevent independent movement of my feet.

'The first time I met him he answered the door wearing a towel that only just covered things.'

'Oh, my God – really? You never told me that.'

'It never came up. Anyway, it was only for a second because then he slammed the door in my face, and I thought, *What a dick.*'

'Oh?'

'Not that kind of dick.' They both laughed and my face flamed bright red. 'Although now that you mention it… No, I thought *What kind of idiot opens the door naked and then rudely slams it shut*? So I was kind of glad not to win the bet. Then I saw him on the side of the road, and he scared off a ride that my friend and I were going to get. And I thought what a wanker.'

'So, not love at first sight then,' Emily observed.

'Not even close. But then something funny happened. I kept running into him and suddenly I was looking at him differently. His smile doesn't always reach his eyes – have you noticed that?'

'Yeah. He's had a rough time.'

'Why?'

'Something happened at high school, with a girl that he was in love with.'

'Heather?'

'Has he told you?' Emily sounded surprised.

'No. Lucky guess. What happened?'

'He fell in love – that deep love only teenagers can feel. And she said she loved him as well, and then she took her life. He doesn't talk about it, but it screwed him up.'

There was another silence. Tears formed in my eyes, the extent of what I'd put Emily through suddenly becoming crystal clear.

'But I'll tell you this. The last few weeks – that's the happiest I've seen him in ten years. So this is important.' Emily emphasised the last four words and there was a pause before Cat replied.

'When I first met him I was carefree. It didn't bother me what tomorrow was going to bring because I lived in the day, and I loved that, I loved my life. Then the attack happened and it changed me. I stopped living in the day and started worrying about what happened yesterday, or what was going to happen tomorrow, or if I was even going to make it to tomorrow. But when I'm with him I don't worry about tomorrow, because if he's in it then I know it's going to be good. So I can enjoy the day. I lost myself, and he found me again. So do I love him? Hell, yes.'

'That's good.' Emily sounded unsure. 'But do you love *him*, or do you just love the things he's done for you?

I pressed harder against the wall, fighting the urge to cover my ears with my hands.

'This is who I am – the real Elissa, strong and getting stronger, independent, often called quirky, or a pain in the arse if you ask Steven. I don't need a knight in shining armour. I'm with him because I want to be, not because I need to be.'

'For what it's worth, I think you two are a cute couple.'

'No, we are a magnificent couple,' Cat shot back, and they both laughed.

Emily said in a warning voice, 'But you know how Troy taught me how to defend myself? If you hurt him I'll kick your ass.'

'Fair enough,' Cat replied. 'So what about you? What's this I hear about a guy?'

'Austin. He's from work. He's sweet.'

'You like him,' Cat stated.

'Yeah, I do.'

'Have you slept with him yet?'

'Elissa!'

'Would it help if I told you about sex with Troy?'

'Eww! God, no – he's my friend. And no, I haven't slept with Austin yet. We've only been on a couple of dates.'

'But he makes you feel good?'

'He makes me relax,' Emily said.

'It's a good feeling, right?'

'Yes, it is.'

'Then I hope it works out for you.'

'Thanks. We were supposed to be going out later, but he got another headache so we called it a night early.'

'Another one?'

'He seems to get them a lot.'

I decided that was enough eavesdropping and crept back along the hallway to my bedroom. As I went out of earshot I heard Cat say, 'Tell him to get his headaches checked out. It could be serious.'

When Cat slipped back into the bedroom I was lying in bed pretending to sleep. There was a rustling as she slid out of the dressing gown and under the covers. She snuggled into my back, wrapping her arms around me and resting her chin on my shoulder.

'Hey, Troy. Emily wants to talk to you.'

'What gave it away?' I asked.

She laughed softly. 'Honey, you'd better get a lot better at pretending to be asleep, because that was shocking.'

'Get off me, you horrible person,' I said in mock anger. She laughed again and kissed my arm before rolling away. Climbing out of bed, I put the discarded dressing gown on, still infused with her body heat, and looked back at the bed where Cat lay with one arm stretched over her head.

'I'll be lying here innocently waiting for you,' she said. I made to jump back into bed and she held up a hand to stop me. 'Uh uh, plenty of time for that later. Go talk to Emily first.'

'How do I know you won't be asleep when I get back?' I asked suspiciously.

'Just go, you idiot,' she grinned.

The end or the beginning

Emily was sitting at the kitchen table cradling a cup of coffee when I walked in.

'I didn't expect to see you for a couple of days,' she quipped.

'I needed a snack,' I replied, opening the fridge and pulling out the cheese. Taking a knife from the drawer I hacked a chunk off one end, much to Emily's disgust. 'Cat said you wanted to talk to me.'

She looked confused. 'I didn't say that.'

I looked off towards the bedroom and frowned. 'Then why would she…'

'Who knows?' Emily replied.

We sat in silence for a moment, then both tried to talk at the same time. I gestured for her to go first.

'Okay, so maybe there was something I wanted to say. Things are changing,' she said unhappily.

'What do you mean?'

She looked around the room. 'Here, us … boyfriends and girlfriends have come through those doors over the years, but in the end it's always been the two of us. Now you've got Elissa, and there's Austin… I can't help thinking this is the end and it makes me sad.'

I reached over the table and squeezed her hand before letting it go.

'Ems, it's never going to be the end of you and me. You're my best friend, and that's not going to change.'

She wiped at her eyes and gave a shaky laugh. 'I know, it's stupid. But things are changing. You know I've been focussing more on photography. Well, there's this exhibition coming up at the Wellington Art Gallery and I've had a couple of pictures accepted.'

'Ems, that's amazing. Why didn't you tell me?'

She fidgeted with her hands, picking at her fingernails. 'It seems I have some sort of natural talent.' She laughed in a self-effacing way.

'About time you were good at something,' I said through a mouthful of cheese.

'Dickhead,' she replied half-heartedly.

I gave her a cheesy grin.

'The thing is, this critic from overseas is going to be here. So what if he doesn't like my work? He's new in the business but they say he can make or break careers. I love taking pictures, and I think it's something I'd like to explore for a living, but if this guy shoots me down then…'

I reached across the table and stopped her hands. 'Ems, he's going to love you. How could he not? You're fabulous.'

'It's true, I am,' she replied with a soft laugh.

'What's this guy's name?'

'Oh, God, I can't remember. Does it matter? Jack something. Jack Cunnington, I think.'

I grinned. 'I think he's going to love you.'

'You have to say that.'

'Maybe, but it's still true.

'Is that a psychic flash?'

I shook my head. 'Personal opinion.'

She looked at me suspiciously. 'Okay, so what if he does love me?

You and Elissa are going to move in together and I'll have to break in a new roommate, and what if they don't like reality TV?'

I raised an eyebrow at the rapid change in subject. 'Hey, don't be in a hurry to get rid of me. Cat and I are new – who knows what's going to happen? Anyway, maybe we'll move in here. Then you'll gain a flatmate, not lose one.'

'Then I'll have to share the bathroom with another girl, and I'm not sure I'm ready for that either.'

I rolled my eyes. 'Then what are you ready for, Ems?'

'What are you ready for?' she shot back. I looked at her in confusion. 'Are you committed to a relationship with Elissa? Or are you still looking for the other side of the hill?'

I considered the question carefully. I thought about the Possibility fresh in my mind – of losing Cat, losing our child, the horrible despair that permeated my entire body. Like all the Possibilities it was frighteningly real. The thought of going through that in real life was almost too much to bear. The urge to run, to put distance between me and the memory was overpowering. For a split second I teetered on the edge, staring down and waiting to fall.

Then I thought of Cat lying in my bed, waiting for me, wanting to be with me. There was something different about her – something about those eyes, the body, the hidden strength – that made me step back.

'That's what I thought,' Emily said.

'What? I didn't say anything,' I protested.

'Not out loud. But you've got this big goofy smile on your face – and you know what? For the first time in a very, very long time, it's in your eyes.

'I need a mirror,' I said abruptly, and hurried down the hall to the bathroom.

I switched on the light and went straight over to the basin. The face staring back at me was unrecognisable. Emily was right – there was a light in my eyes that hadn't been present before. It seeped onto my skin, radiating it with a glow I'd never seen before. This wasn't the face of the moon. It was different, better.

Back in the kitchen Emily hadn't moved.

'Fixed your makeup?' she asked sarcastically.

I kissed her on the top of the head. 'You're going to be fine, Ems.'

'And you?'

'I'm going to be great.'

She studied me for a moment. 'I hope so – but, Troy, keep being patient with her, and if you hurt her I'll kick your ass.'

I laughed and kissed her again. 'You'd better get some sleep, Ems. All this ass kicking requires a lot of energy.'

She looked at me shrewdly. 'Night, Troy,' she said, punching me on the arm.

Suddenly I saw a future where Austin was fine, he and Emily got married and had children, and she was happy.

I closed the bedroom door quietly, shed the robe and slipped back into bed. Cat was facing me, her eyes closed, breathing shallow. For a moment I thought she was faking it, but after watching her for a while I realised she was actually asleep. I kissed her on the cheek, and closed my eyes.

It doesn't matter any more

I woke slowly, becoming aware of sounds and smells and light pushing against my eyelids. I wondered about my age. Some days it was hard to tell. Eyes still shut, I moved first one leg, then the other. No pain. Flexed my fingers; they felt strong and supple. Finally I opened my eyes and looked at my hands. They looked young, wrinkle-free, yet slightly callused. I sighed. That narrowed the age down but not enough.

I became aware of a figure next to me. She lay on her stomach, her long blonde hair draped across her face like a demure mask. It was Cat. A quick check of my phone showed it was the morning after the first time. I studied her sleeping face. It didn't matter if we had a day, or a week, or a million lifetimes. It was time to stop worrying about the future, whatever form it took, and start living for the moment.

I slipped out of the bed, opened the wardrobe door and rummaged around for the shoebox I'd put in there the day Emily and I moved into the house. I grabbed the glass of water from next to the bed and soaked the paintbrushes while I set up. Lacking an easel, I leaned the canvas against the side of the bed. The paints were a little old but hopefully still usable. I squeezed some onto a brush, touched it to the canvas, and began completing the picture.

Occasionally I glanced over at Cat, one time seeing a small smile play across her mouth. Slowly she rolled over and stretched, first one arm, then the other, the movement accentuating the firmness of her breast uncovered by the sheet. Her smile widened as she caught me looking.

'What are you doing?' she asked sleepily.

'Painting the sun.'

She struck a dramatic pose.

'Idiot,' I said and she laughed.

'What are we doing today?' she asked.

'I have to write my resignation letter, but apart from that nothing concrete.'

She looked at me with raised eyebrows.

'Time to start a new life.'

'As a painter?' she asked.

If I'd been asked the same question ten years ago, before all this started, I wouldn't have even stopped to consider it. The answer would have been a resounding yes. But now it didn't seem the right fit. Finishing the painting was important, but I didn't think it was where my future lay. 'No, I think I'd like to do something that helps people.'

She lay back, eyes closed with a smile on her lips.

'I Got You, by Split Enz,' I told her.

'Huh?'

'My walk-away song. It's I Got You by Split Enz.'

She opened her eyes and propped herself up on an elbow. 'Why would you say that?'

I shrugged. 'It's important to have a walk-away song.'

'Are you planning on walking away?'

'Not a chance.'

Her eyes pierced me so I went back to painting.

'Mine is, 'Don't Wait Another Day' by Greg Johnson.'

'Great song. Appropriate too.'

She kept looking at me and finally I turned my gaze back to meet her. 'Cat?'

'Mmm,' she replied.

'I love you.' My voice trembled with emotion.

'And I really, completely, totally love you too.'

We smiled at each other. For the first time in all my lives I knew the way forward. Yet something nagged at me. 'Why did you tell Emily that Austin needed to get his headaches checked out?'

She rolled closer, reached out and traced around my eyes. 'Was it really bad?' she whispered.

'What?' I replied in confusion.

'When I pepper-sprayed you.'

It took a few seconds for her words to register, then my whole world imploded. 'How did you…?'

She gave me the full Cat look, sly and mischievous. 'You'll never guess what life I've just lived,' she said.

About the Author

Rodney Strong quit a 9–5 job to pursue a full time writing career. He lives in Porirua, New Zealand, with his wife, two children, and two cats.

He started working on *Troy's Possibilities* while completing an Advanced Diploma in Creative Writing. The story came about while he was one day thinking about how different life would have been if he had made different decisions at key moments.

Rodney is a member of the New Zealand Society of Authors, and chairs his neighborhood residents group.